ALSO F

Other Blood

Blood's A Rover

Blood Tide

Blood Sisters

Cold Blood (2023)

Saving Sophie Scholl

Guardian Angel

Oral Wars

Damsel

Eco-Freak

Kinky Girls Save The World

Burke And Hare, The School of Death, and Other Stories

Seen The Elephant, Heard The Owl (Alongside I)

The New Kid (Alongside II)

Krampusnacht

For

Fr. Charles J. Scott

Sr. Michael Archangel

Sr. Muriel Irons

Sr. Anthony Mary

Sr. Mary Thaddeus

Fr. Dunstan Curtis

Fr. Bertrand Trautman

Fr. Bede Ernsdorff

Fr. Meinrad Gaul

Fr. Placidus Reischman

Bishop Francis P. Leipzig

And

Mike Contris

GONE AHEAD

BY

D. J. BERSHAW

Published by Sucker's Junk Press
McMinnville, Oregon

August, 2022
Copyright D.J. Bershaw

ISBN: 979-8-88796-885-8

Cover Design by J. Kathleen Cheney
(jkathleencheney@gmail.com)

This book is a work of fiction. Excepting the use of famous deceased persons and Cher, the characters, events, and dialogue are products of the author's lifelong mental situation, which has not always been good (he is of Irish descent). The cities and geography are real, however, except Raptureville.

> We may not doubt that society in Heaven consists mainly of undesirable persons.
> -- Mark Twain

CHAPTER ONE

When the whole mess began, Will Garrison had no idea the blame rested with John Nelson Darby, a man born in the eighteenth century. Will was far more concerned about the cold concrete pressing against his nude backside. That and the young woman bucking and moaning atop him on the floor of what seemed to be an incredibly huge warehouse, dimly-lit by skylights.

He must be delusional, dying. A stroke, he figured. What had started as a simple celebration of his seventieth birthday had gone more than severely awry. The lower end of his spine felt otherwise, however, his hips flexing sharply up, enthusiastically cooperating with what was going on against his crotch. Then, when the woman tensed and let out a low ululating wail, Will recognized that sound. *Katie*, his wife of nearly fifty years.

Younger. Firmer. *Tighter. Holy jumpin' shit*! he thought, even as his own gasping orgasm joined hers and spun his mind away.

"Will?" Katie asked as they came back to themselves, sweaty and breathing hard. Her puzzled blue gaze bored into his, after briefly darting away to take in their surroundings. "Where in *hell* are we?"

"Dunno. Looks like an unoccupied Costco."

Astraddle Will, Katie had a better vantage point. "Bigger. *Lots* bigger. I can see signs on the walls, though." She squinted around them. "Can't make 'em out. The light's not good enough."

"Katie, do I look *younger*?"

She peered down at him again, bringing her face close to his. Her eyes widened. "Mi-gawd!" Her hands flew up to feel her own features, and she gasped.

"Yes," he said, anticipating her question. "You, too. Like when we were first married."

"But...*how*?"

"I don't have the slightest idea." He grinned up at her. "And while I like the view from here, it might be better if we looked for the lights."

Kate returned his smile fondly, then reached down and tousled his hair. "You have a point there."

"*Very* funny."

"That, too." She lifted off him, rose to her feet, and ran both hands through her short blonde hair, kneading her scalp while looking around them in the near-darkness. "As big as a football field," she observed, giving Will a hand up.

"There're lights up on the ceiling," he said, pointing.

"There'll be switches, then. Let's walk toward the nearest wall." She looked down. "Pattern on the floor. Some kind of whorls."

Hand-in-hand, they headed cautiously in what Will's bump of direction told him was north. Within a couple minutes, they found a bank of light switches and threw them all. The place lit up like daylight.

The floor was covered in Celtic patterns, all seeming to coalesce and flow toward an enormous pair of arched bronze doors set into the far wall. Over the doors, surrounded by more knotted designs, were the words, 'Welcome to Raptureville, Cockaigne's Newest Subdivision."

Will grunted, chuckling. "There's your answer, Katie. We've been Raptured."

Without replying at first, her hands on her hips, Katie surveyed the rest of the high walls, all covered with superlatives describing the joys of Raptureville. "Real Estate people wrote these," she said at last, her voice slightly scornful as she read. "'Ten Olympic-sized Pools, Five Indoors! Thirty Kilometres of Hiking and Jogging Trails! Three Eight-plex Theatres! Tribulation Mall!'"

"'Thirty Thousand-seat Stadium,'" Will continued. "'All the Best Acts! All the Best Sports!'"

Katie pointed to the south wall. "'Burns and Allen! Dempsey vs. Tunney! Keaton! Chaplin! Knute Rockne and His 1924 Notre Dame Team!'"

"'World War One With The Original Cast!'"

"*What*!"

"Just kiddin', hon."

Poking him in the chest with a rigid forefinger, she said, "May I remind you that we are in a *very* strange -- apparently deserted -- place, with no idea how we got here, nude, penniless, and without any food whatsoever!"

"But we're kids again, and we just had great sex."

Katie regarded him with blue disdain. "That's nice, dear. Just *so* helpful. And manly." A slow grin spread over her lean features. "*Definitely* manly."

"You've always *liked* manly," Will said, after clearing his throat. He could barely take his eyes off Katie. Damn, she looked *good*!

She snickered. "Manly has its place."

"I'm not goin' there."

"I think you just did, and vigorously."

"Not what I meant."

"I know. Give me credit for understanding how your head works after all these years." She pointed to a set of double doors next to the switches. "Shall we look in there? Maybe it'll be a Wal-Mart."

They opened the doors, turned on the lights.

Will whistled. "Close enough." While the ceiling was nowhere near as high as in the place they'd arrived, the floorspace was close to the same, and it seemed to be *all* clothing and sundries. Signs hanging from the ceiling designated Mens', Womens', Shoes, Underwear, and so forth.

"Underwear first," Katie said, marching determinedly down a wide aisle in that direction. Will trailed in her wake, trying to take it all in, along with Katie's backside.

The selection proved extensive. Will easily found his favorite J.C. Penney's all-cotton three-pack, and Katie collected a half-dozen colorful Donna Karan numbers.

"Those are kind of skimpy," Will said, raising an eyebrow at her picks.

Katie smiled sweetly at him. "I'm not buying for a seventy-year-old grandmother anymore, dear."

"No kiddin'."

From there they went to Womens'. "They've got *Cambio's*, Will!" she exclaimed, holding up a pair of stylish-looking black jeans. She grabbed another pair in the next display. "And *Joseph*! Now I *know* I'm in Heaven."

"Seems awfully organized," Will observed. "Compared to the traditional concept, which was sort of vague."

Without looking away from rummaging through the racks, trying to find her size, Katie laughed. "Maybe it's Mormon Heaven."

Will echoed her laughter. "Then what're *we* doing here? Being Episcopalians and all."

"Maybe it's Open Enrollment day."

He shook his head in amazement. "You're sure chipper and accepting with all this."

"When we're dressed and finish exploring, then maybe I'll be more concerned."

"Sounds reasonable."

They continued gathering garments until they were adequately dressed, packing a few extra things into nylon Nike gear bags from the Sports Clothing department.

"Now I feel better," Katie said, hefting her bag as she grinned at Will.

"Then maybe you both'd be willing to tell me what it is that brings you here in the middle of the freakin' night," said a lilting baritone voice from the end of the aisle.

CHAPTER TWO

Will turned toward the voice, trying to choose his words carefully. This might not be a friendly place. "Findin' some clothes," he answered slowly, his gaze taking in both the tall, barefoot man and the matte black repeater shotgun hanging from one tanned, muscular hand.

"We just appeared in the other room," Katie added, pointing in that direction, "about a half-hour ago."

The man momentarily put his free hand over his eyes. "*Shit*, the techs forgot to turn off the damn computers." He sounded disgusted.

"Computers?"

"Yeah, they ran the first tests yesterday. Brought up four Deer mice, two rabbits, and a real unhappy Spotted skunk." A white grin spread across his dark features. "I understand the skunk presented a problem."

"Can you tell us where we are?" Katie asked.

"Well, yeah, you're in Cockaigne, the Land of the Perfect Life."

Katie's swift glance at Will was troubled. "We thought maybe Heaven," she said.

The man shrugged, and his grin widened. "Close enough. Old Man got interested in the whole Rapture deal. Because of those books. He thought it'd be interesting to actually bring the living here, instead of just the dead. 'A new dynamic' was how he put it."

"Who's Old Man?" Will asked.

"The person in charge. When Old Woman isn't around."

"*The* God?" Katie asked.

The man frowned. "For all intents and purposes. The embodiment of all the male gods, just as Old Woman is for the female."

Katie mirrored his frown. "They co-rule?"

"More or less." He gestured with the shotgun toward the open door between the two big rooms. "Look, why don't we find a place for you to rest for the night. We can talk on the way. I'm Michael, incidentally."

"Michael the Archangel?" asked Will.

Now Michael's grin turned self-conscious. "Folks always ask that, but no, I'm not. Just Michael. Michael O'Conner, actually. I'm one of the foremen on the construction crew. The traditional Archangels tend to keep to the Middle East and Mediterranean basin, where they made their reps. Sometimes they show for nostalgia conventions and Holy Book-signings in North America, but not often."

"I'm Katie Garrison," Katie said, shaking Michael's left hand. "This is my husband, Will."

"Pleased to meet you," Michael replied, shaking Will's hand. He turned and began leading them out of the room.

"How long have you been here?" Will asked. They fell into step with Michael.

"All my life. Born here."

"People are *born* here?"

14

"Just angels. Regular humans can't reproduce. It'd get too crowded. No offence."

"Oh," Katie said, her expression changing to mild awe. "So you *are* an *angel*?"

"Sure am," Michael replied modestly. "One of the numerous heavenly host bustin' their humps to get Raptureville up and runnin'."

As they walked across the room where he and Katie had arrived, Will examined the man more closely. He was a fair bit over six feet tall, handsome, with something akin to Polynesian features, his hair black and moderately curly, and his skin a dark mocha. A sort of everyman, Will thought.

"How many of you on the project?" Will asked. He'd been a structural engineer before his recent retirement, and while his area of expertise had not been subdivisions, he knew something about construction.

"About three thousand total," Michael replied. "A third angels, the rest folks like you two." He sighed. "Lots of people. Old Man Brought Up quite a few catskinners, skip-loader and bulldozer operators, not to mention trackhoe people and dump truck drivers. And carpenters, of course."

"That seems awfully mundane," Katie said. "Couldn't... 'Old Man'...just snap his fingers and make things *appear*?"

Michael shook his head. "He can grant life, perfect health, immortal young bodies, and fiddle with time. That's it anymore, from what He says. Everything else is good old blood, sweat, and tears. And you can't do the necessary fine stuff with tractor beams, molecular compressors, and the like. They throw up way too much dust. On the ground, movin' earth, it's just the same as where you come from." He opened a smaller door beside the large bronze pair.

They stepped out into the warm spring night. The sky was clear, the moon rising from the southeast, the air nearly still. A huge, partially-completed subdivision sprawled over the rolling moonlit hills to the west and south. A lighted heavy equipment lager stood to the north of the homesites, big yellow earthmoving machines sitting behind tall chain-link fence.

"How many homes?" Will asked, unwilling to even try to guess.

"Five thousand."

"That's not very many," Katie said. "How many will be Raptured?"

"Probably fewer than ten thousand, mostly families. Our computer wonks have projected that He'll get bored and go on to something else before the place fills up."

"*He* gets *bored*?"

Michael laughed, the warm, rich laugh Will would expect from an angel. "Think about it. He's been in the business for tens of thousands of years, Bringing Up people he thinks might be interesting. Or fun. He *does* like a good time. This deal must've seemed like a break from the usual and customary. We'll have to see how it goes."

The sound of running footsteps interrupted Michael's explanation. Will and Katie turned to see two small figures in shorts and sandals scampering pell-mell toward them down an asphalt path leading from the nearest completed houses.

"Dad!" shouted one of them. "What are you *doing*?"

"Helping these folks," Michael replied, raising his free hand. "Slow *down*, Mary Pat. You can't see in the dark as well as Bobby."

A little black-haired girl braked to a halt in front of them, her sandals sliding the last few inches. "I'm *fine*, Dad," she answered dismissively. "Hi, I'm Mary Pat," she added to the Garrisons, holding out a none-too-clean right hand, her smudged smile surrounded by faint freckles. She indicated her companion. "And this is Bobak."

Will looked down into a small face dominated by large golden eyes and split by a mouthful of needle-sharp teeth. A rainbow-feathered crest rose from low on the little creature's domed forehead and climbed over its round skull. Will felt his mouth almost fall open as he took the proffered olive-hued hand, felt its warmth even as blunt claws curled against his fingers.

"I'm a dinosaur, sir," Bobak said, his voice no different from any other child his apparent age. His head cocked to one side, and his feathers rose in what Will guessed was the equivalent of a lifted eyebrow. "You *do* know about us, don't you?"

Mary Pat began to giggle. "Bobby *likes* to surprise the new people."

"Some of them think I'm a demon from Hell," the little reptile added, giggling along with his friend.

"*Kids*," Michael said, shaking his head even as he smiled fondly at his daughter and Bobby. "Bobby's parents are part of the construction crew.

They live next door to us. He and Mary Pat are classmates."

"But...*dinosaurs*?" Katie stammered as she shook Bobby's clawed hand.

"Anyone can have Salvation," Michael replied, sounding almost as serious as when they'd first seen him. "Bobby's whole family were Brought Up about five years ago. Another of Old Man's brainstorms. Bobby's a great kid, and his dad does a mean grill on the weekends."

"We're going back to watch Jack Benny," Mary Pat announced. "Pleased to meet you." She and Bobby started to leave.

"Hey, wait a minute," Mary Pat's father said. "Maybe you two could take the Garrisons into town tomorrow, since it's Saturday. Show them the sights."

"During *Rose Festival*?" both children asked, their very different eyes shining with excitement. "Really?"

"Sure," Michael said. "The four of you could have a great time."

"Do I get extra allowance?" asked Mary Pat, looking kid-sly.

Her father laughed. "Of course."

The two children high-fived. "Cool!"

"See you tomorrow," Bobby said, waving a clawed hand.

"Nine sharp, right here," Mary Pat added, grinning. The two ran off. Will noticed that Bobby sported a short tail.

"Nice kids," Katie observed, watching the pair sprint back toward the housing.

"None better," Michael answered, looking momentarily proud. "They've both got terrific moms."

"Are we talkin' the *Portland* Rose Festival?" Will asked.

"No. Boston. When Asa Lovejoy and Francis Pettygrove both died in 1882, they ended up here and reflipped for the town name. Lovejoy won the second time."

Katie let out a loud guffaw. "So it's *Boston*, not Portland!"

Michael nodded. "Yeah. Pretty much the same place, though. Nicer, smaller. Not so many bridges. Only about fifty thousand people."

"Why so few people?" Will asked.

"Well, like I said, not everybody makes the cut, and the population's real mobile, plus there's a certain level of death. People killed other people pretty regularly here until the real scientific breakthroughs in the Fifties. Society kind of mellowed out after that. Boston got to be a cultural center, became relatively peaceful. Some other parts of the world are still wild as hell, though."

"So," Katie asked, "if somebody is killed here...that's *it*?"

Michael nodded. "Exactly. There is no after-Afterlife." He gestured toward the housing area. "Look, you'll have plenty of time to ask questions tomorrow. The kids are both regular chatterboxes. Let's get you settled in for the night. We've got three bungalows which were slated for occupancy, but the six

Mexican-American tile-setters who were scheduled to depart the mortal coil managed to avoid gettin' run over by an out-of-control bus, so we've got some room for now." He smiled down at Will and Katie. "I mean, you're the victims of a screw-up. You're entitled to special consideration."

The three walked up the same asphalt path taken by the children, Michael pointing out the progress made by the construction crews, estimating it would take at least a year before the giant subdivision was completely ready for the first Raptured, and that might require some luck. Katie and Will didn't say much, but exchanged numerous perplexed looks.

Ten minutes and a few intersections later, Michael stopped before a modest stone home on a short cul-de-sac. The roof appeared to be tile, the driveway concrete. "Here we are," he said, leading them up the cobblestone sidewalk to the front door.

"There's a *garage*," Katie said, pointing.

"Nothing in it," Michael replied as he bent over to fish the door key from under the welcome mat. "Most folks use public transit, but some buy the little Ford electrics for short distances."

"What about highways?" Will asked.

Michael shook his head. "No need any more. The Germans were close to anti-gravity during World War II, and John von Neumann was Brought Up in 1957. He founded the industrial group in California that linked the surviving Nazi knowledge with his own studies and those of others. By the early Sixties, we had fusion power *and* anti-gravity. For the first time, we were ahead of Mortal Earth."

"You weren't before then?" Will asked. He thought he saw the reason for that, a person's life going on after an individual had make a scientific breakthrough.

"We had to wait until the person or persons involved with a big discovery died to have the knowledge appear here. But von Neumann and his cronies were different. He'd laid the groundwork for the computer, worked on fission and fusion, and was a real polymath. They just went on creating, and knowledge snowballed." He smiled. "Cockaigne finally truly became Cockaigne in the traditional sense, with all our needs available. Pollution virtually disappeared, the forests re-established, wildlife population rebounded, and a life of plenty was here for everyone. It was the dawn of the Real New Age." He opened the front door and turned on the interior lighting.

The little home had a definite Southwest flavor, Spanish tiled floors with colorful patterns around their edges, rustic wooden furniture, and a surrealistic rooster mosaic on the smaller windowless wall in the living room. Through the living room, Will could see a spacious kitchen. "Is there food in the refrigerator?" he asked.

"Let's see," Michael replied, setting his shotgun on the cushions of a dark blue couch. They walked into the kitchen and opened the refrigerator, discovering a treasure trove of frozen burritos, tacos, and Dos Equis beer.

"Well, I won't have to cook," Katie observed, spying a microwave.

"We'll probably have a barbecue tomorrow night," Michael said. "Grilling season's pretty well under way. You can come over after you get cleaned up, when the kids bring you back from Boston."

"Michael," Katie said. "We're *here*, right? There's no dead old bodies back home?"

"Yeah," the tall angel replied. "You just *disappeared*, then reappeared here, younger. A classic Rapture move."

"We'll be missed."

Michael's habitual smile grew momentarily wistful. "Yeah, I would think nice folks like you *would* be. Probably drive the authorities nuts. Not much you or I can do about that, though. Now, the *big* Rapture, next year or the year after, somebody'll figure that one out." He pointed at the ceiling, his grin returning to normal. "'Oooh, they've been *Raptured*!'"

Katie laughed politely, but Will knew she wasn't going to leave the topic alone until she was satisfied. "Can you think of any way we could get back home, Michael?"

The angel regarded her thoughtfully for a few moments.

"Well...Old Man *could* do that, if you could find him. That's not easy. He kind of comes and goes as he pleases, and doesn't advertise his presence. His show-off years are well behind him. Generally, he's at some 'undisclosed location.'"

"What about Old Woman?"

"She was at the replica restored Stonehenge for *Bealtane*, I know, but that was *weeks* ago. Doesn't get out this way much. Old Man's definitely your best shot." His smile grew sweet again. "Look, you've got some time here. Take it and enjoy it. He can fiddle time. If you can convince him to send you back, you could re-appear the instant after you disappeared, I'll bet."

"Would we still be kids?" Will asked.

Michael laughed. "Oh, yeah. I think he only does *younger*. I mean, that's traditional, except for the Greek gods, who were a little erratic, makin' people *old* or turnin' them into swans or pigs or whatever." He reached out and rested his right hand on Katie's left shoulder. "Think of this as an exciting, exotic vacation, Mrs. Garrison. Kick back, enjoy."

"It's *Heaven*, hon," Will said helpfully.

Katie glared at them. "Don't *patronize* me, you two!"

Michael sighed, letting his hand fall back to his side. "Mary Pat's mom says that all the time, too."

"We'll probably get along, then," Katie replied matter-of-factly, giving Michael a bright smile. "Sorry to be such a bother. Why don't you get home and get some rest, leave us to try to figure things out here?"

"You sure?"

"You bet," Will said. "None of this is your fault *or* responsibility."

"Okay," Michael said. "I'll see the kids get down here on time tomorrow. Though they're so excited, there shouldn't be any problem." He retrieved his shotgun and nodded once as he went out the door.

"Nice fellow," Will observed, grinning at his young wife.

"You're getting that *look* in your eye."

Will thought he must look sheepish, actually. "It's odd to have everything working so *well*." He held his hands up in front of his eyes. "No *glasses*."

"Nice change of subject. Why don't we have some burritos and beer out on the patio? Talk things over."

"Sure."

Five minutes later, they sat companionably close on two chaise lounges, looking up at the night sky as they nibbled and sipped.

"We can't *stay* here, Will. We *have* to go back!"

Will took her right hand his left. "Agreed. Why don't we just take it one step at a time, get the lay of the land."

"You already did that tonight."

He chuckled, and squeezed Katie's fingers. "You're right there, my dear."

"And don't you forget it, Mister Garrison."

"Promise not to."

She laid back and closed her eyes. "Good. We can start trying to find Old Man tomorrow."

CHAPTER THREE

Sometime around seven the next morning, shortly after Will's nose registered the smell of coffee, a be-robed Katie shook him awake. "Will, wake up! There's a Mariachi band out in front of the house! Guitars, singing, the works."

"What?" He strained to hear. Sure enough, spirited Spanish voices came through loud and clear over the horns, strumming, and gourd-rattling. He swung out from under the covers, planted his feet firmly on the floor, and regarded his wife dubiously. "Have you talked to them?"

"No. Get your robe on. We'll go out together. They must think we're the people who were *supposed* to be here."

Will rubbed his nose and shook his head to clear the cobwebs out. "Yeah, you're probably right." He grinned at Katie, admiring her renewed youth. "*Nice* robe, M'am."

She snorted. "Just get yours on, Mister."

"Okay." He went into the bathroom, pulled his robe off its hook, stuck his arms through the sleeves, and belted it up. "Coffee ready yet?" he asked as they went into the kitchen.

"Should be. I'll pour two cups and we'll go out."

A few minutes later, slightly fortified with a couple sips of coffee, Will held the door open for Katie, then stepped out behind her onto the porch. She'd been right, a group of five people stood next to the curb, clustered around a burro-drawn cart with 'Welcome

Wagon' lettered on its side. Two singing guitar-players, two female mariachi-shakers, and a sturdy fellow on horn. All were traditionally and colorfully-garbed, the women spinning on low heels, shaking more than their gourds. At the sight of Katie and Will, the group's eyes widened in surprise and the music subsided, the horn with a final weak "phoot."

In the following silence, the four looked at one of the guitar players, evidently the spokesman. "You are not the Rodriguez brothers," he said haltingly.

"No," Katie and Will admitted, shaking their heads. Now even the burro seemed to be staring at them in disbelief.

"You are gringos," said one of the women.

"Yes," Katie replied, nodding. "The Rodriguez' were...delayed. We were offered their house in the interim. Your playing was very nice, though. Would you like some coffee?"

The musicians exchanged more puzzled glances, then spoke animatedly amongst themselves in Spanish. Finally the spokesman turned back to Katie and Will, smiled and spread his arms widely. "It is decided. We will not waste this good food, *huevos*, *jamon*, and *refrioes*. Let us adjourn to your patio for breakfast. And, *Si*, coffee would be fine."

Taking up his guitar again, he resumed singing, a soft and probably romantic ballad this time, and strolled toward the Garrisons, each step in time to the music. The pearl buttons on his jacket and trousers flashed in the morning sun. The rest of the group followed, the horn player leading the burro and wagon as all of them walked around the house to the patio, the Garrisons in front of the little procession.

The smell of ham, eggs, and refried beans made Will's mouth water, putting him solidly on the side of the spokesman. "You okay with this?" he whispered to Katie.

"Yes, but you need to comb your hair. You've got at least three malignant cowlicks."

"I don't think they mind."

Katie giggled and patted him on the arm. "No, probably not. I'll get some carrots for the burro."

CHAPTER FOUR

The makeshift breakfast lasted over an hour, including a few Tequila toasts to the friendship of all peoples everywhere. They were seriously low on coffee as the band departed after many hugs and an invitation to any and all future performances at the Raptureville Rec Center or in Boston. The burro -- whose name was Pepito -- had exhausted the Garrison's small supply of carrots, but still seemed perky enough as it trundled away with the now mostly-empty cart. It had not brayed once.

"That was nice," Katie murmured, leaning back against Will as they watched the quintet and Pepito disappear around a curve.

"Sure was, but we need to get cleaned up and make it to the Rapture building to meet the kids."

Katie sighed and yawned. "I could just crawl back in bed and sleep for a week."

"And there's the barbecue tonight. Heaven has a hectic pace, all right."

"You *would* say that. I wonder what Boston is like?"

"C'mon. We can speculate in the shower."

* * * * *

Even though the Garrisons were a few minutes early, Mary Pat and Bobby were waiting for them. Bobby squatted quietly on his haunches, playing some kid screen game, his short tail out horizontal behind him, quivering in time to the frantic beeping from the game. Mary Pat stood quietly, apparently much less excited than the previous evening, but Will noticed her right foot tapped the ground every few seconds. He remembered going to the Rose Festival at this age, sometime after World War II, and was certain he'd been a bunch more worked-up than either of these kids. Kids now, even kids *here* he supposed, took things more for granted.

"Good morning!" Katie shouted when they were within hailing range. Bobby clicked off his game and stood, smiling his sharp-toothed grin and waving along with Mary Pat. Will wondered if the dinosaurs had needed to *learn* to smile, that the action might mean something quite different in their culture, like maybe the prequel to tearing out a throat or two. Not that many of the lesser primates didn't behave the same way.

By the time they reached the children, Mary Pat had her little backpack off and was rummaging inside it. She brought out a small shoulder bag and handed it to Katie with a flourish. "Good morning!" she said, "Here's part of your initial draw in cash. Mom transferred the rest to a new account. Debit cards in both your names are in the two wallets."

Katie took the shoulder bag. "Initial draw...?" she asked, unzipping the bag and looking inside.

"Everyone gets thirty thousand dollars when they arrive," Bobby said.

"Kids get less," Mary Pat added. "Unless they were sexually abused and have to be fostered with a family instead of just living in a school dorm. The money's held in trust for them, then."

Katie looked up, pain on her features, the bag forgotten. "Are there a lot of abused children...here?"

Mary Pat nodded, scowling for a moment. "That died at the hands of adults they trusted? Quite a few." She lifted an eyebrow at Bobby. "Wouldn't you say?"

"A dozen or so annually," the little dinosaur agreed. "All Boston -- all Cockaigne -- looks out for them, though. They *must* be cared for and salvaged. It's one of the few things Old Man and Old Woman agree on completely."

"Oh, dear," Katie said, distressed, her eyes brimming. Will put an arm around her shoulders. "Katie, this is a *good* thing," he said softly into her left ear.

"I know. It's just so *awful* that it's necessary!"

"We feel the same way," Mary Pat replied, the expression on her small features warring with her feelings of compassion and her need to get going. "Is everything in the bag? The cards? The RE-FLOAT passes?"

"RE-FLOAT?" Will asked, while Katie turned her attention back to the contents of the shoulder bag.

"Regional Floater," Bobby said. "It's how we get around the area. Low altitude anti-gravity. INTER-FLOAT connects the regions."

"If you wanted to go to Nashville to see Elvis, for example, you'd take the INTER-FLOAT," Mary Pat added.

"So he's really dead?" Will asked, chuckling.

"Definitely, but he still fills the venues," the little girl replied, shaking her dark head in amazement. "My *grandmother* goes to see him every year."

The concept of an *angel* grandmother struck Will as odd. "How old's your grandmother?"

"Over a thousand. You'd think she'd know better."

Katie had found the passes. "Still, it's *Elvis*," she remarked helpfully, as she smiled and held up the heavy cardboard rectangles. "Let's go."

The children led them around the south edge of the enormous Rapture Hall and across a short stretch of wide concrete walkway to a yellow-bordered paved rectangle a hundred feet on a side. A windsock hung from a tall pylon, fluttering fitfully. Otherwise, the day was still, except for swallows darting after insects, and the air already felt comfortably warm against Will's bare arms.

Bobby looked at his watch. "Ten minutes."

"Mrs. Cruikshank's generally early, though," Mary Pat said, shielding her eyes with one hand as she scanned the horizon.

"Mrs. *Cruikshank*?" Katie asked. "Is her first name *Barbara*, by any chance ?"

Mary Pat looked up at her, her brow furrowed briefly in thought. "I *think* so."

"Who's Barbara Cruikshank?" asked Will.

"My school bus driver when I was in grade school." Katie laughed. "But it *can't* be her!"

"We'll know in a minute," Will replied, grinning. "This must be our ride." An elongated silver ovoid, flat on the sides, but its top and bottom rounded slightly, appeared above the trees, moving gracefully toward them. The front looked like a more streamlined version of the nose of a Huey helicopter. Curved windows -- Will counted twelve on the side he could see -- extended rearward from the entry door. In the space between the door and the row of windows appeared a Blitz-Weinhard beer ad featuring two youngish-looking bearded fellows in Nineteenth Century outfits, presumably the original Blitz and Weinhard. A colorful Rose Festival banner stretched along the side of the craft below the windows, proclaiming 'The Year of the Sea-Rovers.'

"'Sea-Rovers?'" Will asked the kids.

"Pirates, mostly," Bobby replied, with his toothy grin.

"Wouldn't they be sort of rowdy?"

"They sign statements of Assured Benign Behavior," Mary Pat said. "No weapons to be used, no assaults against the civilian population."

The floater drifted down onto the landing zone, almost but not quite touching the ground. The entry hissed open, and they began walking toward the vessel. "So they can brawl barefisted amongst themselves, but not go after anyone else?" Will asked, intrigued by the idea of pirates at Rose Festival.

"A *lot* of them are Vikings," Mary Pat replied. "The *real* pirates, particularly the Asian ones, leave Vikings alone."

"There were Vikings all over the news last night," Bobby added, "but then there's a big Odinist temple in Boston."

They stepped up into the floater, and Katie gasped when she saw the driver. Or pilot, or whatever the person was called here, but a young, brunette woman wearing a blue motorman's uniform in any case. "Mrs. Cruickshank!" Katie exclaimed.

"Yes?" the woman said, smiling as she swiveled toward Katie, her eyebrows elevated.

"Do you remember me? Katie McManus. You drove our school bus."

Mrs. Cruikshank laughed, and shook her head. "I remember you as the quiet one, always with your nose in a book. Your brothers were hellions."

"They still are. Older, of course."

"Well, that was sixty years ago, or thereabouts. Right after the war." Her expression softened. "I didn't recognize you when I saw you two on the news at the floater station this morning before my shift." She extended her right hand to Will. "And you're little Katie's man. Pleased to make your acquaintance."

"You sound *just* the same," Katie said with amazed delight, as Will shook hands.

"Well, I'm *not* the same," the floater driver said, still smiling. She lifted her hands in front of her face, wiggling her fingers. "No arthritis, no lower back pain, and it doesn't take me five minutes to stand up, 'cause my knees don't hurt any more. When I look in the mirror now, I see *me*, not some old thing at the tail end of life. Plus I got my old job back, *and* without wheel bearings to overheat. I thank Old Woman and Old Man with every other breath I take."

"Sounds good, all right," Will agreed. "What was that about us being on the news?"

"Oh, they had shots of you in the Rapture Hall. Suitably censored, of course. When you arrived, it kicked on the cameras, and the techs found the discs when the weekend surveillance crew came to work this morning."

Mary Pat held up a newspaper. "Here's this morning's *Oregonian*. You can read it in your seat. You're on the front page."

"*Somebody's* eager to see the parade," Mrs. Cruikshank said, smiling maternally at the two children. Will thought she'd reach out and pinch their cheeks. Though pinching Bobby's cheeks couldn't be that easy, he figured. Mary Pat saw it coming and took a step backward, causing Mrs. Cruikshank to cackle gleefully. "One of these days, Mary Pat," she said, waggling a forefinger at the little girl, who looked about as sour as a freckle-faced tomboy could.

Will accompanied the kids to seats about midway in the body of the floater and belted up, leaving Katie to talk to the driver as the ship lifted smoothly off the pad. He unfolded the paper and looked at the front page. *TWO ACCIDENTALLY RAPTURED IN COMPUTER GLITCH*! read the bold, black headlines. *Mayor Thompson Vows Complete Investigation* stated slightly-smaller letters. If he'd had anything in his mouth, Will knew he would've blown all over the interior of the car.

"Migod!" he said, examining the *very* clear photographs of he and Katie in the altogether, with their privates tastefully obscured by cross-hatched lines. Fortunately, there were no closeups of their faces.

"The afternoon editions will probably feature the Parade," Bobby said.

"That'll be fine with me," Will replied, rapidly scanning the accompanying article, which had their names and everything about them correct.

"The Sunday paper'll have a bigger story," Mary Pat said, grinning as she looked over Will's shoulder. "They called my dad this morning. He told 'em 'no comment.'"

"Thank heaven for small favors," Will said, finishing the piece.

"Somebody from the Mayor's office'll probably be out to interview you on Monday," Mary Pat added in the same helpful, amused tone.

"Worried about lawsuits?" Will inquired.

"There aren't any practicing lawyers in Cockaigne," Bobby said. "It's one of the first rules."

Will chuckled as he thumbed absently through the rest of the paper, then folded it up. "Sounds like a good thing."

"Everybody says so," Bobby replied.

Now the floater had risen enough to give a good view of the terrain below. The gently rolling hills were heavily forested, a few small subsistence farms tucked into clearings, with what appeared to be personal floaters sitting beside the houses. Will figured they were about where Sherwood was back home, and, sure enough, in a couple of minutes they passed over Onion Flats and acre upon acre of newly-planted crops.

"I don't see any stock," he remarked, surveying the countryside.

"We only have chickens and dairy cattle," Bobby said, "and everything's organically grown."

Will nodded. "What about beef and hogs?"

"Protein generators can duplicate protoplasm," Mary Pat said, "so there's no reason to slaughter animals. People still have horses, but not much else of any size."

"The Indians hunt buffalo east of the Cascades," Bobby added helpfully. "And Pronghorn."

"Are the *animals* immortal?"

"No," both kids answered, shaking their heads. "Except *special* animals," Mary Pat said, "like Lassie and Trigger. And my grandmother has a two-hundred-year-old calico cat named Lucy."

Will smiled at her. "That sounds nice. I wouldn't mind that option with a dog I had once."

The young angel made a face. "Lucy's a demanding little shit."

"Most cats are," Will replied, laughing, "given half a chance."

Below, more and larger farms began to dominate the landscape. A tractor worked its way across a huge river bottom field where Tigard was in the real world, turning the soil into dark, gleaming rows. A long, low fieldstone farmhouse and outbuildings lay alongside the field, all looking neat and tidy in the morning sun. A half-dozen kids shot baskets on an outdoor court.

The floater swung left through the hills bordering the Willamette River, and Will caught sight of the familiar broad watercourse to the northeast. An old roadbed, nearly overgrown, cut through the forested slopes below, its slabs of abandoned concrete littered with leaves and fir needles. The remnants of a pre-floater highway, Will decided. "There's just not a lot of people here, is there?" he mused aloud. The kids didn't reply.

Then the outskirts of Boston showed ahead, buildings seeming to rear up suddenly from the Willamette's edge. Nothing over eight or ten stories, from what Will could see, and looking a bunch like the city he remembered from his childhood, the skyline almost familiar.

As they came closer to the town, Will could see the river more clearly, bridges in roughly the same places. Sellwood, Ross Island, Hawthorne, Morrison, and Broadway. The Steel bridge wasn't there, apparently not needed in the absence of railroad traffic.

The water was clogged with ships, including small freighters and what appeared to be fishing vessels, but mostly an incredible array of hulking galleons and graceful schooners, plus a few good-sized dhows and a half-dozen or so seagoing junks. Most numerous, however, were long, low Dragonships, their carven prows pointing out into the river as though ready to receive crews returned from sacking the city.

"Will you look at that!" Will exclaimed, amazed. In the front of the floater cabin, Katie and Mrs. Cruickshank chatted on, oblivious to the incredible sight.

"One of the kings of Norway, Magnus, is here," Mary Pat said, her voice breathless and her nose practically indenting the window glass as they began to descend into Boston. "That big black ship is his. *'Blood Wave*, it's called.'"

"The 'Hound' is here, too," Bobby said, with equal intensity.

"Who's the 'Hound?'" Will asked, curious. "A ship? Or some big-name pirate?"

"He's Cockaigne's greatest bounty hunter," the little dinosaur replied. Will thought he heard a touch of hero-worship in the words.

"Almost no one's ever seen him for sure," Mary Pat said. "Just the people he catches know what he looks like. He's supposed to be seven feet tall, incredibly strong, very quick and deadly, and his sword shines like the sun. No one can stand against him in battle." She seemed much less awed than her friend, however. Maybe angels were natural-born skeptics, Will thought. From what he'd heard of Old Man so far, they might have good reason.

As they passed behind the row of Viking ships, Will pointed at where Tom McCall Waterfront Park would be back home. "What do they call the park here?"

"Tom McCall Waterfront Park," Bobby replied.

"Really? Was he the governor here, too?"

"Still is," said Mary Pat. "Not that there's a lot to govern. Taxes are low, mostly for maintenance of schools, existing state buildings, and public transportation. The militia's nearly disbanded since the border skirmishes with California have trailed off. McCall oversees a peaceful state."

"Does Old Man have anything to do with government?"

Both children shook their heads. "He does his own thing," they said.

"He came to our school once," Bobby added.

Mary Pat nodded. "He has a hard time understanding kids, but Dad says he's genuinely interested. Dad thinks Old Man doesn't remember being a child, and that's why he likes to spend time with us."

"He got all choked up at our Christmas program," Bobby said.

Will couldn't decide if that made sense or not, not knowing if Christianity had any place in this society. He briefly wondered if Bobby had played one of the Wise Men. "Is Jesus here somewhere?"

"No," Mary Pat replied. "He's still alive, in the Middle East. He's a musician."

Now Will was intrigued. "What about Satan?"

Bobby shook his head. "Never existed, except as a job title in the Old Testament. We studied it at school."

"So there's no hell?"

For a few seconds, the kids stared at Will as though he had a screw loose. "No," Mary Pat said at last, with considerable finality.

As the floater descended into what seemed to be Union Station without railroad tracks, Will decided to drop the subject of religion. Besides, close to fifty other floaters sat on the landing zone, he could see crowds lining Broadway, and some of the excitement he remembered from sixty years ago welled up inside him.

CHAPTER FIVE

Like the city's skyline, the Rose Festival Parade echoed Will's childhood. The flower-bedecked floats really *did* float, but other than that easily-accepted small difference, the parade was heart-warmingly familiar. The Rainmakers, over-aged frat boys who hadn't been a feature of the festival for years, soaked themselves and some of the crowd with gleeful abandon, water cannon, and large industrial-strength squirtguns. Will remembered them getting him at least fairly wet a time or two when he was a kid.

"You're really enjoying this, aren't you?" Katie asked, seeing his nostalgic grin.

"I'm findin' I don't just *look* and *feel* like a kid again. I *am* one."

Katie took his left hand in her right, and nodded agreement. "I know what you mean. As much as I want to go home, this *is* wonderful." The float passing them at that moment carried several Rose Festival Queens from the early Twentieth Century in gowns of the period. The young women waved and smiled in the traditional manner, and Will felt perfectly content.

"Oh, boy," Bobby said, pointing from where he and Mary Pat stood in front of Will and Katie. "Here comes the South China Sea Horde!" Sure enough, three lines of burly, barefoot Asians wearing colorful pantaloons and boiled-leather jerkins marched under yellow-and-black banners, strutting and blowing kisses to the cheering crowds. At the group's end walked a large fellow with a long black queue, rhythmically beating a tall drum strapped to the back of a smaller man marching in front of him. Kids and young women -- and a few young men -- ran out of the crowd to have the pirates sign their programs. Will noticed there were no 'X' signatures. Everyone must be literate in Cockaigne, even on the South China Sea.

Next came several bands, restoring the usual Rose Festival atmosphere, then thirty or so huge and mostly blond men wearing traditional Viking garb and carrying heavy swords and axes. Proceeding the men were eight apparent cheerleaders, flipping and leaping over one another. The crowd really cut loose, whistling and shouting along with the cheers.

"This must be the Vikings, huh?" Will asked, though the cheerleaders puzzled him.

"It's the Boston State mens' football team," Mary Pat replied in a near-whisper. "Their *nickname* is 'Vikings.'"

"Oh," Will said, and Katie giggled and punched his arm.

Real Vikings came after another half-dozen floats and a couple more bands. The men were just as big as the football players, and the women only slightly smaller. Their axes and swords looked well-used and functional, with polished-over scuffs and dents in their helmets, armor, and mail.

"These look more authentic," Katie said, practically having to yell over the renewed din. Her grip on Will's hand tightened, though, and Will guessed she was thinking that this bunch could chop through the crowd in about ten seconds.

But they looked friendly enough, waving meaty hands and exposing vast expanses of muscular limbs and white teeth.

Katie bent down to the kids. "Why don't they have any scars or old wounds?"

"Everybody heals in Cockaigne," Mary Pat replied, speaking into Katie's right ear, "Unless the wound is horribly severe and they bleed out."

"Arms and legs even re-grow," Bobby added helpfully. Turning back toward the parade, he put two clawed fingers in his mouth and gave an ear-splitting whistle. One of the passing Viking women with long auburn pigtails grinned at him and flashed the peace sign.

"And to think twenty-four hours ago," Katie said to Will as she watched the powerful woman stride on, "we were having iced tea on the sunporch."

"Seems like a lifetime ago," Will replied, hooking his right arm around his wife's slender waist as a group of swarthy Arab corsairs came into view.

* * * * *

An hour after the parade, Will, Katie, and the kids stood in front of a movie theater in the central park blocks. Mary Pat and Bobby licked ice cream cones and Will read the current movie poster aloud. "'The Three Naughty Guys Go to Baghdad,' starring Benny, Nikita, and Zero." On the poster, three moderately portly young men wearing zoot suits and oversized fedoras danced arm-in-arm and side-by-side along a middle-eastern street, with what appeared to be local fez-wearing gendarmes waving billyclubs in the background. One of the police seemed to be a well-endowed woman, something probably uncommon in the real Baghdad, to Will's way of thinking, even after Saddam.

"I never imagined Khrushchev with *hair*," Katie said.

"Nobody's bald in Cockaigne," Mary Pat remarked around her ice cream cone.

"The Coming Attraction is 'The First Fleet,' with Sir Lawrence Olivier as Lochlann McQuarrie," Will said, peering at a second poster. "The settling of Australia. Even has 'Chips' Rafferty. That might be good."

Katie regarded him with complete amazement. "Will, 'Chips' Rafferty was a *terrible* actor!"

"Maybe he's gotten better," Will replied.

"Maybe when the place that never existed freezes over," Katie said, laughing.

They continued along the street, meandering around groups of people seated at sidewalk cafes. Most of the South China Sea Horde squatted on the Park's grassy expanse on the other side of the street, quietly eating pizza and talking to young women.

Suddenly, Katie clutched Will's arm, pointing to a 'Coming Attractions' board in front of a storefront ticket agency. "Look, Will, it's *Sonny and Cher*! In August."

Will frowned. "I didn't think Cher was dead."

"She's not," Mary Pat said from beside them. "Old Man and Old Woman are huge fans. They bring her up at least once a year, to reunite with Sonny."

"Then they send her *back*?" Katie asked, her gaze bright with interest.

"Yeah."

Will thought that sounded promising, even if he wouldn't mind hanging around here for a few more weeks. "So it *can* be done, like your dad said."

Mary Pat nodded, then laughed. "Well, at least if you're *Cher*."

"She never *has* had any plastic surgery," Bobby added. "She just gets younger every time she's brought up."

"She had to have her *nose* redone the first few times," Mary pat said. "Until Old Man figured out how to keep it from re-configuring."

"Because she got younger?" Katie asked.

"I guess."

Will noticed that some bluegrass group was coming to Boston next month. 'Turkey Trotsky and His Dixie Gypsies.' That seemed far-fetched. What was next? he wondered, 'The Boogie-woogie Piano of Adolf Hitler.'

That gave him another thought. "Did Hitler ever get brought up?" he asked the kids.

"Five times," Mary Pat replied. "But mobs killed him every time."

"I thought there wasn't any after-Afterlife?" Katie asked. "That's what your father told us."

The little girl just grinned and shook her head. "Old Man can be awfully stubborn when he thinks people might be redeemed."

They had just started around another sidewalk cafe seating when a loud, coarse voice boomed ahead of them. "Look, Laddies! There's one of them infernal lizards. A little 'un!"

A trio of large, unwashed, and grinning men blocked their path, dressed in traditional pirate garb, though there were no missing eyes or limbs, and no parrot on any shoulder. There were, however, Will noted, some good-sized cutlasses and modern pistols hanging from wide leather belts.

Will stepped in front of Bobby, placing his left hand on the young reptile's right shoulder. He addressed the speaker. "We don't want any trouble, Mister."

"*Will*," Katie cautioned from behind him.

The big, hairy man guffawed, and leaned forward slightly. "Who said naught about *trouble*, landlubber?"

"We just want to bounce the damned beast around," said one of the others, and all three men laughed.

All the seated diners and everyone else on the sidewalk had halted whatever they were doing and were watching intently.

"No, I don't think so," Will replied, thinking he was going to get the shit kicked out of him in about a minute.

"*Will!*" Katie repeated. Mary Pat and Bobby kept thankfully silent, though Will felt Bobby tense beneath his hand.

"I be Borkan the Mighty," said the menacing pirate, taking a step forward. "Do ye challenge me, lubber?"

As he moved toward Will, Borkan brushed aside the foot of a tall, blond kid sitting with an *Oregonian* in his hands.

"Legbiter," the young fellow said softly, looking up at the huge pirate.

"What did ye say?" Borkan growled, turning toward the speaker.

"My sword's name is 'Legbiter,'" the kid said, still in mild tones. He stood, laying down his newspaper and removing his red baseball cap. He wore shorts and a red 'Vikings Rule' T-Shirt, but nothing on his feet. One of the football players, Will guessed, tall but nowhere near as muscular as the pirate.

"I don't be carin' if yer sword's named 'Cocksucker,' Borkan replied, with a savage smile. "Do ye need a lesson, pretty boy?"

The kid shook his head. "Nay, I *give* lessons to waterborne jetsam such as you."

The pirate roared with laughter, and his comrades joined in. "Do ye, now? What be yer name? 'Teddy the Tender,' mayhap, or 'Bruce the Loose?'"

"My name is Magnus Barefoot. I am a king of Norway, and were it not for my oath taken in this fair city, your head would decorate my bow before sundown."

Behind Will, Katie gasped.

Borkan let out another roar of laughter. "*Magnus*, indeed! Everyone knows Magnus be a giant, stout and powerful, with thews of steel and blue eyes as cold as northern ice."

The kid grinned, without any warmth whatsoever. He cracked his knuckles. "My eyes *are* blue," he said, still speaking mildly. Will felt a shiver go down his spine. He sensed this Magnus, or whoever he might be, was the real deal.

"Aaar!" Borkan yelled, and swung a fist the size of a pomegranate at the kid's head.

Magnus moved casually aside, letting the fist snap past his right ear. He stepped inside the swing, and drove his own right fist deep into the pirate's midsection.

All the air left Borkan's lungs. His eyes bugged out, and he began to fold, just in time to meet Magnus' right knee with his nose, knocking him stumbling backward. Magnus shoved the collapsing pirate aside, grabbed one of the remaining men by his belt and ran him backward into the other, knocking both sprawling. He stood over them, fists cocked, daring them to rise. Both raised their hands in surrender, fear in every line of their faces. Borkan lay curled at Magnus' feet, retching and holding his gut.

"You've not lost your skills, Magnus," said a raspy baritone from Will's left.

Magnus turned toward the speaker, a dark man about Will's size, and grinned and nodded. "Hello, Setanta. I heard you were in town. Do you want this offal?"

"Do you mind?"

"Not at all. He stains the cobbles. And interrupted a fine editorial page."

The smaller man smiled and snapped his fingers. Two burly men stepped from the gathered crowd and levered Borkan to his feet. He hung from their grips, his breath still labored, dazed, with blood streaming down his face to drip on his clothing. Across the street, the South China Sea Horde stood a row, grinning appreciatively. Several waved super-sized beverages and cheered as the beaten pirate was dragged off. A black floater with a stylized grey horse's head emblazoned on its side descended to the street and Borkan was tossed unceremoniously inside.

"The usual thirty percent to the Odinist temple?" the smaller man inquired, lifting an eyebrow, and Magnus nodded. Clearly the two men had conducted business before and were well-acquainted, Will realized.

Bobby spoke up, addressing the dark man, his voice breaking slightly. "Sir, would you sign my festival program?"

"If you would, sir, mine, too," Mary Pat said, thrusting hers forward.

The man resisted tousling any hair or feathers, but he smiled as he produced a pen from his pants pocket and signed both programs after making sure of names and spelling. After handing the programs back, he gave the children two gleaming souvenir coins, and bent down to them. "I pay for tips," he told them quietly, and started to walk away after thanking Magnus again.

"Is it really you?" Bobby asked.

The dark man paused, turned back to the kids, and grinned. "Yes, I'm really me. Always have been." He walked jauntily to the black floater, waved once, and climbed aboard. The floater rose to just above the height of the buildings and sped away to the north.

"Wow!" Bobby said, his golden eyes wide.

"That *was* him," Mary Pat said. "I *know* it was."

"Who?" Katie asked.

"He is called 'The Hound,'" Magnus said as they watched the floater disappear over the rooftops. "A bounty hunter in this time and place, but once he was the most fearsome warrior in the history of humankind. Entire armies died at his hands. I have personally seen him get somewhat peeved and empty a public house or den of thieves in less time than myself and two of my best men ever could, even on a good day."

Mary Pat and Bobby looked at one another, grinning. "It *was* him," they said in unison, satisfaction in every word as they clutched their programs and coins.

"That was *Cu Chulainn*?" Katie asked. Will knew they were getting into Irish history territory, a hobby of his wife's family, especially Katie.

"Yes," Magnus replied, looking solemn. "A tormented man whose misplaced loyalty cost him his wife Emer, his son Conla, and, in the end, his life at treacherous hands. A tragic tale unmatched for sorrow. Now, however they are reunited in Ireland. He journeys away only for bounty."

"What was the horse's name?" Katie asked next. "That was the design on the side of his floater, wasn't it?" *Here we go,* Will thought.

"The Grey of Macha. The steed who carried The Hound into his final battle."

"'The Cattle Raid of Cooley,'" Katie replied.

Magnus looked impressed. "You are well-versed in Irish history. Are your people from the green isle?"

Katie nodded. Her eyes shone. "My family name is McManus."

The tall blond's mouth dropped open, his expression amazed and delighted in less than a heartbeat. "Thor's hammer!" he exclaimed, with a wide smile. "A *Mac Magnus*. You are my descendant."

Katie matched her ancestor's grin, and Will saw their obvious kinship, even after untold generations. "I think so," she replied.

Now Magnus looked thoughtful as he was introduced around. "Perhaps that was why I intervened with that floating dolt Borkan."

"Gosh," Bobby said. "This is like that show on TV, 'These Were Your Lives,' where they reunite ancestors and descendants."

Looking down at the young dinosaur, Magnus laughed. "Is it not?" he said, drawing Katie into his embrace.

"What do I call you?" she asked, her words muffled against Magnus' muscular chest. Will saw tears gathered on her eyelashes.

"I suppose it must be 'Grandfather,'" Magnus replied, sighing as he patted Katie's back. "But in truth, it is your choice." He winked at Will over the top of Katie's head.

Katie remained silent for nearly a minute, then said, with a little smile. "That'll be fine. *Grandfather*."

Releasing her, Magnus' grin included them all. "I will buy the celebratory lunch. As soon as I recover a shipmate who fancies himself a poet." He reached to the back of his chair, pulling up a sheathed sword and buckling it in place on his back, its hilt protruding over his left shoulder. Will decided this must be 'Legbiter.' Magnus set his cap back on his head, adjusted the bill, tucked his newspaper under his left arm, then nodded sharply. "Shall we?"

Will watched Bobby and Mary Pat as they started up the sidewalk, heading in the same direction they'd been going earlier. He guessed you couldn't say 'died and gone to Heaven' here, but both children seemed more than happy to be in Magnus' company. At least some neighborhood and schoolyard bragging rights. And meeting 'The Hound.' That would have to be a really big thing to any kid in this society. Those autographed programs would likely be preserved in mylar envelopes before nightfall.

In the brief time since the incident with Borkan, the street scene had returned completely to normal. Magnus led them along for a pair of blocks, chatting amiably and attracting no notice, until a sign next to the curb caught Will's attention. 'Saturday Afternoon Slam at Globes!' stated in black, block letters. 'Be you Bard, Skald, Versifier, or Creative Rhymer, be pleased to enter our Competition!' Slightly larger letters proclaimed: 'Free Beer!'

"I believe this is it," Magnus said, stopping by the sign, which repeated 'Globes' at the bottom.

"Free Beer?" Katie asked.

"A lubricant for talented expression," Magnus said, with a sly smile. "And the cover charge and food are *not* free."

"Can Mary Pat and Bobby get in?" Will asked, seeing that the windows alongside the entrance were etched with representations of the original Globe Theater in London. He peered into the well-lit interior, which looked moderately crowded.

"Of course. The beer is only an inducement. The food is generally excellent, and the literary competition is genuine."

"Huh," Will grunted. "Whose place is it?"

"Shakespeare's. It's a chain he founded. Well over a hundred sites altogether, world-wide. Very popular with the wish-to-be-cultural set. Publication for national winners."

Entering, they found themselves surrounded by cool tile floors and the faint sounds of a dulcimer.

A young woman in sandals, wearing a long smock gathered at the waist, smiled at them from behind a podium just inside the front door. "Five for the Slam?" she asked, her smile now primarily for Magnus. The smock managed to emphasize her breasts rather remarkably, Will saw, and noticed that the other female employees seemed similarly-endowed. A marketing ploy, probably. Shakespeare, he remembered, had understood commercial ventures. 'Globes' it was.

At Magnus' nod, the hostess led them between tables to a spot beside the left wall, about thirty feet from a low stage. Several people hailed Magnus as he followed behind the hostess. He smiled and nodded, but kept moving.

"Ah, Bjorn's just finishing," Magnus said while the hostess seated them and distributed menus, promising that their server would appear shortly. Will looked toward the stage, where a slim, broad-shouldered man with straight black hair closed a leather-bound notebook to light applause from the ostensible audience.

"Do 'Hebrides,' Bjorn!" someone shouted from the other side of the room. Someone else whistled, and several people stamped their feet until the floor shook.

Bjorn looked at the man next in line to read, and, when the fellow shrugged his acceptance, Bjorn cleared his throat and began chanting:

> The hungry battle-birds were filled
> In Skye with blood of foemen killed,
> And wolves on Tiree's lonely shore
> Dyed red their hairy jaws in gore...
> On Sanday's plain our shields they spy;
> From Islay smoke rose heaven-high
> Whirling up from the flashing blaze
> The king's men o'er the island raise.
> South of Kintyre the people fled
> Scared by our swords in blood dyed red,
> And our brave champion onward goes
> To meet in Man the Norsemen's foes.

"Nothing like the old hits, eh, Magnus?" asked a short, powerfully-built blond man two tables over, raising a mug to Magnus as Bjorn bowed to the clapping and cheering crowd.

"It was nine hundred years ago, in a land far, far away," Magnus said to Katie, Will, and the two children, his tone almost apologetic. "I was scarcely more than a boy." He leaned back in his chair and opened his menu, his expression briefly thoughtful, his voice soft and laden with memories. "But I was *King*."

CHAPTER SIX

Bjorn Cripplehand, whose hands were now quite whole, was Magnus' bardic skald, his verse -- like the piece they'd heard -- honoring the bloody conquests and raids of his king.

"Fairly tough crowd today," Bjorn observed cheerfully after he'd joined them and introductions had been made. The skald seemed to be a lighter heart than Magnus, but the wicked-looking short sword at his waist, along with thick wrists and large, knuckly hands, hinted at some martial prowess. He wasn't entirely a man of words, Will guessed.

Their server, honey-blonde, pretty, and also astonishingly buxom, chose that moment to appear. "*I* thought you were excellent, good sir," the young woman said, beaming at the skald.

Bjorn grinned back. "Could I interest you in a private reading? I give my best performances to small audiences of one."

"I daresay," the server replied dryly. "Let me consider your kind offer whilst your meal progresses. I should hate to neglect my appreciation of the arts, when opportunity is so boldly and generously presented."

When she had taken their orders and departed, Magnus looked at Bjorn the way a parent regards an unruly child. "Late aboard ship tonight, then?"

"One can hope, Boss," the skald replied, looking pleased with himself. "But there are more fit subjects for conversation in this company. Let's not scandalize the younglings, your new grand-daughter, and her husband."

"Are you really a *skald*?" Bobby asked, as the drinks server arrived with beer for the adults and root beer for the two children.

"Of sorts," Bjorn answered, "though not terribly skilled. Let me give you an example: 'Roses are red, and blood is, too. Give me your gold, or I'll kill you.'" As he finished, he grinned hopefully over his mug at the little dinosaur.

Both children seemed underwhelmed, and Magnus laughed. "Ever since we saw Andy Kaufman in New York last year, Bjorn essays humor at every opportunity." He leaned toward the skald. "This evening had best see better verse than that, Bjorn, or your quest for true love will fail."

The skald shrugged, momentarily less cheerful. "Can't match you for the mushy stuff, Boss. Blood and gore are my muses. You always had the better touch with the ladies."

Now Magnus looked uneasy, even blushed slightly. "Bjorn exaggerates," he assured Katie and Will.

"*I've* read some of your poetry that survived," Katie said. "I was moved by your warmth and sincerity." She rested her left hand on her ancestor's right forearm, and smiled at him.

His features coloring still more, Magnus gave Katie a weak return smile, and Bjorn chortled at his king's discomfort. "Thank you, milady," the skald said as he quit laughing, and nodded brightly to her. Then he suddenly cocked his head at Bobby and asked, "What's that in your ear?" Reaching across the table, he pulled a small gold coin from the young reptile's barely-exposed left ear. "Amazing!" Bjorn exclaimed, examining the coin carefully before tossing it back to Bobby. "Can all your folk produce gold from their orifices? If so, a worthy talent, to be sure."

Bobby stared open-mouthed at the coin, turning it this way and that between his blunt claws. Mary Pat began to giggle, and both kids regarded Bjorn with a mix of delight and open suspicion, wanting to believe but not quite able.

"Bjorn also juggles," Magnus said, his expression relieved that any interest in him had shifted to the wily skald.

"Not here, however," Bjorn replied, shaking his head. "My specialty is cutlery, and that might disturb the other diners, not to mention skewering a passerby or two." He turned in his chair and indicated the performer now reading from the low stage. "Let us do this fellow the courtesy of our attention. Perhaps he shall pin the applause-o-meter."

Not having truly heard any of Bjorn's piece, Will had no way of judging the relative merit of the current contestant, the subject of which -- humorously intended -- was the confusion and social change wrought in San Francisco by the Bringing Up of numerous victims of the AIDs epidemic. At the finish, when "the gay wave burst over Telegraph Hill, and the streets ran with a lavender thrill," the audience hooted and clapped with considerable enthusiasm.

"Did you stimulate them equally?" Magnus asked Bjorn when the crowd had quieted.

Bjorn seemed ambiguous. "Perhaps."

"What was the subject?"

"The calamitous aftermath of the tainted salt pork we took aboard in San Clemente after the Big Wave Surf Festival last year."

Magnus nodded, stroking his chin in recollection. "I remember. That food broker with the heavy beard."

"'Reasonable Richard.'"

"Tricky fellow. Perhaps unworthy of our trust. Or custom."

"Worth a brief visit at this year's festival, perhaps."

"Which might result in a better tale than the pork," Magnus replied, laughing as he explained the incident to the rest. "Practically the entire crew lay in the scuppers from San Francisco to Eureka."

"And *that* was the subject of your poetry, Bjorn?" Katie asked. "*Puke*?"

"It may have seemed more amusing in retrospect than it in fact was at the time," the skald admitted ruefully.

Their server arrived with their orders while Bjorn continued to muse. Will had the Antony and Cleopatra salad -- as opposed to a Caesar Salad, apparently -- along with a Blackfriers burger and a huge mound of Falstaff Fries.

"A lot of grub," he remarked to Katie. He looked at Katie's sandwich. "What's that?"

"An 'As You Like It' Club." She took a big bite. "Good sauce."

Will dug into his salad, which had just the right amount of anchovies, and was about half way through it when a chime sounded near the stage. The current performer looked up at the ceiling, startled, as a tall, thin fellow wearing a silk shirt, short pantaloons, and stockings which reached above his knees walked in front of the stage and then paused, smiling. "I'm sorry to interrupt this performance," he announced, "but we have an Official Sighting from Puget Sound."

He clapped his hands and a large plasma screen slid down from the ceiling.

The screen lit up, displaying the deck of what appeared to be a small fishing boat. In the foreground a stocky man with curly white hair knelt on his hands and knees over a bait-box, his back to the camera. The lens basically was shooting at the man's rear, showing an expanse of stained, probably-once-white shorts. A deep, amused voice spoke off-camera, and suddenly the man whipped around, his blue eyes wide. "*Git!*" he yelled, waving his arms and scowling ferociously. "*Shoo!*" He grabbed a nearby deck mop and swung wildly at the camera, which veered smoothly away to continue filming from a different angle. Still yelling, the man took another swing, missed again, and the unequal contest careened around the deck, knocking over chairs and slamming coolers as the camera jinked to-and-fro. A short pause allowed the viewers in the restaurant to read the front of the white- haired man's T-shirt: 'This Ain't No Three-hour Tour.'

Occasionally, glimpses of other people would appear briefly on the screen, arms or legs mostly, as they leapt away from the flailing mop-wielder and his dodging prey. One tall fellow who looked alarmingly like Abraham Lincoln got tangled in a chair and nearly went over the railing before being yanked back onto the deck by a Black man who might have been a young Martin Luther King, Jr.

Most of the rest of the people in the place were laughing and pointing at the screen, but Will could only sit there dumbfounded, totally amazed.

Finally, the mop connected with the agile camera, a glancing blow which spun their viewpoint several times before stabilizing about twenty feet off the starboard railing.

Their final view of the white-haired man showed him still scowling, waving a clenched fist and the mop as the screen went dark.

"Wow!" Bobby said, filling the silence which followed.

On the darkened screen a white-lettered message appeared: 'For a disc of this brief episode or any others from our comprehensive catalog, contact Big Guy Moments at our 800 Number. Have a valid credit card ready.' The number followed.

"That was *Him*?" Katie asked.

"It was," Magnus replied. "He's not a terribly public person at best, and he cherishes his privacy on these fishing excursions."

"The camera was flying?" Will asked, certain that no human camera person could possibly be that nimble.

"They're called Spy Eyes," Magnus said. "All the major market stations utilize them. Another product from Von Neumann and company, manufactured by Hughes Electronics."

Katie was quicker than Will to grasp the implications of what they'd just seen. "He's only a couple hundred miles away, Will! If we could get there somehow..."

60

Magnus chuckled. "We sail north toward Vancouver BC at ten o'clock Monday morning, Granddaughter. If you wish, you and your husband can be aboard. A small detour to find your potential benefactor will not harm."

"Could *we* go?" asked Mary Pat and Bobby, their grins as ingratiating as any kid's could possibly be.

CHAPTER SEVEN

Will slid into second base just under the swift stab of the Red Claw's right hand. His left foot touched the bag an instant before the softball tapped his shin.

"Cursed mammalian agility!" Bobby's father muttered under his breath, throwing the ball back to the pitcher as Will lifted himself to his feet. "Your distant ancestors were not so clever when we hunted them." His faintly-orange gular region pulsed twice, punctuating his words.

Feeling full and wishing he'd eaten less barbequed chicken before the game, Will dusted himself off, grinning up at the taller being. "I'm probably bigger than those ancestors, though."

"Much," the dinosaur admitted, "and much less fur to get caught between our teeth, as well." His own grin expanded, sharp adult fangs larger than Bobby's, his odd laughter like pool balls clicking together. "Interesting that you have come to look so much like ourselves, excepting the feathers, tail, and iridescent scales. One wonders if the hand of the creator sought perfection twice in the long history of this pummeled globe." The pool ball sound repeated.

Will kept his eyes on the next batter approaching the plate, Mary Pat's mother Siobhan, who looked like she'd attack the ball on the first pitch. "Do you believe that?"

"No. Most of the Exodus vessels, with some hundreds of thousands of our people, got safely away during the barrage. Plus, we had settlements on Luna and Mars to aid in their flight. All left the Solar system, to find new homes around Centauri. My hypothesis is that my people eventually returned and upgraded yours from some lesser primate. Genetic studies have found many commonalities far closer than the sixty-five-million-year distance."

Siobhan let the first pitch go by for a ball. Will led off a couple feet from second. "Why not simply resettle here?"

The Red Claw rotated his right fist in his glove and spat in the dust. "Why, indeed? They may have thought that their time here was over, that your ancestors deserved a shot at the gold ring. Or it may have been a business decision, canny capitalists expecting art and science specific to your species to provide a mature market of knowledge, techniques, music, and crafts." He laughed again. "Excepting paintings on velvet, one hopes."

At the plate, Siobhan let the second and third balls go by. Will saw her wrists tense, and figured the next pitch would be the one.

"You and your family didn't make the trip, I'm guessing," Will said, trying for a little distraction, in case Siobhan lined the ball in their direction.

"No. I was in charge of security for the launch site. Spinoffs from the main strike destroyed the launch facility and the final two ships. We died like mammals. "

The short conversation ended when Siobhan tagged the next pitch solidly, right down the third base line, past the third baseman's too-slow response and into the outfield. Will sprinted hard for third, instinctively knowing that Siobhan would try to stretch at least a double out of her hit.

* * * * *

Will and Katie's grandchildren had taken them to see the first X-Men movie, and Will thought that Bobby's mother, Serpent Woman, resembled the character Mystique more than a little. Her nose was more subdued, with wider nostrils, and she had no placental breasts, merely bulging chest muscles, but the similarities were there, nonetheless. After meeting her, Katie had said, "Migod, she's lovely!" and Will had agreed. At least she had on clothes, shorts and a T-shirt.

Now, however, with quite a few fangs in evidence and Mary Pat's mother by her side and in the very-focused conversation, Will felt that he and Katie were on the hotseat.

"Your grandfather has no objection to the children accompanying you?" Serpent Woman asked, tilting her head to one side and flaring her nostrils. Her feathered sagittal crest hadn't lifted, however, which Bobby had told them meant serious trouble.

"He thought there would be no certain danger," Katie replied guardedly. "Just a routine voyage up to the San Juans."

"Probably a little casting about to locate Old Man," Will added, smiling at the two women in a helpful manner.

Siobhan snorted. "On a ship full of giant drunken oafs."

Bobby's mother's golden eyes flashed, and her tail whipped back-and-forth, practically blurring. "And two children who manage to get into mischief on a daily basis even *without* the drunken oafs."

"*We'd* have some peace and quiet, though," Siobhan said, grinning conspiratorially at Serpent

Woman. "And they'd both have their cell-phones. If they get in trouble, Michael and R.C. could go pick them up on one of the company floaters."

Serpent Woman's lashing tail slowed and stopped. She stroked the side of her neck with one clawed forefinger, sending little rainbows rippling across its surface. Her expression altered, resembling Siobhan's, only with more edges. "True, true," she admitted, obviously finding the concept of brief freedom from children appealing.

"We'll do our best to keep them safe," Katie said, her tone one Will recognized from numerous excursions with their own grandchildren. "My grandfather seems quite capable and formidable," she finished.

"The children *did* say he defeated three huge pirates in a matter of seconds," Bobby's mother slowly replied. She and Siobhan traded speculative glances, and Will figured things were going the kids' way.

"We can talk about it over dessert," Siobhan decided. She took Katie's hand. "You can join us. My dear husband is coming this way with a couple of cold ones. The men can chat, and we'll eat."

"Mrs. Turteltaub made some of her fabulous ginger snaps," Serpent Woman said. "They're *addictive*."

Katie gave Will a peck on the cheek and walked off with the other two woman. Siobhan poked her husband in the ribs as they passed one another. "Kicked your butt, big guy!" she teased, referring to the game, which their side had won handily.

"Wait'll next time!" Michael retorted cheerfully, shaking his head as he handed Will an opened long-necked bottle of Blitz. "Siobhan likes to win."

"She seems to know how," Will replied, taking a pull on his beer.

"No kidding. Did they go for the kids heading north with you folks?"

"I think so. The idea of being children-free had a certain appeal."

The tall angel nodded emphatically. "A vacation, sort of. Siobhan would think that way."

"They're nice kids. Remind me of my younger grandchildren."

CHAPTER EIGHT

Monday morning came soon enough. The four voyagers gathered at the Floater stop with both sets of parents in attendance. Bobby and Mary Pat had their necessary items in medium-sized backpacks, and Will and Katie's similar packs were only somewhat larger. Siobhan and Serpent Woman checked their offspring over carefully, asking pointed questions and giving very specific instructions on decorum and behavior.

"Do as the Garrisons tell you, and bear in mind that you will be in the company of people who have a very different lifestyle from yours. Be polite and respectful to Old Man when you meet him," was the joint mothers' refrain. The male parents remained quiet until the final hugs and kisses. "Be sure and call home every evening," Michael told Mary Pat, and the Red Claw echoed him to his son.

Once they were on the Floater and headed toward Boston, the kids seemed relieved. "That went well," Bobby said, and he and Mary Pat high-fived one another.

"I thought for sure they'd be more instructful," Mary Pat said, breathing another sigh of relief.

"They probably know we'll keep a careful watch on you two," Katie told them, giving them a grandmotherly smile.

The Raptureville development fell behind the Floater and a half-hour later they arrived at the Boston terminal, dropping down into an only moderately-busy Monday morning facility.

Bidding goodbye to Mrs. Cruikshank, they climbed down to the open-air concrete waiting area.

Two people were waiting for them, a very tall, slender black woman and a shorter white man holding a 'Garrison' cardboard sign.

"We're the Garrisons," Katie told the pair, holding out her right hand. "I'm Katie and this is my husband Will, and these are Mary Pat and Bobby."

"Fisca," the black woman replied. "and this normal-looking chap is Baker. He is with the local paper, the *Oregonian*. Try not to take him too seriously, and be aware that his Spy Eye will be watching everything you say and do." As she spoke, she smiled, revealing an array of extremely white teeth.

The little recording device, beeping, lifted off Baker's left shoulder and hovered in front of Will and Katie. "Hi," it said, "I'm Sylvia, speaking to you from the Newsroom. The Eye will keep us connected during the voyage. Baker will be the person in charge, but if you're asked to say something regarding some circumstance or other, you'll be speaking with me. Since you two are the current hot news item, there will be times when your quotes will be *very* newsworthy. You both seem to be common sense people, so I expect no difficulties. Baker is experienced, to say the least, but you don't have to take his curmudgeonly tendencies too seriously. Underneath his grumpy exterior is a somewhat pleasant person. Remember that when he starts pitching a fit."

"Oh," Katie said. "Well, thank you, Sylvia. We'll try to be useful subjects. Right, Will?"

"Absolutely. As good as can be."

"Good," the newswoman replied. "We'll be speaking regularly and filming whenever Baker deems it necessary, which should be a fair amount. So, goodbye for now, and have fun." The Eye returned to Baker's shoulder and shut down.

"What is your role in all this excitement?" Will asked Fisca.

"I'm the first officer on the *Blood Wave*. I know I don't look terribly Nordic, but I've proved my worth over the years." Grinning, she indicated her leather pants and top, her lower legs encased in tall sturdy-looking boots. "I do dress for the part, though. In first life, I fought in the Arenas of the Roman Empire. I was the 'Nubian Queen.' Lived through all those exciting years, and died of old age. surrounded by family on the estate I bought with my earnings." The brilliant grin flashed wider. "And here I am."

"So it's worked out for you?"

"Definitely. I'm also the weapons officer, so when the action begins, I run the show."

"What about my grandfather?" Katie asked.

Fisca's smile morphed into a sly grin. "We confer briefly, discuss options, then the crew and I get busy. Despite the Viking lifestyle, we have some very modern weaponry, and the crewfolk are trained in its usage. It isn't all swords and axes."

"We need to get to the ship, folks," Baker said, and the Eye beeped softly.

Fisca nodded, winked at the kids, and gestured to the east, down the slightly sloping street. "Okay, then."

They walked swiftly toward the river, getting to the Park Blocks within a short time. People gave the Garrisons lingering glances and a few smiles, obviously knowing who they were. Several nodded to Baker.

"Are you an important journalist, Mister Baker?" Katie asked.

"I'm well-known, but 'important' might be stretching it some."

"C'mon," Fisca said. "You've been on the job here for decades. Lots of readers turn to 'Baker's Dozen' first thing when they open their daily newspaper."

"Good to know," the newsman admitted, but Katie and Will could tell he knew that already.

After crossing the Park Blocks, the line of ships along the river's edge showed in the distance, but there was a crowd of people milling near the shoreline.

"Well, crap," Baker said. "A religious dispute."

"Here?" Katie asked.

Without breaking stride, Fisca frowned and studied the shouting mob. "Yes, Hellions and BA-BAs. Old and occasional arguments about the nature of Cockaigne."

"Hellions and BA-BAs?" Will asked, as Katie pulled the children closer to her side.

Baker chuckled. "The Hellions believe this is Hell. The Born Again – Born Agains say this is the first step in the born-again process, and someday they will ascend to the real Heaven. These verbal tussles are common enough. Usually just yelling with minor fisticuffs, though this one seems a notch or two up from the normal melee." She shook her head. "We will simply have to deal with it, but I have some options."

At that point, some of the noisy, scuffling crowd noticed their approach. The altercation slowed. "It's The Rapture Babe!" one exclaimed, and the word spread rapidly. Things quieted down, but didn't completely stop. "The Rapture Babe" swirled through the milling group.

Now the four adults and two children were at the edge of the disturbance, Fisca's right hand on the sword hanging from her wide belt. The assorted religious zealots moved aside, but too slowly for the gladiatrix. She raised her voice and shouted: "Karl, Lars! To me!"

Two tall, heavy figures thundered down the ramp connecting the *Blood Wave* to the concrete pier. The Hellions and BA-BAs paused from both their arguments and their excitement over Katie, nearly falling over themselves to escape from the huge Vikings plowing into their ranks, shoving and slamming bodies aside.

"Ve are *hier!*" the slightly larger of their rescuers roared. Both turned toward the subdued disputants with fists raised, glowering.

"Thank you, Karl, Lars," Fisca told them, smiling gently. "Shall we continue, then?"

"Wait!" said several of the now-quiet crowd. "May we have some autographs?"

"They mean you," Baker told Katie. The Eye, already in the air, focused on her.

"Autographs?" She asked. Pens and papers were thrust at her from the nearest bodies.

"Start signing, dear," Will told her, laughing.

The autograph party took almost fifteen minutes, with Karl and Lars vetting each hopeful fan, Fisca growing more and more exasperated, Baker enjoying every minute, and the Eye recording it all.

Finally the small group ascended the gangway onto the ship. Magnus greeted them as they stepped aboard, hugging Katie, shaking hands with Will, Baker, and the children, and very obviously tickled over his first officer's frustration.

The gangway retracted into the great vessel, orders were given, and the *Blood Wave* moved slowly out into the river amid the cheers of the formerly angry zealots. Large Viking rowers manned – and womaned – the benches.

"Not what I expected today," Katie told her ancestor.

He smiled down at her. "Cockaigne is filled with strange moments, granddaughter. This will be only the first of many during our voyage, rest assured." He turned to Fisca. "Am I correct?"

She still looked sour. "Very much so, Mighty King."

Bjorn Cripplehand trotted across the deck, grinning broadly. "Maybe a bit over an hour to Varley's Isle, Boss."

"'Varley's Isle?'" Katie asked.

"Some product to pick up before heading down the Columbia to Astoria," Fisca said. "Killer Herb Varley, a former sea captain, grows some of the best marijuana in the Northwest. We pre-ordered several bales of his highest grade."

"So it's legal here?" Will asked.

Fisca scoffed. "*Everything* is legal here, Mister Garrison, except meth. It's judged too ruinous. Drugs are not terribly popular however, Cockaigne being what it is, but marijuana is a good cash crop."

"Makes sense, I guess," Will admitted, stroking his chin.

"Well, we got off to a good start," Baker said, obviously cheerful after the autograph session and the Spy Eye's documentation.

The *Blood Wave* accelerated to the north, passing under two bridges, Bjorn on the drum. Once out of sight of the Tom McCall Waterfront Park, the rowers ceased their efforts and Magnus engaged the engines.

"Was that just a customary Viking departure?" Katie asked.

"Traditional," Magnus replied. "We enter and leave a port with the rowers working, but once under weigh, the engine takes over."

"It's sure quiet," Will said.

"Around fifty percent power from good-sized Fusion Starcore engines. The *Blood Wave* could move three times this speed if needed, which hopefully won't be necessary."

"What's the fuel?"

"Starcore Fusion Pellets, from Hughes. A few bags see us through a year. Not too expensive, and we get a nice Former Royalty discount."

"This is great!" Mary Pat and Bobby chorused.

"And this is just the beginning," Bjorn told them. "Who knows what excitement awaits us ahead."

"Don't get the younglings worked up, Bjorn," Fisca cautioned, but she smiled as she spoke, more relaxed now they were safely on their way toward the Columbia River.

The Willamette slowly turned to the north before joining the larger watercourse.

"Just a few more miles," Bjorn said. "Killer Herb's operation will be on the left, a fair-sized wharf and the greenhouses and living quarters upslope from that. A very organized facility, in keeping with the product quality. Herb grows good stuff."

"The shorelines are certainly beautiful," Katie said. "Not nearly as grown-up as in our world." An occasional small floating pier jutted out into the river, few and far between amongst the almost unbroken greenery.

Another forty-five minutes and they were moving downstream on the Columbia, much broader than the Willamette.

"Coming up on our left pretty quickly," Bjorn said.

"I can see the wharf," Magnus replied, his voice suddenly concerned. "There's a decent-sized schooner there. I don't remember Herb mentioning another visitor."

"Not just any schooner, either," Fisca said. "That's our friend from San Clemente, Reasonable Richard, and his ship, the *Checkers*. He may be after our shipment, Great King."

"Perhaps you should be on the Bushmaster, then," Magnus replied, nodding in the direction of the big weapon, situated just forward of the mast.

A few long steps, the gladiatrix swung into the seat and unlimbered the Bushmaster, swinging its long barrel toward the schooner.

"That looks dangerous," Katie said, frowning as she drew the two kids closer to her.

"She knows what she's doing," Bjorn assured them. "Richard has nothing to match it. She could blow that ship out of the water in seconds."

"Will she?" Will asked.

"Not likely. If Richard has any brains at all, he'll back down, but there are a bunch of long guns on his railing, so we shall see."

"I don't see Zongo anywhere," Magnus said, shading his eyes with one big hand.

"He's around, Boss. He'll show if they try to spirit our product off the wharf."

"Who's Zongo?" Katie asked.

"A helpful native," Magnus replied, grinning. "Watch and be amazed."

The schooner had spotted the *Blood Wave*, but other than turning a few rifles toward them, didn't seem overly concerned. Hadn't twigged on the Bushmaster or realized what it was. Will figured if they knew what could happen, engines would reverse and they'd leave in haste. Instead, a medium-sized lifeboat lowered into the water, its motor started, and the small vessel headed for the dock and the stacked plastic-wrapped bales of dope.

"Take the mast, Fisca," Magnus said quietly.

The Bushmaster howled like a banshee, and simultaneously something large and furry erupted from the water next to the smaller boat and pulled one of the occupants into the river.

The heavy weapon cut through the mast in fifteen seconds. It began to topple into the Columbia, even as the men in the boat disappeared one-by-one beneath the water, long arms pulling them under.

Shouts came from the *Checkers*, engine sounds bellowed forth, and it reversed back into the main current as the mast jackknifed into the water, the schooner leaving it behind as it fled downstream toward the coast.

"That was Zongo," Bjorn said, his features satisfied. "He's very effective when he gets going."

"He's on our side, I hope," Katie said.

"Always," Bjorn replied.

CHAPTER NINE

Though something over ten feet tall, with the furred, supple body of a long-limbed otter, Zongo was clearly a primate and almost certainly human. He stood dripping on the dock, grinning as he posed for pictures with the captured flag spread across his broad chest, held in enormous webbed hands. A spaniel caught in a playful crouch adorned the checkered background of the ensign.

"Richard must have loved that little dog," Katie said.

"I remember the *Checkers* speech," Will replied. "Fifty years ago. Seems like yesterday."

"Everything does," Katie said, her gaze momentarily far away and her voice much softer. "I hope we find Old Man and convince Him to send us back."

Will put an arm around her. "If anyone can find Him, Magnus can. He may act like this is a lark, but he's one determined fella, or I miss my guess." He smiled at her. "Then it'll be up to us, my love."

Katie smiled back at him. "We'll manage just fine."

"Sure. Now we should have our pictures taken with our savior. The kids are about ready to jump out of their skins, they're so excited."

"Will that be all right?" Katie asked Bjorn, who seemed to be orchestrating the photo-op.

Bjorn laughed. "Karl told Zongo you're the Boss' grand-daughter, so we're not going to get out of here without at least a few snaps. Zongo's been in charge of the island's library for over ten years, and his attention to recording history is exacting."

"My friend Bjorn is correct," rumbled the monster, in a voice even deeper than Karl's. His large golden eyes shone brighter than the fangs in the corners of his wide mouth. "I have given some thought to composition, though Mister Baker might help in that regard. A child on each shoulder, do you think, Mister Baker?"

"Sounds fine to me," the journalist replied jauntily. He'd behaved like a kid in Macy's Santaland since they'd stepped on the dock. Will had refrained from mentioning that this first day might be tough to out-do in subsequent columns. No sense spoiling the man's fun.

Bobby and Mary Pat were duly hoisted up to Zongo's shoulders -- one hand per child -- and pictures were taken of just the three of them. The Spy Eye, which had been vectoring back and forth along the dock, stationed itself just over Bjorn's head, remaining there as Will and Katie moved to stand in front of Zongo. Even with one of the big primate's oversized hands resting on his right shoulder, Will had no trouble maintaining his smile. Virtually the entire crew of the *Blood Wave* were arrayed on the dock behind Bjorn, cameras in nearly every hand, with Karl saying "*Kaese!*" -- German for 'cheese' -- every few seconds, and the hard part was to keep the smile from turning into an outright laugh.

Somehow everything went well, then the cameras were tucked away, and it was time to load the cargo. As large as the containers were, Will was curious as to just how they'd be taken aboard the Viking ship. The ship's rail was a good ten feet above the dock.

The Norsemen's method was simplicity itself. Karl vaulted over the railing and onto the deck, and Zongo tossed the bales one-by-one up into his hands. The entire transfer took less than five minutes. Karl then jumped back down to the dock with a keg of beer under one arm and a tap in the opposite hand, and refreshments were served.

To Will's surprise, Herbert Varley proved to be quite reserved, though he dryly noted that Will and Katie were fortunate to be so photogenic, allowing -- with a sly grin to Magnus -- that Katie's ancestry might be a factor in her case.

"Old Man never ceases to amaze," Varley said, shaking his well-groomed head as he mulled aloud over the concept of the Rapture.

"The children say He just gets bored," Katie said.

The former sea-captain chuckled. "I am always amazed that children seem to understand adults far better than adults understand children." He stroked his tidy beard. "Since we were all children once, the reality is surprising."

"My mom says our minds aren't so cluttered," Mary Pat said around a bottle of Dr. Pepper, several of which had been sent down from Varleylabs for her and Bobby.

"Which makes us able to be more observant," Bobby added.

"I see," said Varley, nodding. "And Mrs. Garrison tells me you two met The Hound at Rose Festival. I have not had the pleasure. How did *he* seem?"

The kids looked at one another for a few seconds before replying. "Nice," they finally agreed.

"Yes, if one is not his quarry, I might suppose that would be true." He turned to Magnus. "Do you agree?"

"As inhuman mass killers go, I find him very pleasant," replied the King, sipping from a paper cup. "Thanks to people like Bjorn and Fisca, my exploits have, in some instances, been somewhat exaggerated. For The Hound, this is not so."

"He is as advertised, then?"

"Oh, yes."

"Fascinating."

"And you don't want to think what the media would pay to have footage of him in action," said Baker.

"A *man* with the power and prowess of a war-god," the tall horticulturist mused thoughtfully. "Something truly unusual even in this incredible place."

Will and Katie looked over at Zongo and Karl, who were playing some sort of game involving beer. Judging from the amount of beer going down, both appeared to be losing. "How about Zongo?" Katie asked. "*He's* unusual."

Varley shook his head as Magnus and the children drifted off to watch the ongoing goings-on. "Not precisely. Zongo is one of two native human species here. Cockaigne is not some special creation. It is merely an alternate Earth where our type of humanity did not develop. Zongo's people are not numerous, living in small villages along this world's watercourses. When Old Man and Old Woman set up shop here, they reached a bargain with the Riverfolk, to trade knowledge and art for tolerance."

"Knowledge and art?" asked Will.

"Opera and Theater have been surprising favorites, particularly the former. 'The Barber of Seville' with an all-Riverfolk cast was staged in Italy last year, moving from city-to-city throughout the season. Tickets were *impossible* to purchase. Former *Popes* were denied, in some instances. Alexander VI was said to be *livid* until John XXIII acquired a few from cast-members, who regard John as their own."

"My goodness," said Katie.

The former sea-captain leaned forward and lowered his voice. "Don't bring up the subject of opera near Zongo. He possesses a magnificent *basso profundo*, and will break into song at the slightest hint of request."

"That sounds interestin'," Will said, and Katie nodded agreement.

Varley's answering smile was gentle. "It is less so on a daily basis, though he has done a CD of traditional Gospel Spirituals which is most uplifting. He is an amazing person. We have petitioned Old Man to grant him immortality."

"Does He do that regularly?" Katie asked.

"There are few petitions, but most are granted."

"So Old Man and Old Woman can confer life and immortality..." Will began.

"...but they didn't actually *create* anything?" Katie finished.

Frowning, Varley considered their words for several seconds. "In past ages, they *may* have, in their former guises as powerful and worshipful beings. My understanding is that they moved beyond the need for acolytes and adoration some centuries ago, becoming both more approachable yet more reclusive." His frown deepened. "A contradiction there, I think. Most odd."

"No fireballs, lightning, or earthquakes, then?" Will asked.

The sea-captain shook his head, smiling. "Not recently, to my knowledge. Perhaps you will discover more during your travels."

"We'll ask Old Man when we see Him," Katie assured Varley, who laughed along with them at that suggestion, but Will knew she would, when the time came.

* * * * *

"You have good instincts," Fisca said, slashing at Will with her slender sword. He parried as he moved to his left on the fore-deck's exercise area, forcing her to half-step back before she could move in at him again. "Not the natural ease which your wife displayed, however," she continued in a conversational tone as she blocked his return cut, "but no panic."

"Yet," Will replied through clenched teeth, watching her dark eyes as he cross-stepped to the right. He'd read as a boy that the eyes would betray intent. Didn't seem to make much difference with Fisca, though. Half the time she seemed to be watching the circle of curious crewmen and not him, yet she still frustrated his every move.

With *Blood Wave* powering steadily down the Columbia toward the Pacific, the benches had emptied for afternoon martial arts practice, the men -- and some of the women -- stripping to their waists. Katie had practiced first, initially with her grandfather demonstrating the basics of simple swordplay, then one-on-one with the smooth and deadly Fisca. Will, Baker, and the kids had watched the gladiatrix in awed fascination as she switched hands and techniques with consummate fluid ease. Now Will was on the hot seat, but found he was having fun, despite the sweat running into his eyes and the afternoon sun glinting off Fisca's blade.

"Give me your best violence," Fisca ordered, grinning as she flipped her sword from her left to her right hand, which Will had decided was her dominant. Will gritted his teeth harder and bore in on her, to little effect. The lean black woman seemed able to read his mind, or nearly, and his attacks were met with easy blocks or empty air.

"Now I shall go on the offensive," Fisca announced as Will retreated, wiping the sweat out of his eyes with a towel Bjorn threw to him.

"Okay," Will replied. He tossed the towel aside and brought up his sword, determined not to look like a complete idiot, but knowing the probability.

She took a couple of probing swipes at him, then her gaze hardened and her moves became much more compact and quick. Will managed to deflect a pair of diagonal cuts, but about a nano-second after the second, found his sword-wrist gripped by Fisca's left hand and her sword passing a hairs-breadth from his left ribs.

"Finis," she said softly in the following frozen silence, her fiercely-grinning face inches away from his. Her nearly-black pupils held amber flecks,

Will noted, thinking that in Fisca's real world, he would now be very, very dead.

"You really did quite well for the first time," she said as the crew began to clap, releasing Will's wrist and lowering her sword. "We can have another session after a light evening meal, when we've reached Astoria." She looked at the crowd, her smile several degrees less dangerous. "Now it's Baker's turn." The crew looked at one another, searching for the journalist.

"He vas chust *hier* a moment ago," said Karl, his broad features contorted with puzzlement.

"*Baker*!" Fisca yelled.

"Yeah, yeah," Baker replied, appearing from below-decks, his voice somewhat muffled by the fencing mask he wore. An epee, heavier than the traditional foil and without a button on its end, hung from his right hand. He'd put on a long-sleeved sweatshirt, but otherwise had on the same clothes he'd worn when he met them that morning. Gro, taller by more than half-a-head, trailed grinning behind him.

Fisca's expression alternated from incredulity to amusement to delight, then repeated. "What is it you have in mind, wordsmith?" she asked.

"Took fencing in college," the columnist replied tersely. "Knew there'd be swords. Thought I might be more comfortable with something familiar."

"Top marks for ingenuity, eh, Fisca?" Magnus said cheerfully from his position in the second row of the observers. Fisca gave him a frustrated glare.

"*Mein* goodness!" exclaimed Karl. "Will that little blade not break easily?"

"Not unless I strike it at right angles," Fisca replied, regarding Baker with a cat's smile. Provided the cat had cream on its whiskers or a canary on its mind, Will thought.

The two opponents squared off in the traditional manner, Fisca emulating Baker's stance, her sword forward. The surrounding crowd moved back slightly, giving them more room to maneuver.

"I've never understood fencing," Katie said to her husband, her right hand cupped over her mouth.

"Me, neither," Will replied. "Guess we'll have to watch and learn, but I'm gonna guess that Fisca's sword is enough heavier that Baker may have an edge on speed."

In the initial exchange, however, a blur of flicks and hissing slides, no advantage for either contestant appeared. Fisca continued to smile her huntress' smile even as she countered Baker's controlled thrusts, and Baker seemed undismayed and unhurried.

"Are they feeling each other out?" Katie asked.

"Probably," Will guessed.

As if he heard them over the exclamations and surprised oaths of the crew, Baker's thrusts began to form a pattern, moving through a series, then repeating, adding an additional modification midway to confuse Fisca's response.

"Fisca will learn his ploys soon enough," Magnus said, having worked his way around the crowd to their sides, the children with him.

In the ebb and flow of the duel, another five minutes passed, bursts of speed interspersed with slower exchanges, before Fisca slipped through Baker's weaving pattern and flipped his blade away, disarming him. One of the crew snatched the epee' from the air, grabbing its hilt.

Baker stood weaponless with his arms hanging by his sides, the neck and wrists of his sweatshirt soaked with sweat, but his expression was anything but cowed. He looked as though he was nearly smiling.

"I *am* impressed," Fisca said softly, flicking sweat from her eyes. "I had thought your *wit* to be your rapier. Nothing like this."

"Thank you," Baker replied, openly grinning. "I wasn't as rusty as I thought."

The crew broke into applause while Gro massaged Baker's shoulders before leading him to the rear of the ship for a sponge bath.

"Give them ten minutes," Fisca said to Katie and Will, wiping her blade on her shirt. "Then we shall have our turn."

"Could you have ended it sooner?" Magnus asked his First Officer.

"Certes," she replied, nodding, "but he still did well. And we shall need all the internal good will we can muster if we are to prevail if and when we catch up to Reasonable Richard. Mister Baker now feels good about himself and better about me."

"Teamwork," Magnus said, chuckling. "And, you're correct, I do hope to deal with Reasonable Richard after we locate Old Man."

Will turned to look at Magnus, and over the taller man's shoulder he noticed a thin pillar of dark smoke rising almost straight up from the forested heights south of the mighty river. "Look!" he exclaimed, pointing.

"A mishap at Bulgey Wood, methinks," Fisca said.

Magnus shielded his eyes with one large hand. "So it would appear. Another battle for supremacy among the ego-burdened."

"'Bulgey Wood'?" Katie asked.

"A colony of would-be scientists and philosophers living around the shores of Lake Mee," Magnus replied. "Their nominal leader, a woman named Schwartz..."

"Whose motto seems to be: 'May the Schwartz Be With You,' Fisca interrupted.

"...and frequently," Magnus continued, laughing. "Her followers contend for her sexual favors, and occasionally jealousy rears its green head."

"Pitched battles ensue," Fisca added. "Cabins are set ablaze, and so-called great inventions and greater works of literature put to the torch, until the combatants exhaust themselves and peace regains its unsteady feet."

"Then the cycle begins anew," Magnus said.

"That doesn't seem very productive," Katie observed, frowning at the thickening smoke along the distant ridgetop.

Magnus shrugged. "Even here in Cockaigne, as you may have heard Fisca remark ere now, common sense is not always so very common."

CHAPTER TEN

Seated on the seaward veranda of the Astor House after a seven-course Salmon dinner, Will, Katie, Fisca, Magnus, and Baker sipped glasses of Oregon Reisling and watched the crew of the *Blood Wave* playing volleyball on the broad beach below the restaurant. Four long nets were strung along the sand, a vigorous game going on over each of them, with stacks of swords and shields beside each group of players. Just in case, Will supposed.

"How much longer will the trip take?" Katie asked her grandfather.

"Two days will see us around Cape Flattery, then another through the Strait of Juan de Fuca to Godsend, where Old Man generally resides. Should he not have returned from fishing, they will at least know where we can find him, or when he plans to arrive home."

"Is 'Godsend' on the mainland?" Will asked.

"No, on what you know as San Juan Island."

"Big place?"

Magnus shook his head. "A small fishing village, with his sprawling stone home on a headland overlooking the ocean."

"It's quite beautiful, however," Fisca said, pouring herself another glass of wine. "Bright, airy, with the sun and the sea seeming practically at one's fingertips."

"Where do we stop the first night?" Katie asked.

"A truly amazing place," Magnus said. "Levinsk, a colony of artisans and scholars."

"Founded by Russian Jews, the Levinskis," Fisca added, "who gathered from around the world to create one of the most tranquil and learned settlements in the history of the Afterlife. In Cockaigne, one frequently hears the phrase, 'Well, I'm no Levinski, but...'"

"Are they part of the original Russian influx into the Pacific Northwest?" Will asked.

"The founders were fur traders, yes," Magnus replied. "Led by the great Lev Levinski. When they were Brought Up, they remembered the potential of the region, and colonized what you know as Hoquiam, Washington."

Fisca leaned forward toward Will and Katie. "What the King is not saying is that if Reasonable Richard sailed north rather than south to safety in California he will go to Levinsk."

"Why?" asked Katie.

"They are shipwrights nonpareil. They could have a new mast affixed on his ship within half-a-day or less."

"Then he could be there when we get there," Baker said, with a hopeful journalist's smile. The Spy Eye, perched on his right shoulder, gave a tiny bounce of interest, and Will heard its lens whir. It grew increasingly hard not to regard the little mechanism as some sort of artificial life form, a kind of small, round, and thankfully mostly silent sidekick, beaming back pictures and information to faithful readers and viewers across Cockaigne.

Magnus shook his head. "Richard's ship has significant speed on the *Blood Wave*. Should he have gone north, we would have to catch him in Gray's Harbor before he reaches the open sea."

"Still, one can hope," Fisca said.

"Indeed," Magnus replied, and the two exchanged knowing predatory grimaces.

Hoping to direct the subject away from the usual mayhem, Katie turned to Mary Pat and Bobby and smiled warmly at them. "Well, children, are we going to have dessert?"

* * * * *

The *Blood Wave* left New Astoria in early mid-morning, after the crew completed an up-at-dawn five-mile run down the beach and back in full gear. Will had thought his lungs were going to burst, and Katie had remarked that it was hard to appreciate the scenery when all one could see was large Viking butts. Baker, of course, had agreed with her, though in less polite terms. Will was glad the kids had stayed back on the ship, helping with breakfast.

Once underway, they rounded Point Brown and entered Gray's Harbor shortly after three in the afternoon. The vista of gleaming tidewater flats and hillsides mantled with giant fir proved stunning. Rowers took their places on the benches once more, and the big dragonship sped swiftly toward the far side of the huge bay in time to Bjorn's drumming.

"There's *smoke* over Levinsk, Magnus," Fisca said, peering through her binoculars. "Take a look."

"Perhaps they've re-started the old foundry," the King said, putting the glasses to his eyes and scanning the distant shore. Will could barely even make out the town. He, Katie, Baker, and the kids crowded to the rail.

Fisca grunted and shook her head. "The foundry's up near the main gate. The smoke seems to be coming from the waterfront."

"Right," Magnus agreed, frowning. "I can see it clearly. Perhaps Richard *has* been here."

"And gave the town a few parting shots on his way out of the harbor."

Now the King seemed puzzled. "To what purpose?"

"Maybe because he's still a complete asshole," Baker put in.

Magnus grinned and turned to his First Officer. "What is it you always say, Fisca?"

"He is an evil fuck."

"Just so," the King replied, and a certain anticipation spread over his features.

* * * * *

Three-quarters of the way across the harbor, damage on the Levinsk waterfront was evident, even to the naked eye. Smoke wreathed some of the larger buildings, and fire-fighting equipment sat on the long concrete quay, thick hoses dangling down into the water. Small figures bustled about, though no streams of water arced into building fronts.

Taking his turn with the binoculars, Will saw no flames. "Any fires must have been extinguished several hours ago. Looks like they're just mopping up. There's folks going in and out of the buildings who're not wearing fire-fighting gear."

"Then Richard has certainly escaped us and reached the sea," Fisca said grimly, her jaw muscles knotting.

Baker tapped the Spy Eye on its metallic carapace. "Do you have enough of a charge to go take a look?" The little device bobbed up-and-down in assent, then flew rapidly away toward the town as Baker took a palm-sized viewer from his belt-pack and flipped it open. The screen, about the size of a postcard, lit up. Crouching down with the afternoon sun at his back, the journalist motioned the Garrisons and the two children behind him so they could see clearly. "The Eye'll go in on survey mode, over the town. That'll give us a better idea of the extent of damage."

"Neat-o!" Bobby and Mary Pat said, their eyes wide as they peered down at the screen.

"Give us an overview, then scan the waterfront," Baker instructed the Eye.

As the Eye climbed higher, Fisca appeared beside Will's left shoulder. "May I look, also?" she asked, and Will moved closer to Katie to give her room. When the town appeared in its entirety, the First Officer frowned almost immediately. "They appear to have blown the main gate on the landward side. Can we have a closer view, Baker?"

The Eye swooped down on the big gate, half of which lay flat while the other half hung diagonally from battered hinges. To Will's eyes, the high stone wall looked undamaged, however. The wall encompassed the entire settlement down to the shore, with watchtowers set along it at regular intervals, a broad graveled road leading into the forest. "Why do they need a wall that big?" Katie asked Fisca.

The tall black woman's answering smile was thin. "Remember that this is an alternate world, without destructive humanity. Zongo's people are not the only form of mega-fauna." Her lips pinched together tightly for a moment before she spoke again. "This is *bear country*. And I *hate* bears."

From the rail, Magnus laughed. "Fisca had a bad experience in the Arena with a bear. She has *not* forgotten."

"They have *Grizzlies* here?" Will asked.

"That and worse," Fisca replied. "Short-faced Bear. Larger, faster, more aggressive, almost completely carnivorous, and *very* opportunistic, alone or in groups. By now, they will have been attracted by the sounds of Richard's shelling. Some may already be within the town." She pointed down at the screen, where a heavy tracked vehicle ground along the main route through Levinsk toward the gate, accompanied by a dozen or so footsoldiers. A few other armed men and women waited at the gate. "Although the Levinskis have a mobile howitzer approaching the gate, which should effectively hold them off until repairs can be effected."

"*Bear* are that smart and aggressive?"

"These are," Fisca answered, turning to Bjorn and his drum and raising her voice. "Up the count. The sooner we arrive, the better. And the rested should be first off the ship."

"We go directly to the gate," Magnus said. "A handful on board to protect the ship." He looked down at the children. "I'm afraid you two will have to remain here until the gate is repaired and the town secured."

Both kids nodded, for once not looking disappointed at the prospect of being left behind.

* * * * *

The *Blood Wave* slid smoothly alongside the highest part of the long pier and the engine reversed to bring them to a halt. The rowers had ceased their labors a half-mile out so they could kit up, and Bjorn brought the ship in on fusion power. Heavy ropes were thrown to the dark-haired men on the pier, and the ship wound in on capstans. The moment they were snug against the dock, crewmen and -women sprang onto the concrete and thundered into the town, shields at their sides and swords at the ready.

"It's a *pretty* town," Katie said.

"*Ja*, it is most lufly, with the flower windowboxes *und* the stately elm trees," Karl rumbled as he, Katie and Will stepped off the ship, "but we must protect it from those *verdammt* monsters, for without the Levinskis, the Vorld would be a vorse place." The huge Viking looked down sharply at the Garrisons. "Your shields are correctly buckled?"

"Yes," they answered.

"Then we go. Stay close behind me. I <u>haf</u> much bear experiences."

Will didn't doubt it, but Fisca had told them the Short-faced bear weighed up to three thousand pounds and could run a steady thirty miles an hour. Even for Karl, who probably tipped the scales at over five hundred pounds, that sounded like a formidable foe. The bear didn't have a sword, however, he reminded himself.

The locals who'd tied the ship up had rapidly followed the crew in the direction of the damaged gate, and Karl, Katie, and Will jogged along behind them after saying goodbye to Bobby and Mary Pat and the few crewmembers still aboard.

"Should we be attacked," Karl said as they entered the town, "I will take the front and you two stick the *Schwanz*."

"What if the bear is female?" Katie asked innocently.

"*Mein Gott in Himmel!*" Karl replied, roaring with laughter even as his broad features flushed in embarrassment. "Not *that Schwanz*. The *correct* word. *Tail*." He continued laughing, grinning at Katie. "You did not tell me you knew German."

Now it was Katie's turn to blush. "I took two years in college. I guess I still remember the naughty things." She glared at Will as they crossed the first cobble-stoned intersection. "You, Mister, will not say a *word*!"

Will shook his head, winking up at Karl. "Not me, M'am. I'm just loaded for bear here."

They paused at each cross-street for Karl to scan their surroundings. After the third or fourth time, the big man hefted his sword and said grimly, "Perhaps good fortune is ours today. But if Richard's sappers blew the gate during the shelling, the gate explosion would have been covered by those sounds. *Und* if the city folk pulled their people from the watchtowers to fight the fires *before* the gate went down...then maybe we have problems."

A hundred feet into the next long block, a gaily-painted steel garbage can rolled out from a narrow alleyway to their left and wobbled to a halt in the middle of the street. Bright gouges marred the colorful beach scene depicted on the can, and loud grunts of something feeding came from the alley.

"Shields up," Karl said quietly, not looking at the Garrisons. "Take a firm grip. I will go first, one of you on each side just behind me. *Und* try not to be killed. Our *Koenig* would be most displeased."

Will and Katie had only a second to exchange a brief glance before the giant bear erupted from the alleyway and launched itself snarling at the trio. An instant's impression of a broad, flat, fanged head registered as he and Katie sprang by the charging monster, one on either side.

Roaring even louder than the bear, holding his sword in both hands high over his head, Karl smashed the flat of the blade on top of the bear's skull, slamming the beast to the cobbles. Then, before the bear could recover, he scooped up the garbage can and jammed it over the creature's wide head, wedging it onto the thick neck.

"Now I *haf* you!" the tall Viking yelled, hammering the end of the garbage can with his shield, forcing the bear to retreat even as it clawed at the heavy can.

"Do not attack it," Karl shouted breathlessly as he forced the frantic animal backward up the street past the astounded Garrisons. Muscles stood out on his thick legs, and the cleats on his boots rasped on the stone surface. "Now it is frightened, but pain would enrage it. *Hier*, grab the handles. Help me push! It is nearly too much for me."

The bear made sounds like a giant hog, amplified by the confining garbage can. Coupled with Karl's roars, the noise filled the street and reverberated off the walls of the rowhouses and shuttered businesses lining their route.

When he had a good grip on the left handle, his hands and face only inches away from the blind flailing of a clawed front paw as large as a pizza pan, Will gasped, "Why not just kill it?"

"*Nein*," Karl grunted, shaking his head as he strained to hold the can in place while the bear scooted rapidly rearward. "They keep down the mastodons and forest bison, which can become a nuisance." He continued beating the end of the can. "Push harder! The gate is not far."

Will occasionally caught glimpses of Katie around Karl's bulk as they proceeded up the street at close to a full-on trot. Her eyes were narrowed with determination, her fingers white on the sturdy handle they gripped. Once or twice he saw her bend her helmeted head away from a wildly swinging paw.

Just when Will thought his legs would give out any second, he saw the gate ahead, surrounded by the open-mouthed crew of the 'Blood Wave' and a dozen or so equally astonished Levinskis. The crowd parted as they forced the bear around the right side of the mobile howitzer. "Let go now!" Karl shouted to the Garrisons. He planted his shield against Will's side of the garbage can and shoved the bear around to face the open country on the other side of the gate. Then he swung his right leg in a wide arc and kicked the enormous animal's rump. "*Los*! Run free, little forest creature!"

With a final loud, echoing squeal, the bear sprinted off, weaving slightly, still blinded by the can. Panting, bent over, his hands on his knees, Will saw that it ran without the waddling gait of most bear, more like a monstrous wolverine. It dislodged the can a hundred yards or so into its flight, paused briefly to shake its dark head, then accelerated away to disappear into the denser timber.

Laughing with relief, Karl put his arms around the Garrisons and hugged them until Will thought his ribs would snap. "*Lieber Gott!*" the big man said to Magnus and the assembled crew, grinning widely, "They both were magnificent!"

"Are you uninjured?" Magnus asked, frowning as he stepped closer and examined the three of them.

Will and Katie could only nod from within Karl's confining embrace, their lungs too compressed to exhale. "Karl...could...you...let...go?" Katie managed to get out.

"Oh, *ja*, sure," Karl replied, releasing them, his smile broadening still further. "Sorry."

"We're fine, Grandfather," Katie said, as she and Will slowly straightened up, flexing the kinks out of their shoulders and backs. Will's ribs creaked.

"Jeez, and I thought *yesterday* was going to be the highlight of the trip," Baker said from atop the mobile howitzer, beaming down at them. "The Eye got it all, I think."

As the journalist spoke, the little device dropped out of the sky to hover in front of Will and Katie, and Sylvia's voice asked, "How about a quote for the listeners and readers?"

Katie mopped sweat from her blond bangs with her right hand and grinned at the Eye. "How about a dry towel and a cold beer?"

"I'll second that," Will said, trying to look less exhausted than he felt, glad he could lean unobtrusively against his wife.

Sylvia chuckled and asked, "Weren't you terribly frightened? That bear was monstrous."

Katie removed her helmet and shook her head. "We didn't have time. Karl needed our help. He could have been hurt."

In the moment of stunned silence that followed her words, the crew began to laugh, the volume swiftly growing until it drowned out Sylvia's next question.

When the laughter subsided to a few muffled guffaws, Katie said, "Maybe that wasn't a good answer."

"*Nein*," Karl said, holding out one long, beefy arm. "I *haf* a *scratch* on my wrist." He scowled ferociously at his shipmates. "It could *haf* been *much* worse without the *Koenig's* fearless grand-daughter and her brave husband!"

Will had never seen so many people try to stifle laughter in his life.

CHAPTER ELEVEN

When the gate had been re-hung to the exacting standards of Levinsk workmanship and the *Blood Wave's* crew had passed through the local baths, a feast of thanksgiving was held on the concrete terrace in front of the Great Hall of Levinsk. Various Levinski elders made short speeches, including a Rabbi, and a string quartet played classical pieces as the meal progressed.

"This is certainly the *quietest* meal we've had with the crew," Katie said, surveying the crowded tables around theirs, each table about equally divided between locals and Vikings. Subdued conversation and laughter floated over the terrace. It seemed normal and civilized. If one's eyes were closed.

"It is always thus with the Norse," said their host, Jason Levinski, as he dipped a piece of thick-crust bread into his soup. "Polite and soft-spoken to a fault. Though I have heard in battle their behavior is less restrained."

"Oh, yeah," Mary Pat said, "and you should see them on the *ship*."

"Truly?" Levinski's eyes were a dark, soulful brown, deep and intelligent. As he spoke, his neatly-trimmed beard bounced with amusement. "In any event, the arrival of your ship proved very timely with regard to the safety of our community, and I understand the entire episode will be on the evening news."

"What do *you* do here, Mister Levinski?" Katie asked.

"I am a naturalist, just now specializing in raptors."

"Birds?" Will asked.

"Yes. Usually I am in the field observing, but for the next few weeks I will be here in town, correlating my notes on the Golden Eagle, which should occupy one small segment of a book my colleagues and I are putting together for publication next year."

"Are the species the same here?" asked Katie.

"Roughly. There are small differences in the familiar species of which we know, and more species in total. Mankind might as well not exist in this world for all its effect on the wildlife, so this is a paradise for those such as myself." Levinski's symmetrical features colored slightly with enthusiasm as he talked, and his eyes danced. "I must confess, though, that my true joy in my work is the months spent in the out-of-doors, a food fabricator and mini-computer in my backpack, a walking staff in my hand, and my dog, Daniel, at my side."

Will could picture that. "Sounds like heaven. Where's Daniel now?"

The naturalist looked at his watch. "Probably sleeping, or possibly watching 'Lassie.' Rud Weatherwax and the original dog remain popular, although the pool of children capable of playing the role of Lassie's human companion is quite small. In the current series, Jack Elam has the part of Uncle Charlie, while the child is a preternaturally-cute blonde girl named Melinda."

As Levinski finished speaking, a gong sounded loudly from the direction of the Great Hall, and a voice announced the beginning of the evening news from Boston.

"Oh, boy," Baker said. "Here we go, Gro!"

The tall, lanky woman put her right arm around the journalist's shoulders, and murmured into his left ear so softly that Will barely heard her, "Whichever of us has the most screen time gets to be on top, my dearest wordsmith." The music booming out of the big screen on the side of the Great Hall prevented Will from hearing Baker's spluttered reply.

"That's lovely music," Katie said, as the screen showed the 'Blood Wave' setting sail from Astoria, the morning sun glinting off swords, shields, and helmets as the dragonship headed out to sea.

Levinski nodded. "It's Bach. He does work for commercials, travelogues, and nature films. Mr. Baker's employers must have great faith in the viability of your mission. Bach is spendy."

Five minutes worth of scenes from the previous day's journey flickered swiftly over the screen as large black letters appeared: 'The Raptured.' Katie and Will's smiling faces formed behind the letters, which gradually faded away as the announcer's deep, mellow voice described today's events, beginning with John Jacob Astor seeing them off at the Astoria Quay and finishing with their encounter with the giant bear.

"I didn't realize the Eye was *behind* us when the bear came out of the alley," Katie said, fifteen minutes into the program.

"Or how *big* the bear was," Will replied, wincing as the huge animal's claws narrowly missed ripping open his head.

"The camera's programs position it perfectly for maximum effect," Levinski stated, shaking his head as the bear was forced backward toward the gate.

"That's one *crazy* Viking." He smiled at Will and Katie. "And you two went along with him."

"We didn't have time to think," Katie answered.

"Good point," the naturalist said, smiling and nodding.

"He knew what he was doing," Will said, as, on the screen, Karl kicked the bear in the rear and it sped off.

Levinski continued to chuckle as Katie's and Will's faces re-formed on the side of the Great Hall, and the announcer asked, "What will tomorrow bring for our intrepid travellers? And what of *this* man?" Reasonable Richard's blue-jowled features glowered out at them. "A simple provender and outfitter suddenly turned Scourge of the High Seas. Will his reign of terror be brought to an end?" The 'Blood Wave' was shown at dockside, provisions being carried aboard. "Tomorrow the quest goes on!"

"What do *you* do about the bears and other predators when you're out in the wild, Mister Levinski?" Katie asked, her own bear experience clearly refreshed by the news clip.

"I have learned to climb both rapidly and well," the naturalist admitted. "And I have weaponry and sufficient ammunition."

"What about Daniel?" asked Will.

"Daniel weighs two hundred and fifty pounds and has the disposition of a mean drunk. He knows when to fight and when to run. So far he's survived handily."

"A useful companion," Will said.

"He's saved me more times than I can count," Levinski said, with a wide, unaffected smile.

* * * * *

Sunset had dwindled to a faint orange glow on the western horizon when Will and Katie strolled hand-in-hand along the promenade above the Levinsk sea-wall. Tall Norfolk pine set beside the cobblestone walkway whispered softly in the gentle sea breeze off the harbor.

"This is *so* peaceful, Will," Katie said, leaning against him as they walked.

"And me here with the 'Rapture Babe.'"

"You could go the rest of both our lives without bringing *that* up."

He kissed her cheek. "Gotta stay in character. But I'll admit spending more time here has a lot of appeal. Baker says their historical archives are so complete they replicate most of the information in the Great Library of Alexandria."

"I was thinking more of evenings like this," Katie replied, turning to face him, slowly pacing backward. She clasped both hands behind Will's neck, and they paused to share a long kiss.

Time passed, a minute or two, then both of them became aware of an intermittent rather liquid sound just slightly louder than the susurrus of wind in the trees.

"Is that some kind of nightbird?" Katie asked.

"Dunno," Will replied. "Maybe we should meander over and take a look."

Still holding hands, Katie and Will walked slowly in the direction of the sound.

"It's coming from behind that low stone wall," Katie said, pointing with her free hand.

They stopped ten feet from the wall. "Everything okay over there?" Will asked. The sound had acquired a certain familiarity.

"Will," Katie cautioned, "it might be an *animal*!"

"Oh, I'm sure it is," Will replied, grinning.

"Go *away*!" came a male voice from behind the wall, practically hissing.

"*Baker*?" Katie said. "Is that you?"

"Go away!" the voice repeated.

"Findin' any nightcrawlers?" Will asked innocently.

"Just one so far," said a feminine voice, giggling. "A small one."

"*Ha-ha*!" Baker said. "Everybody's a comedian."

"We'll just keep walking, then," Katie said, giggling herself, her left hand pressed over her mouth in case she lost it completely.

"You do that," the journalist replied.

"This gonna be in your column?" Will asked, as he and Katie strolled away. Baker didn't reply beyond a low muttered growl. The initial sound which had caught their attention, however, didn't resume again until Katie and Will were quite some distance away.

* * * * *

Morning found a low fog bank covering the harbor entrance, even though the rising sun warmed the rowers as the 'Blood Wave' stroked for the open sea and the route north. Standing beside Will, Katie, and the children, Fisca regarded the looming fog speculatively, stroking her delicately-cleft chin. "North or south, which direction did Richard sail?"

"Why would he go north from Astoria, except for Levinsk?" Katie asked.

"Good thinking," Fisca admitted. "So you believe he would now sail south?"

"What else?" asked Will.

"How to predict a megalomaniac, then. What appears to us as dirt-common sense may not matter one whit to Reasonable Richard. He may not have access to television, and thus not view the nightly spectacle of your sacred quest, but *'Checkers'* will have radio communication." Fisca shook her head. "We cannot know what he knows, and certainly not what takes place in his cunning and demented brain, but we did not see him as we approached the harbor from the south, yet he had reached the ocean, so we may have chased him north without realizing."

"He afraid of Magnus?" Will asked.

"Certes," Fisca replied, her eyes half-lidded with anticipation. "Excepting The Hound, and Old Man and Old Woman themselves, *everyone* fears Magnus Barefoot. Richard, however, did us less harm than we him, so he may let a desire for revenge skew his reasoning."

"He's done *that* before," Katie said.

"Until now, however, he has maintained a low profile in San Clemente, buying and selling drygoods and provisions." The tall black woman peered off into the fog again. "From whence comes this change? Somehow, I'll wager, Arnald Almaric has convinced Richard to undertake some vile evil." A slow smile formed on her lips. "I wonder what it could be?"

* * * * *

They broke out of the fogbank just before noon. A low skiff of pale grey clouds remained off their port bow, barely above the horizon, perhaps promising rain later in the day, but otherwise the sky was gloriously clear as the monster Dragonship churned powerfully north.

Fisca had held weapons practice while the ship was still fogbound, declaring that the cooler weather would make their work less strenuous. Now, after sluicing off the sweat and briefly drying in the warm sunshine, Will and Katie sat on the deck near the starboard rail, carefully cleaning and oiling their weaponry. The children were with Bjorn.

"Baker's certainly been quiet this morning," Katie observed, forcing a line of oil into the tang of her sword. As she worked, she suppressed a full-on smile, and Will felt his own lips curve up in response. He knew what his wife was thinking. At least on this issue.

"He did okay at practice, but he might be a smidge tired, I suppose."

Then a long shadow fell across the deck, and a barefoot Gro hunkered down to squat in front of them, laughing softly. "He *should* be tired, don't you think?" she asked, her grinning features recalling every blonde pig-tailed, freckled urchin Will had ever seen. Provided said urchin topped six feet by several inches and handled a sword as though she was born with one in her callused hands.

"I hope we didn't embarrass him too much," Katie replied.

Gro reproduced the giggle they'd heard last evening from the other side of the stone wall. "He'll survive. He doesn't like people to think he's susceptible to mundane urges which give such joy to the rest of us. It isn't *professional*!"

Katie nodded swift agreement. "He tries *so* hard to be stuffy and opinionated about nearly everything, but he has a good heart." She glanced at Will. "Don't you think?"

Will sheathed his sword, laid the weapon beside him on the deck, and thought for a few moments. "Oh, yeah. He just needs to be generically grumpy and oppositional for a while. Gives him time to consider. He's been pretty chipper about the stories for his column and the rest of the media, though. Gettin' away from his desk at the newspaper has probably done him a world of good." He smiled at Gro. "You haven't hurt him, either."

The big woman looked briefly sheepish, then shrugged. "Warrior's work doesn't feed all the soul. We must connect with one another or risk losing our humanity. That's why I asked Baker for advice about a web-log I'm doing for our voyage." Her white-toothed smile flashed. "And it worked! He's been most helpful."

"Your web sounds the same as ours," Katie said. "Do you have satellites?"

Gro nodded. "Put into orbit by Hughes anti-gravity ships."

"You must have space travel, then," Will said.

"Colonies on the Moon and Mars. H.G. Wells even lives on Mars. I've been to both places. The Moon's only real draw is the low gravity and the view of Earth, but Mars is lovely beyond belief, and now that the atmosphere is getting thicker, the sunsets are breathtaking."

"The atmosphere is getting thicker?" Katie asked.

"Particularly in the valleys, of course, part of the reconstruction. Old Woman Brought Up some Martians and they led us to the ruins and the atmosphere machines. Von Neumann's people jumped on those with both feet and hands. A destination resort. Money to be made."

"A vanished race given back their world." Katie said, her eyes shining. "What do the Martians look like?"

"Dark-skinned, very tall. Human, though no one's discovered how they got there. Their creation myths are somewhat vague. They're rather Asian-looking, no body hair except on the crotch, and the men are, shall we say, *quite* something." Her wide grin left no doubt what the 'something' was.

"Do you think it's because of the low gravity?" Katie asked, arching an eyebrow at Will, who did his best to look put-upon.

Gro laughed. "One doesn't ask about such things. One merely accepts the offered gift and celebrates the giving."

* * * * *

By late afternoon, approaching the mouth of the Sooes River, where they planned to anchor for the night, fog closed in again on the 'Blood Wave.' Fisca turned on the sonar to aid the GPS, and the ship continued at the same pace. All five of the travelers stood behind the tall black woman and studied the GPS screen.

"Anybody live around here?" Will asked Fisca, seeing the dark line of the river emptying into the Pacific near the top of the screen.

"Some indigenous peoples, native tribesmen who have embraced the land and lore of their ancestors. They still have modern conveniences, however, and prosper through cultural trade with other similar groups throughout the world. Just now, I believe they entertain several dozen primitives from northern Europe who longed to experience life gleaning the plentiful bounty of the sea."

"Like a summer camp?" Katie asked.

"Exactly," Fisca replied. "Days afloat with spear and net. Stringing shells on plaited cord, brewing potent native drink, and learning rituals undreamed of in their former lives."

"Will we get to see anything?" Mary Pat asked, and Bobby looked hopeful.

"Certes," Fisca said. "Magnus and I know the guests' leader of old. He will doubtless welcome a chance to renew acquaintance and come aboard this evening, along with the Native chief, a powerful shamaness named Mary Thunder Elk. Which thought reminds me..." She raised her head and shouted toward the vessel's stern. "Lars! Time for the horn."

When they were nearly at the mouth of the river, and Will felt the spreading outflow pressing against the hull of the dragonship, one of the men who'd accompanied Karl during their confrontation with the Hellians and the BA-BAs went to the vessel's prow carrying a large, long brass horn. After briefly inspecting the instrument, he took a deep breath and blew. A low, mournful note echoed away through the fog, then repeated.

"Probably hear that for miles," Will observed.

"On a clear day, close to five," Fisca replied, "and with the fog, twice that distance."

As Lars continued to sound the horn at fifteen second intervals, about half the full complement of rowers took their places, and the 'Blood Wave' began to swing directly into the river's current, heading upstream. "Can we go watch Lars?" the children asked.

"Of course," Fisca said, beaming down at them. "Lars will likely even let you blow. He has adaptors for different-sized mouths. Take the biggest breaths you can imagine." They scampered eagerly off.

"Did you have children?" Katie asked Fisca.

The tall black woman's eyes seemed to dwell inward for a few moments, and her smile softened. "A daughter and two sons. They led unremarkable but good lives, with me in my retirement, managing the family's lands, but were not Brought Up. My irritating grandmother was, however, as was a great-grandson who became a successful Legionnaire. They reside in New Rome."

"What percentage of humanity are Brought Up?" Will asked.

"Overall, less than one percent. And, as you have doubtless heard, many died a second and final time in the lawless years before the Twentieth Century. Old Man and Old Woman Bring Up the interesting and vibrant, who are not necessarily the peaceful and meek. As Cockaigne became more culturally-deep, however, the new arrivals were less violent individuals, and the death rate fell. With increased technology and freedom from want, societal calm has become the norm."

"Except for people like Reasonable Richard," Katie said.

Fisca's smile changed again, barely turning up at its corners. "Whose existence provides occupation for such as Magnus, myself, and our fellow crew-men and -women."

"And the 'Hound,'" Will added.

"Setanta is a special case, I believe," Fisca replied. "One of Old Man's early personas was the Daghda, the Chief of the Tuatha De Dannan. Cu Chulainn's father was purportedly divine, thus explaining his supernatural nature and his superhuman prowess in battle. One may speculate a possible connection between the great god and the great warrior."

"The 'Hound' that good, huh?" Will said, recalling Magnus' words at their first meeting.

"He is the ultimate human weapon. Single-handed, he destroyed entire armies."

"But not here," Katie said.

Fisca shook her head. "No. Here he has been relatively sedate. Occasionally, when his identity becomes known, someone will challenge him, but the ending is always the same."

"What about guns?" Will asked. "He just shrug bullets off, too?"

"I have not seen him shot. Magnus has. Setanta only became more irritated, with the usual result. Magnus said there was no visible injury to the 'Hound' when the brief exchange was over."

When neither of the Garrisons responded to her statement, Fisca asked: "Can you hear the drums in the distance? We are approaching the village."

* * * * *

Giant Tiki torches illuminated the floating dock on the river's north shore, flickering haloes outlining the flames and the tall, thick totem poles standing in silent vigil behind the torches. A crowd of milling humanity jammed the pier, most waving vigorously and shouting as the 'Blood Wave' slid to a halt. Many wore fur capes adorned with colorful feathers and beads, or cedar bark coats and hats, but few of them seemed even close to the size of the Vikings.

"There are a lot of blonds and red-heads," Katie remarked.

"Those are the Europeans," Fisca replied, grinning widely. "Their leader is approaching with the vast shamaness." She pointed to a tall, powerfully-built woman and a short, squat, blond man moving through the crowd, the woman breaking path for her smaller companion.

By the time the pair reached the water's edge, a wide gangway had been lashed to the dragonship's side, and the two slowly mounted it.

"Let us greet them officially," Magnus suggested, smiling and taking Katie's arm as he strode to the ship's end of the gangway. "Mary expects it, and Oog will find it amusing."

"*Oog?*" Will asked, standing just behind his wife.

"His real name is 'Morning Flower Petal,'" Fisca replied, laughing, "but he feels his adopted name gives him more recognition in societies which tell caveman jokes."

"This is so cool," Mary Pat and Bobby said together, their eyes wide at the spectacle on the dock.

"He's a *caveman?*" Katie asked.

"That and more," Magnus said as the big woman and much smaller man stepped onto the 'Blood Wave's' deck. "Mary! he shouted, embracing the dark-skinned woman, who was nearly his height and broader.

"Magnus, Great King," she replied in a warm contralto voice as they hugged. "It has been much, much too long since you and yours graced our lodges." She turned to the stocky blond man at her side, bowing graciously. "And here is the illustrious Oog, famed throughout the civilized world, as well as the less civilized."

"Hotcha, hotcha, hotcha," said Oog, snapping the fingers of one hand and doing a little two-step, his wide features radiating modest innocence. Beneath beetling brows, his bright, blue eyes danced. "Magnus, my man!" As he shook the king's hand, Oog's fur cape parted enough to reveal a white T-shirt displaying the message, 'Proud To Be Primitive.' Seeing the surprised expressions on the Garrisons' faces, Fisca put a hand beside her mouth and softly said to them, "Neanderthal."

"This is so *cool*," the children repeated, their eyes even bigger.

"And here are The Raptured," Mary Thunder Elk said, looking Will and Katie up-and-down as she paused for a moment, hands on hips, before taking their hands in hers and embracing them each in turn, Katie first.

"Boy, gotta get me one of them DVDs of your arrival," Oog said as he pumped Katie's hand. He shook his crewcut head and winked up at her. "For only twenty-three chromosome pairs, you're a real looker."

Katie laughed. "Thank you, Mister Oog."

"Hey, just 'Oog.' Our people don't stand on ceremony." He shook hands with Will, then turned to Bobby and Mary Pat, spreading his arms wide. "Somebody shorter'n me! That's *good*! Come give your Uncle Oog a hug!"

The children readily complied, while Katie and Will exchanged amazed glances.

"One wonders how they ever went extinct," Fisca observed, a gentle smile flowing onto her full lips.

"He always like this?" Will asked, watching the stocky Neanderthal with the kids. The man was built like an oak stump, with heavy shoulders, enormously muscular arms, and outsized hands and feet.

The Gladiatrix nodded. "Mostly, yes, as are the rest of his people. In the right cause, however, they are fearsome warriors, combative and stubborn unto death. You can imagine the havoc Oog could create with an axe, and their dexterity with such weaponry is impressive."

Mary Thunder Elk folded her arms over her chest and regarded Oog and the children with a fond and maternal smile. Will suspected she did that a lot, and wondered if Old Woman might not resemble this large yet infinitely gracious lady. If not, she should, he decided.

As he had that thought, Mary turned to Magnus with a coy smile. "Is my great friend Karl not with you this trip?"

Will craned his neck and looked over the shoulders of the closest crew members. No sign of Karl, but, being reserved by nature, he must be near the back of the group.

Before Magnus could reply, Karl's booming voice came from behind his shipmates. "*Ja*, I am *hier, Liebling*!" A considerable commotion ensued as the big man struggled through the ranks and people shifted aside to give him passage.

Magnus began to smile even wider and Katie giggled. "I think we just found out something about Karl."

"Gives the story a human interest angle," Baker said from behind the Garrisons, as the monster Viking and Mary Thunder Elk embraced, with the Spy Eye hovering just over their heads. "Today's been a little quiet in comparison to the first two."

Oog, who'd moved close to Katie and Will to give Karl more room, turned to Baker. "Tomorrow might be more excitin.' We were out fishing late yesterday, just after sunset, when this big schooner comes stormin' by between our dugout and the shore, headin' north. Damn near swamped us. Had to be your pal, Richard."

"The best news of the day, then," Fisca said, practically purring.

"Guy's a butthead," Oog replied, scowling. "We took a little vote last night after supper, decided if you folks headed after Richard on your way to see Old Man, we'd tag along for back-up."

Fisca's brow furrowed in thought for several long moments, her gaze contemplative. Then she began to laugh. "It may be strenuous. Have you plentiful Root?"

The Neanderthal gave her a fearsome smile, baring large incisors. "You <u>betcha</u>."

"What's 'Root?'" Katie asked.

"Super-duper cave person energy snack," Oog replied, winking at them. "Never dive into the deep shit without it."

Before the Garrisons could question the Neanderthal further, Mary Thunder Elk gestured to the ramp and said, "Let us continue our conversations ashore. Mother Ocean has been kind to the children of man today, and we shall feast on her largesse tonight."

An impromptu procession wound off the ship, over the wharf, and up a broad cobblestone path. Beyond the gentle rise lay a cluster of lodges set in a grassy clearing hemmed by old growth fir. The fog, thinner here away from the water, still lent an otherworldly cast to everything, like looking through a lightly frosted lens. Until they drew closer to the lodges, the trees' height and massive trunks made the buildings appear neat and compact. Nearer, however, the fog thinned even more, and their perspective changed. The lodges were revealed to be nearly gymnasium-sized, constructed of Red cedar logs milled flat on two sides and notched at their ends, fitted together so precisely that the joins were difficult to pick out.

"They're majestic," Katie said, somewhat breathlessly, as they walked between two lines of the bulky structures, each fronted by a single colorful totem pole depicting salmon, eagles, bear, wolves, and the occasional portly beaver.

The main lodge, larger even than the others, sported three taller totems, two to the right of the open entrance, and a much bigger one on the left topped with a winged Thunderbird.

"Is this going to be another whopper of a meal?" Will asked Fisca. "Seems like every day ends with a real chowdown."

"They're only being hospitable, Will," Katie admonished, before Fisca could respond.

"It is more than that," Fisca added. "Magnus is known for righting wrongs with great zeal and attention to detail, and the crew are large, loveable oafs capable of enthusiastically punishing considerable numbers of miscreants in very short order. In a word, we are *appreciated*."

"That makes sense," Will agreed, watching the kids ahead of them, walking beside Oog, hanging on his every word.

"How did Mary Thunder Elk get her name, I wonder?" Katie asked, as the Shamaness and Magnus drew closer to the entrance of the main lodge. "Do you know, Fisca?"

The former Gladiatrix threw back her head and laughed loudly. "Oh, yes, indeed. A few minutes after coming into this world, cleaned and wrapped in swaddling furs, she was laid in the loving arms of her parents. In the profound silence of that sacred moment, gazing up at the faces above her wreathed with looks of fond adoration, Mary gave a resounding fart!"

CHAPTER TWELVE

When the *Blood Wave* rounded Cape Flattery the next morning, Katie glanced back at the three large dugout canoes trailing them, each filled with burly blond figures paddling steadily. "Should we be going slower so they can keep up?" she asked Magnus.

The King shook his head. "No, they would sense our reduction in speed and begin shouting to either go faster or pull over and let them by. They are proud of their strength and stamina, not without reason."

"Do we *need* them with us?" Will asked.

"It cannot hurt. I feel Richard lurks somewhere ahead along our route. This is why Fisca sits at the Bushmaster, why we have no rowers on the benches. Oog's plan is to keep us between his boats and the *Checkers*, should we flush out Richard. Then, while Fisca and their gunners exchange fire, the canoes, low in the water and difficult to target, will swoop in and attack. *I* would not want Oog and his people swarming over *our* rails with their axes. Unless he is completely mad, Richard has to feel the same."

"But they have only axes," Katie said, her brow furrowed. Will knew she was concerned about the Neanderthals' safety.

"Each of them carries an automatic pistol, a stout club, and a sharp knife. On a deck, among enemies, they are the equal of anyone and far better than the riff-raff attracted to Richard's promises of easy plunder."

"That makes me feel better for them," Katie said, visibly relaxing.

"What about Arnald Almaric?" Will asked Magnus.

The King massaged his neck with one thick-fingered hand, his expression mildly perplexed. "Aye, *there's* the unknown. As Fisca has told you, Richard has been content in San Clemente for the long years since being Brought Up. Now, perhaps at Almaric's urgings, he ventures into the sea lanes, seeking something. But what?"

"Maybe Almaric just wants to talk to Old Man," Will suggested.

"No, the misguided fool is truly holier-than-thou, even holier than a partially-retired god, at least in his own mind. Almaric purportedly views Old Man as something of a fraud or imposter."

"Don't you think that's a mistake?" Katie asked.

Magnus shrugged. "So little is known about the motives of these men, any speculation means little. *I* believe Old Man is no different than he has ever been. Challenge him and he is capable of massive reprisals. He has only stepped away from the use of power. He has not abandoned it. We shall see."

"Does Richard have any allies who'd be this far north?"

The King smiled down at his many-times-removed granddaughter. "An astute question. My blood truly runs in your veins, my dear. Did either of you notice two men wearing sunglasses and dark clothing standing with Richard on the deck of the *Checkers*?"

Katie looked at her husband. Will shook his head. "No, I don't think so," she finally said.

"Ah," Magnus replied, his grin widening to sharklike proportions. "That is because they were *not there*. In my experience, these men, who served Richard so ably during his lifetime, are never far from their former master. Since they were not aboard ship with Richard and Almaric, they must be elsewhere."

"San Clemente, maybe?" Will offered.

"Possibly, but that distance is too great for their comfort, I would opine."

"So they could be up here somewhere?" Katie asked.

"A myriad of estuaries, bays, and islands dot the passage to Puget Sound. Any one -- or two -- could hide vessels capable of attacking us with speed and maneuverability we cannot match. The Bushmaster might provide more firepower..."

"And I have an almost infinite amount of ammunition, I might point out," Fisca called cheerfully from her seat behind the powerful weapon, thirty feet away. Clearly she'd been listening to their conversation.

"...but our methods of warfare -- up close and personal -- still must involve being ashore or on a deck with room to swing an axe or a sword, or throw a short spear. The *Blood Wave* is armored against all but the heaviest weaponry available on Cockaigne, yet were an enemy to stand off and rake the deck with automatic fire, our response would of necessity be limited to the Bushmaster and a handful of .50 caliber sniping rifles."

"How long until we reach Godsend?" Will asked.

"Four or five hours. Old Man resides on what you call Pile Point on the southwestern shore of the island, just above False Bay, so our route is a gentle northerly curve.

"How close to Vancouver Island will we be?"

"A mile or two offshore. Any attack will likely come from that source, before we swing north around Victoria. Here the Strait is wide and the shoreline free from hidden places. There is a different tale."

"What about the U.S. side?"

The King shook his head. "We will be ten miles distant. Far for an undetected assault over water."

"I don't like the waiting, Grandfather," Katie said, hugging herself.

Magnus smiled down at her. "Patience is a virtue, my dear." His smile grew grim. "As is massive retaliation."

* * * * *

Three hours later, the Neanderthal dugouts clustered together on the starboard side of the *Blood Wave*, hopefully unseen by observers on the northern shore. Lines secured them to one another and the dragonship, alert crewmen with waiting blades at each end. Other crewmen scanned the forested bulk of Vancouver Island with binoculars, and Fisca sat relaxed and waiting behind the Bushmaster.

"How you holding up?" Will asked the tall gladiatrix. He and Katie stood beside her, with Baker and Bjorn midway on the port side of the ship, watching the Spy Eye's field of vision on the journalist's laptop. The kids were belowdecks.

"When we are completely past Victoria, then I shall judge us safe," Fisca replied, looking down at them. "Not until then. We are directly north of Port Angeles now. They must strike soon or lose the moment."

"Will there be traffic in the harbour?" Katie asked.

"Certes, cloaking any strike at us for a time."

"Something black and low coming west out from the harbour, moving slowly," Baker called out from the rail.

"Ah," Fisca said, with an anticipatory grin. "Prepare to drop to the deck when I give the word," she told the Garrisons as she swung the Bushmaster's barrel toward the shore.

"Another ship coming up behind and to port!" shouted one of the stern observers.

"These will be Richard's former aides, I suspect," Fisca said. "One on each vessel. Odin grant I send them to their final deaths."

"They're speeding up!" Baker yelled. Will could scarcely hear him over the crew's scrambling for weapons. After a moment's pause, the newsman continued. "Some kind of armored Cigarette boats. *Really* fast!"

One squat, beetle-like shape could be seen in the distance, skimming over the water, a high rooster-tail plume behind it. The masts and main cabin prevented Will and Katie from any view of the second boat to the west.

A puff of smoke suddenly appeared above the vessel coming at them from the harbour, followed a few seconds later by a dull explosion.

"Mortar," Fisca growled.

"How are they going to get a range on us?" Will asked.

"If they fire every few seconds, each blast will simply walk nearer as they close on us. Eventually, they'll either hit us or come near enough to have our range."

"Turn into them, Lars!" Magnus shouted, 'Legbiter' held defiantly over his head.

Solid 'thunks' came from the starboard rail, as the lines linking *Blood Wave* to the dugouts were cut away.

A shrill whistling fell out of the sky behind them, the mortar shell exploding astern, throwing up a geyser of water.

"Full Power!" bellowed Magnus. Impossibly, the monster ship accelerated, rising at the bow, slanting straight at the oncoming enemy vessel, snipers settling in behind shields, preparing to fire.

From off the starboard side, the Neanderthals began to chant loudly: "Root! Root! Root!" Despite the Dragonship's steadily increasing speed, they didn't seem to be falling back.

"Get down!" Fisca said, and fired to the west at the second black ship, short bursts that nearly deafened Will and Katie.

"I'm going to see to the children," Katie shouted into Will's right ear, then ran bent over toward the rear of the ship.

"Help with the ammunition at the bow," Fisca told Will between bursts. "You can't do me any good here."

As he sprinted in a crouch to join the snipers, Will caught a glimpse of Fisca's foe still speeding toward them, slaloming slightly now to make targeting difficult. A second glance showed Baker and Bjorn seated with their backs to the port rail, intent on the laptop, ignoring the developing battle around them.

Another mortar round detonated well behind the ship. The Neanderthals continued to chant.

Will slid to a halt between two of the snipers, both men nearer his and Bjorn's size. "How can I help?"

"Keep the magazines filled," the man on Will's left replied. Two bulky opened ammo boxes sat in front of Will, tucked up against the base of the railing, gleaming rows of shells up to the rims of the boxes.

"How many rounds?"

"Eleven. These are Barrett Model 82A1 semi-automatics. We can't penetrate their armor, but if we put a few through their view ports and into their upper decks, that'll discourage 'em."

Will looked around them. Six snipers, including two women, knelt at their stations, ready to fire between armored panels bolted to the rails and deck. Each had two additional magazines lying beside them, but, even so, he was going to be hopping. He took a deep breath and tried to compose himself.

"Commence firing!" Magnus roared from right behind Will. The heavy Barretts crashed as one, then settled into a ragged pattern of a shot apiece every ten seconds or so.

The first empty magazine clattered to the deck on Will's right, and he scuttled on all fours to grab it. It took a good half-minute to re-fill the magazine, and by then, another empty was ready. Seconds later, two more hit the planking.

The battle became a blur of cartridges and magazines, the only other constants being the booming rifles, the steady howl of Fisca's Bushmaster, Magnus' shouts, and the rhythmic chanting of the Neanderthals. Occasional enemy bursts slashed through the air above their position, or clanged loudly into the armor around them. Will, lacking the time to think about any of it or even feel any fear, just tried to maintain his footing on the increasingly sweat-slippery deck and keep the snipers supplied with fresh ammo.

Then Fisca gave a triumphant yell, and a massive explosion rolled over the foredeck from the left, nearly knocking Will off his feet. Seconds later, something heavy smashed into the port side of the hull. The *Blood Wave* shuddered for an instant, then shook off whatever had struck them and surged forward.

Oog's people stopped chanting. Will heard the brief crackle of small-arms fire followed by horrific screams, the sounds swiftly dropping behind them.

The man on Will's right snapped a fresh magazine into his weapon and chuckled wistfully. "The Cavies are havin' fun now, you bet. Lucky little devils!"

The renewed roar of the Bushmaster, firing forward toward the other enemy vessel, drowned out any response Will could've made, but he remembered the wicked axes the Neanderthals carried and felt a shiver go down his spine.

Then an empty magazine hit the deck to Will's left and he got busy again.

Will had scarcely filled that magazine and slid it to his left when the sniper on that side said, "Now we've got her. Fisca's breached her hull." Behind them, Magnus raised his voice: "Pour it to her, lads and lasses! We'll send 'em off to Hel!"

"Please keep your sword down and out of my line of fire, O Great King!" Fisca yelled between bursts, laughing, and Will heard Magnus grumble in response.

The snipers shut down and peered around the armored panels. Will joined them.

The enemy vessel, black and streamlined, lay dead in the water two hundred yards away, at a forty-five degree angle to the *Blood Wave*, listing slightly. A thin curl of smoke rose from the rear of the low cabin. There was no sign of life. A lone corpse hung limply in harness behind a heavy machine gun mounted to the rear and above the cabin.

Magnus regarded the disabled Cigarette boat in silence for a few moments. "It appears to be settling in the water. Wait five minutes to be certain, then we decide to board or not."

"If anyone lives, boss," Bjorn said, "they'll have to fight, parlay, or swim for it." He and Baker had joined the king, Will, and the snipers at the prow of the Dragonship. The remainder of the crew were slowly appearing from belowdecks and out from under the rowing benches.

"Aye," Magnus agreed. "When Oog and his jolly band are finished with the first vessel, their thoughts and conclusions shall guide our actions."

"I can have the Spy Eye reconnoiter," Baker suggested.

Magnus nodded. "Good thought, Scribe. Keep your device well away from the vessel, however. There may be timed explosives on board, and your employers can neither afford the expense of the mechanism's loss, nor we its invaluable services."

"Sure," Baker replied, swiftly tapping instructions on his keyboard, and the Spy Eye soared to the north, curving back toward the south and hovering to survey the disabled Cigarette boat from opposite their viewpoint.

"Pretty quiet," the journalist said slowly, his gaze on the laptop screen as the robot camera scanned the enemy craft. "No sign of life."

"Then we wait for Oog," Magnus said.

Their wait wasn't long. Within three minutes of Katie and the children's rejoining them, two crewmen hoisted the grinning, dripping Neanderthal over the shieldwall on the port side of the *Blood Wave*. Oog stamped his feet heavily as he approached them, jarring water from his clothing and hair. "Hadta wash the blood off," he announced cheerfully.

"How many on the vessel?" Magnus asked.

"Five accounted for. Number six had SCUBA gear, got away."

"Richard's minion."

"Musta been. Left behind a seabag with a classy dark suit, nice shoes, and a coupla pair of sunglasses inside."

"Then the other has likely escaped also," the king replied, taking a deep breath and releasing it. "I see

132

no purpose in examining the second vessel. Let it sink. It may be booby-trapped."

"But not with real boobies, I'm guessin'," Oog said, his grin widening.

Magnus raised an eyebrow at the shorter man. "The *bird*?"

"No, the..." Oog paused, catching sight of the children and Katie. "Uhh, yeah, the *bird*," he finished lamely, looking sheepish.

"Then it's off to Godsend!" Magnus boomed, clapping the chagrined Neanderthal on the back as the second cigarette boat slipped beneath the waves.

When the dugouts were securely lashed to the dragonship, their journey recommenced, and shortly after that, Will caught the odor of cooking meat coming from the direction of the Neanderthal vessels.

"Oh, that smells *good*!" Katie exclaimed, then stopped, looking at Will, her features both puzzled and suspicious. "You don't suppose..?"

"Best not to ask," Will replied.

CHAPTER THIRTEEN

We are going to see a god, Will reminded himself as he, Katie, Baker, and the children followed Magnus, Fisca, and Oog up a seemingly endless series of broad, stone steps curving toward the top of the headland. Two dozen of the crew walked behind them in the bright sunshine, Bjorn and Gro in the lead. A large cloudbank had shrouded the interior of Vancouver Island as they docked next to Old Man's fishing boat, but here, out in the Sound, the weather was clear, though tiny puddles in the hollows of most of the steps indicated recent rainfall, and the moss between the massive trees dripped.

"A week ago, this would have been a real workout," Katie remarked as they trudged steadily upward, and Will agreed.

"Welcome to Cockaigne," Fisca said, smiling over her shoulder at them, her mood much lighter now that she'd shot up Richard's support vessels and killed a few people.

"Race you to the top, Mary Pat!" Bobby said suddenly, swatting her on her right arm.

Without replying, the young angel sprinted off. Bobby tore after her, his short tail sticking straight out behind him as the pair flew up the steps to disappear around the curve.

"Kids," Oog said, shaking his heavy head, but he smiled as he spoke.

"Spare me," Baker added sourly.

"Those children *adore* you, Mister Baker," Katie admonished.

"Yeah, well, they're good kids," Baker admitted. "I'm just a little down, is all." He'd been muttering about their quest being nearly over, which would bring him back to his desk job in Boston, and the thought seemed to mark a return to the mood he'd shown at their first meeting.

"Allay your fears, good wordsmith," Magnus said companionably. "I shall ask Old Man to authorize our pursuit of Richard, thereby lengthening your task. The timeline for our delivery of Killer Herb's product in Vancouver is somewhat flexible."

"Fame," Fisca said, grinning as she nudged Baker with an elbow. "Maybe even a book deal!"

"*And* more time with me," Gro said, stepping up behind the newsman and pinching him on the rear.

Baker jumped, covering his butt with both hands. "Stop that! It's undignified!"

Gro pulled one of his hands loose and pinched him again. Baker scampered up a few steps to escape, and Katie began to giggle.

"You're not gonna win this one, Baker," Will advised the spluttering columnist.

"Sometimes I really wonder how you people ever became the dominant species," Oog put in.

No one seemed to have a response for that remark, and in the following stillness, what sounded like cursing floated down to them from the crest of the headland. The words weren't loud enough yet to discern individually, but the anger in them was clear.

"My goodness," Katie said, her expression worried. "I hope the children didn't provoke that."

"No," Magnus replied. "One doesn't simply walk in on Old Man. He has handlers. But that is certainly his voice."

"Boy, he sounds really pissed!" Oog said.

"Perhaps some difficulty," Magnus said, his eyes narrowing as he drew 'Legbiter' hissing from its sheath. "Perhaps *Richard*! Let us hasten." He charged up the steps, Fisca beside him, with Oog, Will, Katie, and Baker on their heels, and the rest of the crew a few steps behind.

They reached the ridgetop in less than two minutes, and slowed to a walk on the concrete path, scarcely out-of-breath. There was no sign of anyone, even the kids. The shouting was clearer now, but Will couldn't understand it. It seemed to be coming from a low stone building visible through the trees, perched right at the edge of the headland.

Oog saw Will's confusion. "Pre-exists the Gift of Tongues. Even I get only about every third word. He just said something about jamming a tuber up someone's fundiment. I think."

"Many of the very early religions involve gathered plants or crops," Fisca added by way of explanation. "The gods of fertility and harvest are invoked. No one knows exactly when Old Man became involved with creation, or even if he had anything to do with it directly."

"Doesn't *he* know?" Katie asked, as they quick-stepped toward the distant building.

"Vague early memories only," Fisca replied. "Similar to what most of us recall from just past infancy."

"He told me once -- the beginning of his memory -- he remembered cave paintings," Magnus said, his sword back in its sheath for the moment.

They drew closer to the slate-roofed building, and a grassy sward appeared beyond the northwest edge of the structure. Twenty-foot-wide stone steps led from the building to the walkway. A man wearing black robes rested on the steps, animatedly conversing with Mary Pat and Bobby. They appeared to be enjoying themselves.

"There's a man who knows how to talk to kids," Will told Katie, as the children's laughter drifted to them.

"Jonathon Elbunn, the Vicar of Skyppenbirg," Fisca said. "Old Man's Major Domo, for all intents and purposes. Or perhaps facilities manager and secretary. Old Man is not good with his time."

"Old Man is really angry over something, and this priest is entertaining two children?" Katie asked.

"The Vicar will doubtless explain," Magnus replied, his narrowed blue gaze roving guardedly over the terrain. "Nothing appears terribly amiss."

"Two gold pieces say you're wrong," Fisca said.

"Ah, Magnus, Fisca!" the priest exclaimed, bouncing to his feet and striding to them. "And most of the crew! The children said you'd be here momentarily." Not much taller than Oog, he pumped Magnus's hand with great vigor and obvious delight. "Just the people we need to solve our dilemma," he told Fisca as he took her hand.

"What?" Fisca asked.

"They've taken Jape."

"*Who's* taken Jape?"

"Richard. He and his crew came ashore while I was in the village purchasing bread and fresh vegetables. Some locals saw them coming and going. Old Man was fishing on the other side of the island. Jape was recording his Saturday night radio program when I left. My hypothesis is that Jape finished his work, strolled outside, and was spirited off. They thought, of course, that he was Old Man."

"Who's Jape?" Katie asked.

"Old Man employs several doubles. Jape was here during the most recent extended fishing expedition. He's quite convincing." The priest frowned. "Too much so, apparently."

"So they think they have Old Man?" Will asked.

"Yes." Though he'd answered both Will and Katie's questions, Elbunn now seemed to notice them for the first time. "Ah, the Raptured. The famous Garrisons. My apologies for not realizing. The nightly chronicles of your quest have been most entertaining, most entertaining indeed. May I shake your hands by way of congratulation for your excellent ratings?"

"Of course," Katie replied, stepping forward with Will. The Spy Eye dropped out of the sky to hover behind the priest, scrupulously recording.

"You've worked unscripted?" the Vicar asked as they shook. "If so, it's wonderfully well done." In the background, the shouting continued, somewhat less stridently, Will thought.

"Spontaneity seems best, don't you think?" Katie replied.

"Always," Elbunn agreed, "as with Old Man's current state. His outrage seems to be abating, however. Initially, I truly thought he might Manifest, he was so upset. We always have to re-decorate when that occurs."

"I've heard tales," Fisca said.

The Vicar shook his head. "It's quite a stirring sight when the stained glass blows out from the window frames."

"Not today," boomed a resonant bass voice from the vaulted entry. "What a fool I was to authorize Bringing Up that disgusting pissant!"

"*Which* disgusting pissant?" Elbunn inquired innocently, turning toward the shorts-and-T-shirt-clad figure striding purposefully toward them on sandaled feet.

"*Almaric*!" Old Man exclaimed, his broad tanned features still flushed with anger as he approached. "Richard only agreed to go along with him in hopes of attaining more power. He tires of San Clemente. Almaric wishes to discredit me, Old Woman, and the entire belief structure of Cockaigne. That I can deal with, but they've kidnapped Jape." He paused on the bottom step, looking momentarily chagrined as his blue gaze studied them. He pointed at them in turn with a thick index finger. "Good to see you, Magnus, Fisca. Good columns lately, Baker. Putting on a little weight, there, Oog."

"Too much protein," the Neanderthal replied. "We had a little dust-up out in the Sound." Behind them, Will heard the Dragonship crew grunt approval.

140

Old Man regarded them all appraisingly for a moment before stepping forward and taking Will and Katie's hands in his. "I'm truly sorry for your being Brought Up in such an untidy and untimely manner. When this sorry business with Richard is over, I shall send you back to your earthly lives."

"We really haven't minded," Katie said, not the least taken aback by having her hands held by a god. "It's been fun."

"But...the *bear*," Old Man said, looking incredulous as he released their hands.

"Karl would *never* have let anything happen to us," Katie replied.

"I...see." He looked around at the assembled Vikings for a moment, his brow furrowed. Will thought he could practically *hear* the crew grin.

"It's sort of like going to summer camp," Will said.

Old Man nodded thoughtfully, stroking his beard between one thumb and forefinger. "I'm sure you're only putting brave faces on your circumstance." He turned to the Vicar. "Jonathon, would you call down to the village and have a meal sent up? We can save the bread and veggies until the morrow. Get a head count. If needs be, I can multiply a few things."

"Just so long as the incident with the pizza doesn't repeat," the Vicar muttered under his breath as he disappeared into the building.

* * * * *

One thing Cockaigne possessed in abundance, Will decided, were beautiful sunsets. A giant fan of streaked gold stood above the western cloud mass, backlighting Old Man as he attempted to explain why he didn't want to directly involve himself with bringing down Almaric and Reasonable Richard. "I do not wish to ascribe that level of importance to their actions."

"Almaric may say your lack of reprisal shows lack of power, the implication being that you *cannot* strike back at them in a traditional Judeo-Christian manner," Magnus said, taking a swallow from the longneck bottle of Olympia in his right hand.

In the following silence, Old Man appeared to consider the thought for a long moment. The crew had gone back to the ship to prepare for tomorrow, leaving Oog, Magnus, Baker, Fisca, Katie, and Will with Old Man to formulate a plan of action. The children and Jonathon Elbunn played hopscotch on the flagging in front of Godsend, the Vicar holding up the hem of his robes and skipping nimbly over the chalked design.

Sighing finally, Old Man nodded agreement. "Or that I am too cowardly, or too unsure of my powers after these long years."

"They might *wish* that," Fisca said in a low, dangerous voice. "They can only hope, great Lord, that you will not personally pursue them. Even Almaric, madman though he may be, knows in his heart of hearts you *can*. Grant their wish. Remain here. Send *us* to do your bidding and rescue Jape."

"When they are subdued," said Magnus, "and Jape is free, you come down from on high to render final judgement."

"'News at Eleven,'" Oog said cheerily.

Old Man let out another, deeper sigh. "All right," he said resignedly, before turning to Baker. "Can you spin that?"

"Easily," the columnist replied. "'Benign God Deigns To Punish Evil-doers, Hopes For Their Repentance.'"

"'Requests Non-denominational Prayer From Populace,'" said Oog.

They all turned to stare incredulously at the squat Neanderthal. "*What?*" Old Man said finally, thick hands on his hips.

"Forget it," Oog replied, shrugging. "It don't compute anyhow. Who would they pray to?"

Old Man glowered down at Oog. "Nobody likes a smartass."

"How about another beer, Your Benevolence?" Oog said hopefully.

CHAPTER FOURTEEN

"This is like one of them 'Quest' things, ain't it," Oog said, surveying their little group as they stood on the beach of Cadboro Bay, on the eastern shore of Vancouver Island. The longboat which landed them was already halfway back to the *Blood Wave*. Will could see crew lining the Dragonship's rail two hundred yards offshore, Magnus and Fisca standing out from the others on deck in their tense postures and crossed arms.

"We need a wizard," Katie replied, laughing.

"*Herr* Baker is a wizard with words," Karl rumbled happily as he shouldered a huge pack loaded with provisions for their trek across Saanich Peninsula to the inlet of the same name where the *Checkers* was believed to be anchored.

"And we're the halflings," Bobby and Mary Pat chorused.

"Just so long as Katie and I didn't beam down with the wrong color jerseys," Will said as he and Katie adjusted the straps on their own packs.

"I hate to sound optimistic," Baker said, looking up at the Spy Eye hovering fifteen feet overhead, "but the timber's so thick they're going to have a hard time spotting us if we use any reasonable amount of caution."

"And your little peeper don't accidentally send anything back to your newspaper," Oog said, popping the quick-release on his pack and stepping forward, axe at the ready as the pack dropped to the ground behind him. "How'd that look, Karl?" he asked the massive Viking. "Quick enough, you think?"

"Very *schnell*," Karl said, nodding his helmeted head in approval. "You vill take them off at the knees."

"We're ready," Gro said, brushing down her long skirt. She, Katie, and Mary Pat all wore dresses, adding to the hoped-for illusion of a simple Norse family pursuing a leisurely journey to the Vancouver Moot on Mid-Summer's Night. "Who knows some good marching songs?" she asked, grinning brightly at her companions.

"*Gut* idea!" Karl enthused, clapping his large hands, startling a small covey of quail which regarded them from up the beach's grassy border. The pudgy little birds turned tail and scuttled swiftly into the undergrowth.

"No marching songs!" Baker and Oog shouted in unison.

* * * * *

Ragged cloud cover lay over the island when they set off into the interior on a wide game trail, the sun fitfully visible to the east, but within an hour a light mist began to fall. The travellers donned waxed cotton ponchos and slogged on into the gloomy timbered depths.

"Good thing it's warm," Baker observed. "This could get depressing if it was wet *and* cold." The Spy Eye, squatting atop his pack, chirped as if in reply.

"*That* certainly sounded optimistic," Katie said, smiling over at the journalist.

"It's me," said Gro, elbowing Baker in the ribs, earning a dirty look. She and Karl, with their long legs, could have easily out-distanced the rest, but had allowed the children to set the pace, much of which had so far involved interactions with frogs and salamanders.

"Ve are making good time," Karl said, examining his wrist GPS. "Elk Lake is just to the south, through the trees. By full nightfall we should be in the hills overlooking Hagan Bight."

"What made this trail?" Will asked, looking up into the green dripping canopy above them.

"Anything that wanted to," Oog replied. "Bison, pigs, the occasional migrating mastodon family."

"*Und* the Liddle People," Karl added.

"Oh, yeah, I forgot about *them*," said Oog. "Mean little farts."

"'Little People?'" Katie asked incredulously. "Is there no end to weirdness in this place? What are 'Little People?' Leprechauns?"

"Menehunes," Karl replied. "But *Herr* Oog exaggerates. They are no worse than *Herr* Baker."

"Hey, now!" Baker objected.

"Damn territorial, you gotta agree," said Oog.

"How small are they?"

"Three feet or less. Call themselves the 'Floresians.' Serious attitude problems, an' stronger than shit. Travel in packs of several dozen, real good with knives, just swarm their prey. Ya don't wanta piss 'em off."

"My *goodness*!" Katie exclaimed.

"In their defense, they *haf* a strong sense of justice," said Karl. "Innocent travelers need not fear."

As Karl finished speaking, a large clearing appeared before them, and the dark waters of Elk Lake shone dully to their left under leaden skies. The trail curved to the right around the borders of a reedy marsh.

Simultaneously, Will saw a dim light in the clouds to the west. "That's not the sun," he said, pointing.

"A *floater*," Gro growled, glaring up into the murk.

"Back to the trees!" Karl shouted, waving his huge arms.

Will grabbed Bobby, Katie scooped up Mary Pat, and they ran for it. Oog passed them, accelerating, as they re-entered the forest, his stubby legs blurring.

"Find a log!" yelled Gro, swinging in to their rear. They dove for cover, Karl huddling by a giant root wad, the others seeking shelter behind a downed snag.

"They'll have infra-red-capable tracking systems," Gro snarled from beside Will, frustration clear in each word.

A deafening chain gun opened up seconds later, ripping long chunks of cedar bark from the nearest trunks. Pieces showered down around them, heavy branches crashing to the forest floor. Oog muttered a steady torrent of curses in between bursts.

After five minutes which seemed to last forever, the firing stopped. A deep infra-hum slowly traversed the clearing, passing over their hiding places.

"Come to earth and die now, please Odin," muttered Gro, fingering the hilt of her sword, her smile a rictus of frustration and anger.

The humming passed overhead again, then disappeared away to the west.

They waited another fifteen minutes before cautiously peering over the torn-up top of the snag. The stink of gunpowder and smoldering duff permeated the humid air.

"God *damn* it!" said Baker, slamming his right fist into the mangled snag.

"You okay?" Will asked.

"I'm *fine*. But we can't *broadcast* this."

"Yet," said Oog, hefting his axe. For once, he looked deadly serious, his blue eyes angry.

"Bastits," a soft high voice said from somewhere behind them.

"Bastits," another voice repeated, away to their left. It seemed to echo among the trees around the clearing as other throats took up the call. "Bastits, bastits, bastits."

"The Liddle People," Karl said, turning to face the forest, his face wreathed in a broad smile. He raised his arms in welcome. "Every<u>vun</u> look happy. Or maybe *ve* all die today."

CHAPTER FIFTEEN

The rest of the company turned to face a seemingly empty wall of towering trunks and dense understory. Will strained to see something -- anything -- human, but couldn't.

Then, suddenly, they seemed to materialize from the undergrowth, tiny compact furred men and women with determined expressions on their small features. Dozens of pairs of deepset golden eyes studied the travellers curiously from beneath beetling brows.

"They look sort of like Zongo," Katie whispered. "Only small."

"No clothes and a knife on every hip," Will added.

A woman nursing an infant the size of a hamster stepped from the crowd. "Are you uninjured?" she asked in a high, musical voice. At her words, a groundswell of "bastits!" came from those behind her. She silenced them with an arm-chop in the air.

Mary Pat put her right hand on Karl's left wrist. "Let me and Bobby talk with them." She and the young dinosaur walked deliberately forward to face the little woman from three feet away. Both bowed deeply. "We are all fine," Mary Pat said. "Greetings to you and your people."

The woman's eyes widened fractionally, then she smiled and shifted her child to her other breast. Beads of milk strung across her furred chest. "Child of the Gods. Child of the Distant Past. Viking warriors. A Mediast." Her smile widened. "*The Raptured. And* the Amazing _Oog_."

Oog knelt before her on one knee, his head briefly bowed. "You're very kind, your grace. 'Amazing' ain't been on my *curriculum vitae* for a while."

Her laughter was song. "Yet they tried to kill you, and you escaped. Is that not amazing?"

"Quick reflexes and dumb luck," the Neanderthal replied, grinning at the small leader. The infant released its grip on his mother's breast and peered intently at Oog, perhaps intrigued by his deep voice.

Another chorus of 'bastits' rippled through the crowd of Floresians.

"Call it what you will," the little woman said. "My name is Jo, and we do not care for uninvited violence in our lands. We will do what we can to aid you if you tell us what you seek. And I would like to hear it from you, Mr. and Mrs. Garrison."

As Katie began to explain the kidnapping of Jape, Will wondered how this tribe of miniature humanity even *knew* about him and Katie. The packs and bedrolls on most of their backs argued against any sort of permanent settlement, and children and adolescents were dotted amongst their elders. They must be nomadic hunter-gatherers.

Whatever they were, they weren't shy. The younger members of the tribe clustered around Karl and Gro as Katie spoke, more interested in the tall Vikings than the litany of their travels. By the time Katie had finished, Karl was festooned with a dozen small bodies, the smallest perched cheerfully atop his helmet, and several clung to the more horizontal parts of Gro. The Spyeye lifted off Baker's shoulder and captured the amusing tableau for what Will hoped would be an eventual broadcast at the successful conclusion of their mission. After all they'd been through thusfar, a happy ending at least seemed *possible*.

* * * * *

Will hadn't thought it was possible to go *deeper* into the forest, but he'd been wrong. Just after noon, clouds thinning overhead, near-darkness enveloped them at ground level, a kind of perpetual twilight. They trudged on mossy paths, their footsteps muffled, with Jo and most of her people ahead of them practically trotting.

"Good thing there's nothing to film," Baker groused. "The lighting's terrible."

"It isn't too much farther, sir," said one of the larger Floresian children sitting on Karl's broad shoulders. "Perhaps two more hours and we'll be into the blackberry patches near the inlet. It's much more open."

"No berries yet, though," Gro said, grinning over at the dozen or so kids occupying the upper reaches of Karl.

"Not to worry," the big Viking replied confidently. "We *haf* plenty of foodstuffs in my pack. No one will starve."

"Is there a plan when we get there?" Katie asked. "Or do we just radio back to the ship?"

"The *Eye*'ll sneak in over them and send pictures back to Magnus and Fisca," Baker said. "*If* the *Checkers* is there, the *Blood Wave* will try to cut them off before they can escape out the bight to open water. The main problem is the floater situation. The one that attacked us might be somebody unconnected with Richard and Almaric, but if it's theirs, we're in trouble."

"If they had a floater earlier," Will said, "why didn't they use it?"

"They're great weapons platforms, but only the big ones carry much armor or shielding. Fisca's Bushmaster has more range and firepower. Coming in low over the trees like the little one which hit us is practical and effective, but out in the open is a different story. They're vulnerable."

"Karl hit one with a rock once," Gro added. "Screwed up the gyros and it crashed."

"A lucky throw," Karl said, but he grinned as he spoke, and the young Floresians looked impressed.

An hour or so later, they paused for lunch, the Floresians happy to partake of some items from Karl's backpack in addition to their own foodstuffs. As they ate, the juvenile 'Little People' conversed with Bobby and Mary Pat, who were nearer their own age and size. The idea of school created a lot of questions, since hunter-gatherers were essentially home-schooled during their wanderings, and while they knew what classrooms were, they had never experienced them. The idea of books and being warm and indoors while learning intrigued them. Surprisingly, they learned to read at a young age, and most families carried personal libraries in their bedrolls and backpacks. They also had satellite uplinks, different portions of which were carried by older tribe members who were childless or whose children were grown. They also held seasonal gatherings around Vancouver Island, and some had even attended the big Vancouver Moot itself. The children who'd been there shared how intimidating the sheer number of larger humans had been, and Mary Pat and Bobby agreed completely, though the little kids all thought that Karl seemed nice enough, and Gro was attractive. The concept of blonde pigtails fascinated them, and some of the tinier Floresians thought they were handy to go up and down Gro's broad back, not to mention swinging on them.

When everything was tucked back into packs, they set off again, moving to the northwest and Hagan Bight, and by mid-afternoon they were weaving through a sea of freshly-green blackberries. In the softer areas, prints of elk, deer, the occasional Forest Bison and Mammoth or Mastodon showed clearly, but no sighting were made.

Karl and Gro led the way behind the natives, with Will, Katie, and the Raptureville children just ahead of Baker and Oog. No Floaters appeared, which was fine, since the berries had no real cover for anyone the size of Karl, let alone the other conventionally-built humans. Conversations continued with the kids hanging on Karl and Gro. All the younger natives were inordinately polite and respectful to Katie and Will, but more open with Bobby and Mary Pat. Since Bobby was the only living dinosaur any of them had seen, more of their questions were directed at him. Being the kind of open kid he was, none of them were disappointed. He answered all their questions and then some. He and his parents may have died a horrific death sixty-five million years ago, but he seemed unaffected by it.

Eventually, as the afternoon waned, they walked out of the blackberries and into a thick stand of cedar bordering the inlet itself. A half-hour later, cautioned to silence, they could see the water. Baker sent the Spy Eye up over the Bight, moving it slowly to the south, keeping it right at the edge of the tree tops until the inlet began to narrow, then bringing it back and sending it to the north. Within a half-hour, it located the *Checkers'* anchorage, marking the spot on Baker's screen.

The group, still led by the Floresians and speaking only in whispers, walked along the eastern margin of the Bight. The ground rose slightly as they went, until they reached the anchored vessel in Brentword Bay, keeping well back out-of-sight of the water. The Eye kept position in the upper branches of a particularly large Cedar, sending back a good view of the ship and its crew's activities.

Huddled in a depression about fifty feet from the edge of the high bank, Baker, Gro, and Karl studied the small screen after sending a report of their findings to the *Blood Wave*, waiting in Cordova Bay to the east and slightly south. A back-and forth whispered conference decided to wait until first light the next morning to move to the hopeful interception.

Night was beginning to fall as their troop retreated a half-mile into the heavy timber and settled in for the night. Fortunately the air was warm, since any sort of campfire might have betrayed their presence. The huge trees also shielded them from both the weather and the cooler night air.

"I think *ve* should disturb their tranquility tomorrow *morgen* once Magnus gets moving up to the mouth of the inlet at Deep Cove," Karl said as they ate. "The Checkers has a turn of speed on the Blood Wave, but *ve* may be able to distract them for a time and keep them from departure, giving the King a better chance to block them from the open water."

"Easy agreement on that," Baker added, "but if we rain a storm of rocks down upon them, they just might up anchor and speed away, not bothering to try to battle us."

"When you say 'us,'" Katie said, "you mean Karl, since he's the only one of us large and strong enough to throw anything of any size, right?"

A chorus of 'Bastits' came from the gathered crowd of Floresians, who were drinking some sort of herbal concoction from tiny cups as they listened to the bigger people plot the next day's actions.

"I've got a fair stock of root with me," Oog said. "That means I can join in the rockfest, for what that's worth. Two of us throwing, with the Spyeye giving us feedback on our efforts, we could really rain on their parade. If we piss them off enough, they might stick around for some retribution."

"Or flee rapidly," said Gro.

"We know Richard has a temper," Will said, "but we don't have much knowledge about this Almaric fellow."

"Depends on how much influence he has on Richard," said Katie. "'Kill all. God will know His own' indicates he has a reactive mindset."

"He gets mad easy?" Oog asked. "Or does he just pull that kind of crap when he's safe and surrounded by the Papal Armies?"

"Perhaps we wait until the Blood Wave is on the move," Baker said, "then try the rocks." He looked around himself. "At least there's quite a few rocks available."

Jo spoke up from the ranks of the Floresians. "We can readily gather rocks shortly after sunrise. How large do you need?"

"Four to five inches," Karl replied. I can throw that size a hundred yards easily."

"They'll send up their drone again," Will cautioned.

"We saw it on the open deck," Gro said. "If we can target it, a few good hits will disable it enough to prevent an aerial response."

"Sounds necessary," Oog said, occupied at the moment with some type of crusty bread.

"Too bad we can't have a singalong around the campfire," Baker said, drinking from a flask of cold coffee.

"I can offer a better activity for us," Gro told him, draping one long arm over his shoulders, and grinning in obvious promise.

"There you go, Baker," Katie said, smiling at the amorous pair. Baker hated to admit to human motives, so he tried to look uninterested, but Gro would run over that minor difficulty in seconds. Everyone, including the adult Floresians, said nothing, merely smiled at the hapless journalist while he looked put-upon.

Bedrolls under the massive Cedar worked well enough, except that Oog snored.

* * * * *

The duff under the tree was cushiony and comfortable, so everyone slept well, despite Oog. The pervasive mist was dissipating when the dawn woke them. A quiet breakfast of something like MREs from some provider in Boston proved palatable. Baker called the *Blood Wave*, explained the rock-throwing idea, of which Magnus approved. They would be under weigh shortly, since they had nearly twice the distance to travel if they were going to stop the *Checkers* from escaping to the north between Salt Spring Island and the main island.

When they'd finished breakfast and packed up everything, the group went closer to the water, taking turns studying the view from the Spy Eye. People were up and about on Nixon's ship, but most shown were breakfasting on-deck. The former President looked as though he could use a shave, but then he usually did.

By the time the *Blood Wave* sailed north, a goodly stack of rocks had been gathered, Oog was working on a length of root, and Karl was doing stretches, limbering up for his rock dispersal efforts.

One more check-in with the King, and Karl and Oog both picked up two rocks, one in each hand, and made an initial throw, keeping well back from the high banks so as not to expose themselves to the almost certain return fire from the *Checkers*.

"Oog went over their deck," Baker said from the monitor screen. "but yours landed about three feet from the drone, Karl. Up your firing rate. Keep them busy dodging rocks."

A virtual rain of stones commenced, the vast majority now hitting the anchored schooner squarely on its deck. Four hit the drone, knocking it sideways and clearly damaging it. An attempt was made to get it into the air, while several crewmen commenced firing above the bank's crest, the rounds passing well over the attackers' heads.

"They're bringing up the anchor," Baker announced as more rocks were brought to the diminishing pile of missiles. "The little guy with the priestly robes is running around yelling at everyone. Nixon's looking at him like he doesn't approve, since his guys are doing what they can. Several got bonked by rocks, a couple are down on the deck. The drone is incapacitated. Good job so far. Keep it up!"

When the anchor was safely up, the ship's engines roared to life and the *Checkers* began to move.

"Throw more to your right now. They're still firing, at least two of them, but we have to compensate for their movement. Oh, good, another one down!"

A dozen rocks later and the schooner was out of range, already moving at a fair number of knots.

"Up to Magnus and the *Blood Wave* now," the journalist said as the attack ended. "A pretty good job. Too bad they didn't stay and fight."

"Probably realized they couldn't get to whoever was shelling 'em," Oog said, flexing his shoulders, getting the kinks out.

"*Und* they had no idea who *vas* the source," Karl added, looking quite self-satisfied.

"Nice work," said Will and Katie.

"If our moms knew about this," Mary Pat and Bobby said, "they'd shit a brick."

"Such language!" Katie told them, but she smiled.

A small wave of "Bastits!" went through the Floresian ranks.

"What now?" Gro asked.

"We keep talking to the Dragonship," Baker replied. "Regardless of what happens at their end, they're going to have to pick us up. If they blow Nixon out of the water, they come here. If he escapes back through Sansum Narrows, Blood Wave still picks us up before resuming the chase. We can relax for now."

CHAPTER SIXTEEN

Baker and Oog kept in touch with Magnus and crew as they attempted to cut off the *Checkers* flight to the north, but the speedy schooner slipped away, and the *Blood Wave* sailed south to pick up the overland troop, accompanied by the big Neanderthal canoes. Magnus was unhappy, Fisca looked to be grinding her teeth, and the rest of the crew were unusually silent. Only Oog's people were cheerful, standing in their dugouts.

"Did you see them at all?" Baker asked the King.

"No. When we turned south, in this direction," Magnus replied, "both Fisca and I thought we might have trapped them, but no such luck. They beat us to the junction and sailed up the Narrows before our arrival. Beyond that, they could have gone anywhere."

"His two main minions in his past life have to be in Victoria or perhaps Port Angeles, so he will end up going there," Fisca said, running her right hand through her tight black curls. "The question is, will he turn south again when they reach the open sea, or will they circumnavigate the island and approach the Capital from the west."

"Circling the entire island is a vast journey. The other option will be much shorter." The King turned to the Floresians. "What do you people think?"

Jo pulled on her stubby nose while looking around at her gathered kinfolk. "We can radio ahead to our relatives on the north end of the island. The human towns are much sparser on that part of the island. I can make requests."

"Contact the satellite array, Magnus," Baker said. "They have sails. That marks them. I think they'll make for Vancouver, on the mainland, rest up and provision, then sprint for Victoria after a few days, thinking they've eluded us."

Magnus brightened considerably at that thought. "Aye, a plausible idea. His blue eyes narrowed. "Can you deceive them in your daily column, imply we are going around the island, then instead swooping down upon them on the open sea, where the Bushmaster can assail them."

A slow dangerous smile spread over Fisca's dark features at that last thought, though she said nothing.

"Our walk across the island didn't really grab my readers, I'm sure, and I couldn't tell them about the drone attacking us. Somebody on the *Checkers* might have put two and two together, known we were out there and heading in their direction. Not a good thing. I can make up a phony travelogue, spice it up with some amusing encounters as we go north and west around the island. That'll work, I think."

"My blog can do the same," Gro said. "Maybe some bear incidents or a rampaging bull Mastodon high on seasonal male hormones."

"They do that?" Katie asked.

"A little late in the season now, but it might work," Gro replied. "I could also drop in some hints about Baker's manly nature, his burgeoning lusts."

"Old news here," Katie replied, "but maybe not in Boston. "He is quite virtuous in the paper?"

Gro nodded. "He tries to capture the moral high ground, implying the rest of us are ruled by base instincts and regrettable actions."

"He remains a pinnacle of human decency?"

"Exactly. This allows him to prattle on about the potential lewdness of his readers. Looking down his very moral nose."

"You do that, Baker?" Will asked. "That seems so unlikely."

The columnist shrugged. "Part of my writings are slight exaggerations. On occasion. The purpose, after all, is to entertain."

"Did you tell your readers about the incident in Levinsk?" Katie asked. "Behind the wall?"

"With me," Gro added.

"My loyal readers would never believe such a thing," Baker replied.

"Perhaps it would be more appropriate in my Blog," Gro mused, running the ball of her left thumb over her lips.

Baker looked horrified. "You wouldn't. Would you?"

"It could happen."

"What happened behind the wall in levinsk?" Bobby and Mary Pat asked.

"Nothing you two should learn about," Katie told them.

"Parareproductive entertainment activity, I'll bet," Bobby said, showing most of his sharp teeth in his version of a grin. Mary Pat joined him.

Baker regarded them uneasily, uncertain of a good response. Gro held up her right thumb in approval. The adult Floresians laughed.

"We should rejoin the hunt," Fisca said. She bowed to the Floresians. "You were most kind to help us. Is there anything we can do in return?"

"Mention our aid and intrinsically kind natures in any columns or Blogs." Jo replied.

"You really helped with the rocks," Karl told them. "Oog and I *vouldn't haf* been so effective without that."

"Thank you," Jo said, amid a few 'Bastits' from her companions. "Glad to be useful."

"Could Old Man do anything to make your lives easier?" Katie asked the little natives.

"Give us your radio wavelength, and should we think of something, we'll let you know."

"More of the steel spearheads," a male Floresian said. "We trade for those. A couple dozen extra would be good."

"Do your people have villages?" Katie asked.

"We have a Winter den in a cave complex not far from where you met us. It's warm and comfortable. Dried nuts and berries gathered in the Summer and Fall sustain us, with some Winter hunting excursions."

"You have such hard lives," Katie said, looking troubled.

"Don't be sad," Jo told her. "We have lived thuswise for thousands of years. We acquired needed upgrades when Old Man began bringing the deceased up from your Earth. A gradual process of things we could use to make our lives easier. That will continue, but for now we are quite satisfied."

"Time to board," Magnus said, bowing to the Floresians. Hands of various sizes were shaken, several Floresian children hugged Mary Pat and Bobby, and their group mounted the gangplank onto the *Blood Wave*. The engines sprang to life, and the dragonship pulled away from the shore. Will, Katie, and the two children waved, along with Karl and Oog. Gro blew kisses.

"They were *so* nice!" Katie said as the crowd of small bodies receded in the distance.

"Content in their lives, seems like," Will said.

"*Ve* were fortunate not to upset them," Karl said, "but *ve* were not at all disturbing, and having two children with us helped."

"So we were useful?" Mary Pat asked, grinning up at the huge Viking.

"You're both very nice children," Katie assured them. "No one will think otherwise."

"I'm trying to figure out how to bring you into my Blog," Gro told them. "If you have any suggestions which won't disturb your parents, please let me know."

Thoughtful expressions appeared on two young faces. Inner wheels turned. "Okay," they replied.

"Any luck finding the *Checkers*, Baker?" Will asked the journalist, who sat on a bench studying his Pad.

"They went north, as we suspected, then tuned east." Took me a while to locate them. If I had to guess, they're going to Vancouver."

"Our home port," Magness said from his position at the wheel.

"Really?" Katie asked.

"Most of the Scandinavian Dragonships berth there. Port taxes are low. There's an actual part of the port called Scanditown. We have quarters."

"Quite plush, too," Gro said, glancing at seated columnist. "We'll have a good time, Baker."

"Now that we'll be locked into a lengthy pursuit," Fisca said from her position standing beside the King, "we can continue our weapons training." Her dark features broke into an anticipatory smile, flashing her array of white incisors.

"Wait until we break out into the main waters," Magnus advised. "Then you can have at one another."

"Good thing we brought plenty of root," came Oog's voice from the cluster of Neanderthal canoes beside the Dragonship. "This is going to be a long haul, looks like. Course, we can replenish at Vancouver."

"Is this 'root' only effective for the Neanderthals?" Katie asked, keeping her voice down.

"They think so," Fisca said, "and they're probably correct. It doesn't have a very pleasant taste for our kind of humanity, and their jaw musculature can handle its texture better than ours. Very chewy."

"And if it's cooked, it loses its effectiveness," Magnus told them, keeping his gaze ahead of their path though the passage.

"Has anyone tried to synthesize the active ingredient?" Will asked.

"Maybe," Baker said from his seat. "Problem is, there's not that much of a demand, since Oog's people aren't that numerous."

Another half-hour found the *Blood Wave* out into the open sea and pointed directly at Vancouver, which lay slightly north across the Strait of Georgia.

"Where will they berth?" Katie asked Baker. She sat down beside him and peered at his Pad screen.

"Good question. Not where we'll be going. Then there's always the issue of the damage they did in Levinsk. That's got to be out there on the airwaves. Richard's not well known this far north, but unless they're paying for what they need with gold, providers will be loath to deal with them."

"We have some time for the weaponry now," Fisca said. "Who's first?"

Baker raised his right hand, went to get his weapon.

Fisca remained impossibly skilled. Baker was sharper than his previous outing, but the slender gladiatrix prevailed in the end, though the columnist retained his weapon this time.

Katie went next, and her improvement was noticeable. Fisca smiled throughout, complimenting Katie several times. "You will be able to hold your own against most swords within a few more sessions. I'm pleased."

Will thought he did better after watching Baker and Katie defend themselves against a wickedly efficient opponent. He hadn't really learned many of Fisca's moves, but enough to parry some of her lesser efforts, and she was pleased when they were finished.

"If this continues, I am going to think I have a good future as a teacher," Fisca said. "Baker, of course, has considerable experience, but you two tyros have made real progress in a very short time." She turned to Magnus. "What say you, Great King?"

"My descendant has some good genes in her past, apparently. May I take some credit for that, Nubian Queen?"

Fisca laughed. "You may. She has a nice, supple wrist and good instincts. After many generations, your bloodline may still take some credit, as you suggest. A few more sessions and you might contest Mrs. Garrison yourself to better gage her skills."

Magnus appeared to give the concept some thought, looking off into the distance for a few moments, his features frowning slightly. "If she wishes," he said finally.

"A future destined," Fisca told Katie, nodding emphatically.

"Are you sure?" Katie asked, clearly dubious.

"When the time comes. I will sponsor you against your revered ancestor. You will be ready, never fear."

"If you say so," Katie replied, with a nervous grin.

"I can see our destination," Magnus said, some time later. "Another hour. And no need for rowing as we enter the bay, Bjorn. We will be on our home grounds."

"Water, actually," Bjorn replied, laughing.

"As you say, good Skald."

"Do you have an assigned berth?" Will asked.

"We do."

"This is more fun than the rock throwing," Mary Pat said, and Bobby echoed her.

"Are there restaurants," Katie asked.

"Oh, yes," Fisca assured her. "Decent food, too. Not just salt pork and watered grog, the traditional seaman's fare. Good beef, venison, and well-brewed beer. The gardens to the east provide not just vegetables, but also the creatures which attempt to plunder the crops. No bear, no lions, but forest hogs, deer, elk, and the occasional Mammoth or Mastodon. Poultry is also available, both eggs and meat. Fields of plenty, as is said. Fish, also, as you might imagine."

"Newton's, let's don't forget," Bjorn said from his post by the King.

"Do you two remember Robert Newton, the actor?" Fisca said, "He has a quite decent establishment here. 'Treasure Island,' usually referred to by the locals as Newton's."

"Long John Silver," Baker said. "His classic role. Arrrr!"

"We both remember him," Katie replied. "Right, Will?"

"The gold standard for pirate jargon, for sure."

"We'll berth in," Magnus told them. "get you four settled in quarters and cleaned up, then see the sights and hit Newman's."

"Good thing our folks gave us credit cards before we left," Mary Pat and Bobby said.

"We still have our initial funds," Katie said. "You youngsters shouldn't have to pay a penny for what you need."

"Don't even think about it," Will added.

"Okay," the two replied, grinning widely. "But we'll pay for any souvenirs and gedunks."

"Fair enough," Katie said. "We have to return you two to your parents in one piece and keep you safe and well-nourished."

"Karl and Oog will keep us all safe."

"You two weren't with us during the bear episode," Will told them. "That was close to being *too* exciting."

"Karl did what he needed to do," Katie said, "and we all survived. Although there were questionable moments."

Hearing his voice, Karl hauled himself upright from where he sat on the deck, and stumped over, slipping his game console into his wool vest, showing most of his teeth in what passed for a smile.

"It *vas* a rollicking adventure, for sure," the cheerful monster said, patting both children on their backs. "But it *vas* good you liddle ones were not there. There were short moments of danger."

"You think?" Katie said, giving Karl an arch look.

There was no putting Karl off his good mood, his default attitude. He chuckled warmly, nodding agreement, seeing the irony.

"This is your home port," Will asked. "What will you and the other crewmen and women do?"

"We won't be here long enough to do much more than refresh ourselves," Baker said, hunched over his Tablet and speaking up. "Richard has landed at Williamson Slough, or nearly. He'll spend a night or two there and then head for Victoria to rendezvous with his two main minions, assuming they got there safely. My understanding is that they're resourceful rascals, so they'll be waiting for him. And that clerical wretch, Almaric, who seems to be directing the operation."

"What the journalist said," Karl replied. "An overnight or two, *zen ve* are off again."

"Whatever happens, I guess," Katie said, squeezing Will's left wrist.

"It'll work out," Will said. "Your ancestor won't let us down."

"Don't be too sure," Magnus said over his right shoulder, from his position at the wheel.

"We *are* sure, Grandfather," Katie told the King.

"Having faith and certainty is good," Fisca said, laughing softly, her right hand kneading Magnus' neck.

The conversion died down as the Blood Wave neared the entry to the main port and Lionsgate bridge, or what passed for it here.

"Do we have to go through Customs?" Katie asked.

"Since it's their home port, I wouldn't think so," Baker said. "So, no Customs, Fisca?"

"Not here, as you said. We're home, we're well-known, and all is well until we sail away again."

The *Blood Wave* slipped under the bridge, closely followed by the Neanderthal canoes, then slowly advanced to a line of Dragonship slips which were about half-filled. Magnus deftly slid the big craft inside an enclosing spot, barely touching the wooden edges. Karl sprang onto the dock and tied up to a large brass cleat.

"Hey, Great King," Oog yelled from behind them. "Where do we go?"

"Either side," Magnus replied, walking to the port side and pointing to that berth. "How many of you are there?"

"A dozen-and-a-half," came the reply, "and we're all mighty hungry." A rumble of guttural voices followed his words.

"We'll find you quarters as soon as our crew is on the dock, Oog. Did you bring a change of clothes?"

"Sort of. We'll be fine after a shower, ready for some chow."

The *Blood Wave* crew walked down the gangplank, greeting the Neanderthals, all agreeing their adventure had been worthwhile, the best part maybe even yet to come. Katie, Will, and the kids, along with Baker and Gro, kept to the rear of the throng, the Spy Eye hovering over the group, missing nothing.

Karl gathered Oog's cadre and took them to the Bachelor Sailors Quarters. Each of the Neanderthals carried a medium-sized seabag, and they kept close to Karl's massive back as he led them up a short flight of stairs and through a tall door marked BSQ.

"This way," Fisca told the Garrisons and the two children.

"Where do I go?" Baker asked.

Gro grabbed his right arm. "Where do you think? You'll bunk with me in my humble apartment. Don't worry, it's not a study in pink." She glanced up at the Eye, shaking an index finger at it. "And you, clever device, will not record the goings-on inside." The little mechanism peeped twice, bobbed in the air once, and lit on Baker's right shoulder, where it rested silently, watching the tall Viking woman.

Another, longer flight of stairs led the crew and their guests up to a broad walkway below a large carving of a Dragonship's prow, then through a set of double doors into a large central area with chairs and couches providing ample seating for a couple dozen over-sized bodies.

Fisca took them down a long hallway to a set of guest quarters and opened a door exposing a nice-sized room furnished in what Will and Katie thought must be Viking chic, dark woods and sturdy chairs with surprisingly modern facilities, a large sink, a set of shelving with towels, and a bathroom with a shower, a toilet, and a bidet side-by-side. A king-sized bed stood near one wall, with a bunk-bed on another.

"Did you call ahead, Fisca?" Katie asked, studying the bunk-bed, upon which Mary Pat and Bobby had already dumped their bags. Mary Pat took the top bed.

"I did," the gladiatrix replied. "Everything had to be prepared for the King's descendant. Does this arrangement seem adequate?"

"It's perfect," Katie replied. "Thank you so much, Fisca."

"Just part of my job, sort of like picking up after the King's minor messes."

"I wouldn't have thought he would be creating messes."

Fisca smiled and sighed. "To be fair, our Magnus does not leave much to chance, and he is expert at finishing issues shortly after they begin. Still, he sometimes requires help, I which case, I am there." She turned to Bobby and Mary Pat. "Does this set-up seem adequate?"

"Oh, yes," the two replied. "It'll be a relief to get clean again," Bobby continued.

"Do you sweat?" Katie asked him.

"Some. Not like your sort of mammals, maybe half as much. Our lungs are more efficient, and that helps. We can exert for longer periods of time before we begin to sweat."

"Well," Fisca said. "The four of you get cleaned up, then come down into the main room, we'll meet the Neanderthals and do a walk-around, then eat at Newman's. If there's nothing more, I'll go check on the Great King." She went out the door, closing it gently behind her.

"Okay," Katie said, "you children get showered first, then you both should call your folks while Will and I get cleaned up."

"Gotcha," Mary Pat replied, heading for her backpack, with Bobby doing the same. Both were shortly in the bathroom, and Will and Katie could hear the shower begin.

"This is pretty darned nice," Will said, embracing Katie.

"Too bad we can't do anything more while we're here," Katie replied, kissing him.

"We can't scandalize the kids," her husband replied, "but these new younger bodies do make demands, don't they?"

"Really? Do you think so? Or is it just a male thing?" As she spoke, Katie leaned back in his embrace and frowned at him.

"My memory reminds me that I was not always the instigator during our early marital days."

"If you say so. I was never the blushing bride, was I?"

"A lithesome maiden, as I remember."

"Dear God, William! I wasn't a maiden when we married."

"Just a figure of speech, then." They held each other tight between kisses until they heard the shower stop, then stood and waited for the bathroom door to open.

The kids came out five minutes later, wearing clean clothes.

"Well, you two didn't do anything disturbing while we were in there, did you?" Mary Pat said, with a young hoyden's smile. Bobby gave her a puzzled look.

"No," Katie told her. "We have some reservations, even if we are young again."

"We're still old in our minds," Will added, grinning at them.

The two kids looked at one another. "We didn't think of that."

"Let's go get cleaned up," Katie said, taking Will's hand leading him to the bathroom, each carrying a change of clothes and Will's shaving gear.

When they were safely inside the privacy of the bathroom, Katie shook her head as she undressed. "That Mary Pat is a little stinker."

Will chuckled. "I guess Angel kids aren't any different from our sort of human then. They're both terrific children." As he talked, he lathered up and shaved, Katie watching with a smile on her youthful features.

"They are. I wish they could meet our grandkids. They'd all get along, though ours wouldn't know what to make of Bobby."

"Left to just themselves, they'd be fine. The parents would be the issue. Bobby's pretty much a regular kid, he just doesn't look it."

"Shower time, William." They started the water and stepped inside.

"This feels good," Will said. "That trek through the boonies left me somewhat grubby."

"Sometimes grubby is good," Katie said. "I like the salt." She soaped both of them up.

"That sounded kind of earthy, young lady."

"You know, we need to decide how to face our own children when we look younger than they do. Do you have any thoughts on that subject?"

Will thought a bit as he shampooed his hair. "Maybe Old Man will have some suggestions. He's spent a lot of years at his job, though I kind of doubt he's had a lot of this sort of issue."

"Don't forget Cher. People must notice when she comes back younger from a gig with Sonny in Cockaigne."

"She's a show business legend. People see her as an ever-youthful icon. They expect her to look great. When she does, they just accept it. We won't be so lucky. Our kids will take one look at us and the questions will start."

"You think they might see us as imposters?"

He turned off the water, gave Katie a tight hug. "No, don't think so. If we wear familiar clothing and act glad to see them, they'll accept us as Mom and Dad. Also, we will have the knowledge of our relationship with them."

"The grandchildren will push us, asking the expected questions," Katie told him, as they toweled off.

"Not to mention your Aunt Mildred. She may be in her nineties, but she's sharp and doesn't hold back. We have to concoct some sort of answer."

"Mildred McManus is a force of nature. I love her dearly, always have, and she thinks the world of you, but there won't be any easy answers for her, Will. She won't be deflected."

"Particularly if she's had a glass or two of wine."

"Probably wouldn't hurt to ask Fisca and Magnus. They're both sharp."

"Sure, but Old Man will be the final word."

They dressed in silence, each lost in their own thoughts.

Back out in the bedroom, they found the kids playing games. Bobby's was 'Trouble in the Triassic,' which gave Will half-raised eyebrows. Mary Pat was playing 'Angry Angels,' maybe more unsurprising.

"You having fun?" Will asked.

"We decided we were hungry while we waited," Bobby said, "but the games distract us a little bit."

"Bobby's metabolism is jacked up compared to mine," Mary Pat told them as she flipped her game off and tucked it away inside her backpack.

Bobby looked apologetic, but still smiled his sharp-toothed smile, as he closed his pad.

"Let's go down to the main room and see what's going on," Katie said.

"You're doing mom-stuff," Mary Pat told her, laughing.

"She is?" Bobby asked, genuinely perplexed.

"I am," Katie replied, laughing along with the young angel. "Does your mother do that?"

"A little, but my Mom is 'tougher than boiled owl shit.' At least that's what my Dad says."

"I agree," Will said. "Having seen her in action."

The quartet went out into the hallway, shutting the door behind them, and headed for the main room. When they arrived, most of the Vikings and all the Neanderthals were waiting, the latter dressed in colorful Hawaiian shirts.

"Pretty nice," Will told Oog. "Not what I would have expected, but still special."

"Homo sapiens approval," Oog said, addressing his companions. "What do you guys think?"

Rumbles of approval spread though the stocky group, all of them smiling at Will.

Karl arrived, with Magnus and Fisca at his heels, and the rest of the crew behind them.

"We can walk down the promenade to Newman's," Magnus said, leading the way out of the quarters, the others in his wake, Fisca beside him. Once down the stairs, he turned left and walked purposefully to the west. The few people going the opposite direction greeted the King warmly, but no conversations ensued, and shortly the whole bunch went into 'Treasure Island,' the true name of the place.

Robert Newton, wearing a version of traditional pirate garb. greeted them as they entered. "Arrrh, Mateys. A goodly group destined for the best of victuals in great volume at low, low port prices."

"You old devil," Magnus told the actor, grabbing his extended hand with both of his. "You never change, a taste of Cornwall we all look forward to."

Newton guffawed as he greeted Fisca, but his merriment ratcheted up several notches when he saw the Garrisons. "The Raptured! My gracious. Such a pleasure."

"We loved your films," Katie told the ebullient actor.

"Thank you. For the most part, I enjoyed making them. I still think of myself as a stage actor rather than the movies, but one takes fame from whence it comes and accepts the accolades as they arrive."

"Well put," said Will.

Newton winked at him. "Words possibly stolen from some production or another. I still tend to chew the scenery on occasion." He spread his arms wide. "Nonetheless, welcome to my humble establishment, take seats and the staff will satisfy you every culinary need." He lifted an eyebrow at Bjorn. "And you, Sir, please do not use your honeyed tongue to tempt my female staffers to errant activities of a carnal nature, as you have in the past."

Bjorn placed his right hand over his heart, his eyes wide and innocent. "I never would. Your lascivious hirelings always made the first move, if you recall. I am not without urgings of a sexual nature, but I rarely make the first effort, a true Norwegian. We are intrinsically a shy folk."

Newton roared with laughter. "A true pity I have no garden, else I could utilize some of that for fertilizer."

"You impugn my nature, good sir. Were it not for the excellent cuisine and compelling servers, I should be deeply hurt."

"Perhaps you would be more at ease at the local Globes. Shakespeare is expanding to the north, and will shortly open here in Vancouver." A brief frown crossed the actor's features.

"No," Bjorn replied, "Your establishment is my favorite by far. Even your unkind thoughts about my demeanor will not dissuade my patronage. Also, the Boss is picking up the tab, I'm thinking."

Magnus gave the rascally skald a harsh look. "I take care of my associates."

Newton saw to their seating, remarking on the colorful shirts worn by the Neanderthals, introducing himself to each of them. Oog's reputation had preceded him, and Newton told him where to buy a supply of fresh root.

"Wasn't sure you folks would have any," Oog replied, "but we're running low, and these adventuresome Vikings are leading us all over the ocean, trying to catch our elusive quarry."

The actor nodded. "I understand it's Reasonable Richard, an unpleasant fellow in life, and unchanged in Cockaigne."

"Just so," said Magnus, "but we will hunt him down and recover Old Man's associate."

"I hope that isn't Jape or the practical curate."

"The former, I'm afraid."

"Not a happy captive, then."

"No sign of him on the *Checkers*, either," Baker said. "and we had hours of observations. They must be keeping him below decks."

"I suppose we will be missing his enjoyable Saturday evening hour of music and witticisms, then, at least until he is freed."

"Old Man will be stuck doing that himself," Baker replied, chuckling.

"It won't be the same. Our revered Creator and Maintainer doesn't have the same touch, I'm afraid, but don't tell him that, please." He paused briefly. "But enough chit-chat. Let me get menus and send out a pair of servers to take your requests."

"We're right here," Two skirt-clad young women said from behind the proprietor, their arms full of menus and welcoming smiles on their fresh faces. Both smiled particularly at Bjorn, who smiled back. Magnus rolled his eyes, seeing the inevitable. Newton glared at the skald before departing.

While there was beef and pork on the menu, seafood dominated, and most of the diners ordered Sesame Crusted Albacore Tuna or Arctic Char, with the Neanderthals going for the Sandbarge, a mix of prawns. Oysters, Ahi tuna, and Dungeness crab. Magnus listened carefully to the requests, fully realizing this festive outing was going to damage his finances to some extent. Fisca gave him a concerned glance or two, finally shrugging and saying it was all in a good cause, which seemed to mollify the King.

When the food arrived, hearty appetites went to work, and Mary Pat and Bobby held their own against the adults, showing their crusted tuna no mercy. The

Neanderthals set high marks for speed, volume, and additional orders. No surprises there.

Where the meal ended, the desserts vanished, and the bill settled, Oog and his canoe mates went off to get a new supply of root, while Karl and the other Vikings saw to the delivery of most of the marijuana bales, leaving some for personal use and bartering.

"Shall we go to the Long Branch then?" Magnus said when they were back on the Prominade. "Amanda and Jim are always happy to see us."

"Plus they have the best local gossip," Fisca added.

"Grist for my news mill, too," Baker added, his right arm linked with Gro's left.

"Are we talking 'Gunsmoke'?" Katie asked.

"Yes," Fisca replied. "Two of our favorite people, plus many of the other actors from the show are also here. Old Man was a huge fan, and as the players died, He brought them up to similar circumstances. The interior of the Long Branch is virtually identical, albeit modernized and enlarged."

"Is James Arness the Marshall?" Will asked.

"For the city and surrounding terrain. Ken Curtis is his deputy, Burt Reynolds is one of the local blacksmiths and machinists, and Milburn Stone practices locally."

"Milburn Stone wasn't a physician, he was an *actor,* for goodness sake!" Katie exclaimned.

"His skills and knowledge were upgraded," Baker told her. "When he is not fishing, Old Man is fairly attentive to details. Vicar Elbunn also keeps track and does the reminding when necessary." He gave the Spy

Eye a tap on its carapace. "Be ready. We may get some good worthwhile info shortly." He was rewarded with a shrill 'beep.'

The saloon was a couple blocks away, though the natives who were out and about stopped to talk to Magnus, and all seemed delighted to meet 'The Raptured,' which was marginally embarrassing for Will and Katie.

"You're the 'Rapture Babe' even here," Will teased her. "That's what you get for being so good-lookin', I guess."

"You *guess*? Have you forgotten my looks when we first met, William?"

Will regarded her fondly. "I only have to look at you now to jog my memory. You're darned easy on the eyes."

"Best you say things like that," Mary Pat and Bobby said, grinning up at Will.

"Right you are," Will replied, nodding at them. Magnus, Fisca, and Baker kept quiet, merely smiling.

"Here we are," the King said, leading them through a pair of traditional swinging saloon doors.

Amanda Blake greeted them from behind the bar, and James Arness, Ken Curtis, and Milburn Stone waved from a table in a corner.

"How long will you be in Port, Magnus?" 'Miss Kitty' asked when she came out from behind the bar and hugged the King and Fisca, giving Baker a dirty look.

"Hey!" the columnist complained. "I didn't deserve that."

The saloon owner patted him on one cheek. "Tradition must be observed, Baker. You've spilled a few of our beans over the years, so you deserve the occasional hard look."

"I was only doing my job," Baker protested.

"Sort of like 'I vas only following orders' for the Germans, eh, Baker?" Arness said, chuckling.

"That's too harsh, Jim," Milburn Stone said. "Baker's not a bad sort, especially when compared with some of those people you deal with in your official capacity."

"Granted," the Marshall replied, shrugging, "but he's so easily picked on."

"I keep him in line," Gro said, putting an arm across the columnist's shoulders.

"One can only imagine," Arness said, with his famous lop-sided grin. "I can well believe you're pretty darned good at it, too."

Baker wisely kept his mouth shut during the exchange, even with the two children and Will and Katie staring at him, expecting some sort of rebuttal.

"Would the group of you like something to drink?" Amanda Blake asked.

That was agreed to readily enough, seats were taken, and the conversation continued, mostly about Katie and Will's impressions of Cockaigne.

"It's all been good except for the bear," Katie told the locals.

"Watched that on television," Ken Curtis said. "Half expected a sadder ending. Since Karl was involved, though, it worked out well. Most people probably expect a guy that size to be not as smart as he is, what with the way he talks and all, but he seems to come through when he has to."

"He has been a real stalwart over the years," Magnus agreed, and Fisca echoed him.

"He's treated us really well," Bobby and Mary Pat said. "Looks out for us, makes sure we'll all safe.

"Oog has been good, too," Bobby added. "He acts less seriously, but he's right on top of things as they happen."

"Always joking," Mary Pat told them. "except he's mostly just trying to distract us from the bad stuff."

"He shot right by everybody when that armed drone showed up," Stone said. "As short as he is, that was a surprise."

"He made sure we had the children safe first," Katie replied.

"So, what's with Richard?" the Marshal asked.

Fisca was ready. "He's been convinced by Almaric that he can expand his power base somehow. They kidnapped Jape when Old Man was out fishing, which did not sit well with our Creator. Only the presence of Jonathon Elbunn kept a lid on his anger, and that was a near thing."

"I think he didn't want to lose control with Mary Pat and I there, too," Bobby said.

"Does Richard think they have the real Creator captive?" the proprietress wondered.

"Maybe," said Baker. "It depends on whether Jape can keep his natural level of humor suppressed, instead acting outraged and indignant the way Old Man would.

If he continues pitching fits and throwing stuff, they may not wonder why he doesn't manifest his powers and just blow the crap out of everything. Almaric is likely convinced Old Man is just a has-been god whose powers have diminished over the years. As long as Jape continues his charade, they'll just figure Almaric is correct and they have no worries."

"Do you think Old Man will do the show on Saturday?" Curtis asked Baker.

"At first, I thought so, but if He does, that'll give the game away. They'll know the one they've got is the wrong one, or they'll think the substitute is doing the program. But I think Albunn will advise him not to broadcast."

"They could get Rush Limbaugh to come on as a substitute," Arness said, still smiling, "except he's in Florida."

Baker's expression shifted to introspection for a long moment. "Rush's standard message doesn't resonate in this society. This is, after all, the Perfect Life. No societal discord, people free to explore their dreams and go into a life very different from their earthly one."

"You didn't," Gro said, tweaking the journalist's right ear.

"There was a need here for what I do. I didn't have to start over. Gossip, minor turmoil, very small societal ills, those things are my meat and potatoes. Go with what you know. Boston's got enough weirdness to keep me focused and busy." His smile widened. "This little jaunt has let me expand my game some. Having The Raptured and these two kids along just adds to the mix."

"Don't forget Oog," said Mary Pat.

"Even better. He's a whole 'nother ball game. Plenty of good quotes, some excellent action. His interaction with everyone else, along with the other Neanderthals, is good general interest." Baker spread his arms. "It's a journalistic smorgasbord."

"So what's next," Amanda Blake asked Magnus.

"Richard has to go to Victoria to reconnect with his two lead minions if they're there. They are capable and clever, true sneaky buggers, manipulative and persistent. Once they're back in the fold, he will have to decide how to proceed."

"I wonder how they interact with Almaric?" Stone asked.

"Good question. Their loyalty is to Richard, not the former Papal advisor. There is also the presence of the false Old Man. Jape will probably succeed in fooling them, so will Almaric try to show Jape – as Old Man – is no longer powerful? That seems likely. Will there be some sort of public disgrace or confession or – Heaven forbid – a public execution. Hard to guess at this point."

Baker held up his left arm for attention. "At that point, if a public spectacle is announced, Old Man will be incensed, just totally pissed off, and he will leave his home and rain shit down on them. Johnathon Elbunn will agree with him, and make no attempt to hold Old Man back. Jape will be rescued and Richard and his cadre seriously punished."

Arness nodded. "No collateral damage?"

"Elbunn will be right there with advice and suggestions. Old Man will listen to him."

"Father Elbunn was really nice to us," Bobby and Mary Pat said. "He told us about his imaginary friend, Skippy, a magic wagon. And we played Hopscotch."

"I didn't think priests had imaginary friends," Gro said. "On the other hand, there's all those saints, and even Jesus, so maybe it's normal. At least we have Odin, who's totally real."

"You don't actually believe that, do you?" Bjorn asked.

"I have some sincere doubts," Gro replied, "but only intermittently." Her usual smile expanded to its limits. From the right angle, an observer could count the rugae on her palate. "If a believer is going to be true to their theology, occasional doubts can creep in, right?"

Magnus looked skeptical. "I'm quite certain Odin takes a dim view of back-sliding in faith. His corvid associates keep him well-informed, not to mention the wolves. If he keeps a notebook of doubters, Gro Forsberg's name may well be in it."

Now Gro's tanned and freckled features grew concerned. "You won't rat me out, will you, Great King?"

"He will not," Fisca said, giving Magnus a reproving look. "We need people like you, Gro, and our leader realizes that. Your good nature and sunny disposition buoy us all, plus your sword work is both skilled and helpful when things get grim."

"Also you keep Baker on an even keel," Bjorn added, his smile nearly matching Gro's.

"I feel better now," the lanky blonde replied. "I have no desire to be called out by our premier god, carried off to a back room in Valhalla and spending eternity peeling potatoes or slicing onions instead of battling other warriors and leading an eventful afterlife."

Magnus grew serious. "If we are not in Valhalla here, Gro, where do you think it might be? Granted this does not fit all the descriptions from the Eddas, but it's close enough for most of us, and much more varied than those rather dreary circumstances with daily strife, bloodshed, and pain, made bearable only by the banquets and good ale each evening."

"Maybe sex, too," said Bjorn cheerfully.

Everyone, even the Long Branch crew, looked at him quizzically.

"The Valkyries?" he asked, eyebrows elevated.

"The bottom line for our skilled skald, as always," Magnus said, tipping his mug up for a long swallow.

"So when do you think you'll be leaving port again?" Arness asked.

"Probably not tomorrow," Fisca replied. "Richard will have re-provision, and Karl and Oog's stones injured some of his crew and damaged their drone, so that will slow their departure. So the day after the morrow at the earliest, I think."

"His bad boys from his earthly life are in Victoria?" Amanda Blake asked.

"Yes," said Baker, "or so we believe. Maybe Port Angeles. We blew their boats out of the water, but there was no sign of them after the fight. They must have had scuba gear and submersible powered devices of some kind which got them away from us quickly. So they've probably been busy formulating some new mischief to keep the *Checkers* and its crew out of our clutches."

"They know we are a formidable foe from our last encounter," Fisca said, "and Oog and his bunch were scarcely involved except for taking out the crew of the one disabled vessel, which they did rather nicely. On the other hand, they know we cannot utterly destroy them as long as they have the ersatz Old Man on board. He's their survival insurance."

"Wouldn't they all die and Old man survive?" Katie asked. "They have to at least consider that, right?"

"We know next to nothing about Almaric, except he wishes to usurp Old Man," Fisca replied. "There is also the question of Old Woman, who though she is less confrontational than Old Man, is certainly no pushover on any level. She could easily arrive here."

"Being our philosopher, Milburn, what do you think?" Arness asked.

"Jim, I'm a doctor, not an expert on the doings of powerful eternal beings."

The Marshal grinned in response. "A little Star Trek going on there, eh?" He turned to Magnus. "Have you thought of asking Keiko's help?"

"The famous Orca? No. I forgot he hangs out around here. Have they found a way to communicate with his Pod?"

"They have," Bobby said. "They announced it at school just before Summer Break. Von Neumann and Hughes perfected a device which enables communication between the two species."

"What did the orcas want to talk about?" Magnus asked.

"Easy enough," Baker said. "Fish and sex. And they want to meet Robin Williams. Something about being on the same wavelength."

"What could they do to help us?" Katie asked. "They have underwater stealth, I guess. Are the translators portable?"

"If we go to a local electronics shop in the morning, a program can be downloaded into a laptop with vocal enhancement and a submersible feed. The program won't be cheap, but the gadget won't break the bank, so we can see what sort of educement might strike Keiko's fancy, besides what I mentioned. It's worth a try."

"First thing in the morning, then," Magnus replied, nodding thoughtfully.

The conversation turned back to local gossip and goings-on further into the interior, continuing for another hour. Since the Pacific Northwest was the primary traditional home of the legendary Sasquatch, numbers of them had been brought up and were settled in the massive forests of Cockaigne.

"Do they come into the city?" Katie asked.

"On occasion," Amanda said. "Going to the movies, primarily. They love comedies, apparently. There aren't many of them, so getting to know them is something new. I understand the theaters have had to put in a number of larger seats to accommodate them."

"Cockaigne is full of surprises," Katie said.

"For as much time as He spends fishing," Baker said, "you'd think He wouldn't have time for bringing people up, but He still does. Of course, the tech wizards keep making our lives easier, so maybe He has more time for his own endeavors."

"He sure seemed nice enough," Mary Pat said, "though He was kind of short-tempered, which was understandable under the circumstances, His friend Jape being kidnapped and all."

"Jape is also His friend and companion, someone who is more light-hearted and playful than Johnathon Elbunn. They play a lot of cards in the evenings. He brings up people in his spare time. Elbunn keeps lists of likely candidates."

"Time-efficient then," Will said. "Makes good sense, and it keeps his time more open for fishing."

"The Vicar is very dedicated."

"Well, we should see the sights," Magnus said, standing. "What's the tab, Amanda?"

"On the house. It's not every day we get a King of Norway in the door, and the girls will be happy to know Bjorn is in town, even for a short time. They all look forward to him."

All eyes turned to the skald, who looked both uneasy and proud. "Tell them I'll be in later, when the evening draws down a bit." He avoided looking at Bobby and Mary Pat, who seemed to understand the situation but said nothing.

Back out on the promenade, Magnus led them along the waterfront, remarking on new shops which had opened since their last time in port.

"This is surprisingly upscale," Katie said, looking in the windows and the street displays."

"Wait until you see Victoria," Fisca told her. "It's much larger and has a greater variety of products. A few decades back, before the real scientific advancements, both cities were awash in competing businesses and gang activity. Boston settled down much more quickly, thanks to Tom McCall and the work of von Neumann and his scientists. Manufacturing began in Boston and spread north rapidly, advancing societal norms and pushing the unruly out from their alleyways and dark basements. It's much quieter now, getting more genteel by the year."

Magnus nodded. "Used to be we couldn't stroll around town like this, had to be armed and on our guard at all times. I've lost track of how many brigands and seadogs we had to throw in the harbor on every visit. James Arness and his deputies have made a remarkable difference, but the manufacturing and construction jobs have helped greatly. Affluence is a cure of sorts, that's for certain."

"There seems to be a lot of art objects in the stores," Katie said. "Handwork, and very nice."

"Old Man brings up skilled artisans, primarily painters and sculptors."

"Don't forget the writers and composers," Baker said. "The number of concerts, Opera, and big-budget musicals grows every year. Movies, too."

"And we kids have Jim Henson, Walt Disney, and Disney's creators," Bobby said.

"Chuck Jones, too," Mary Pat added. "And Walt Kelly and Carl Barks. We've really got all the best."

"Elbunn is a real comics fan," said Baker, "and he does make up the lists of prospective individuals to be brought up. We got Mark Twain, Bill Porter, Edgar Allen Poe, and the members of the Algonquin Round Table. It's a continual upgrade, a lot of great talents."

"We got to see Tim Conway and Harvey Korman last Summer," Bobby said. "My dad had to have some of the historical references explained to him, but my mom laughed through the whole show. We're really lucky."

Katie and Will looked at one another, each knowing what was going through the mind of the other. "If we stay here," Will told her, "the kids will never know what happened to us/"

"And the grandchildren," Katie replied, taking Will's hand.

"You are unique in our experience," Fisca told them. "People who shouldn't be here, yet are, and have contributed to our lives. It is very strange."

"When we're back home," Katie said, "Maybe we can return for visits. We'll miss all of you. Even Baker."

Fisca flashed her bright smile at the journalist. "Old Man might do that. He has moments of true compassion."

"We have a lot of ground to cover before then," Magnus said. "First we deal with Reasonable Richard and his evil advisor, then we solve the great complication of the Garrisons."

"Elbunn will be on top of the problem in a heartbeat," Fisca said.

"And he will do the right thing," Baker added. "We have nothing to worry about. Solve the problems we have and go from there. Old Man may love fishing, but when push comes to shove, he will always do the right thing."

"So we deal with Richard and go from there," Katie said. "Is that right?"

"'Free Willy'!" Bjorn exclaimed, his right fist in the air.

"So you think we are only one magic Orca away from success?" Fisca asked, laughing at the Skald.

"No, but that would be nice."

"What can one troublemaking Cetacean do to stop Richard and his shipload of thugs?"

"Their intelligence is different from ours," Magnus said. "They cannot manipulate objects as do we, but they still have spatial abilities, incredible reflexes, and great strength. Also a wonderful sense of humor. We have heard the stories."

"Tomorrow we try to contact them, after we purchase the means to do so," Magnus continued. "What happens after that depends on the winds of fate and time."

"You were always better than me with words," Bjorn said, shaking his head.

"Our King is best with the words of love," Fisca added, looking fondly at Magnus, who seemed profoundly embarrassed.

"His love poetry was beautiful," Katie said, putting the King even more ill-at-ease.

"I do not enjoy being the subject of even mild taunting," Magnus replied, his features flushed.

"Accept it for what it is, Boss," Bjorn said, "sincere admiration. We should all be so lucky."

"You may well be on intimate terms with some local former maidens later this evening," the King told his Skald.

"The honeyed words," Fisca said, regarding Bjorn with something akin to friendship.

"Go with what you know," the Skald replied, shrugging.

"You are a true rascal," Katie said.

"Better him than me," Will said.

"You were never a rascal," Katie replied. "You were – and are – a good person who is a real man of decency. Your humor is ironic and occasionally snarky, and I love you dearly."

Will sighed deeply, trying to escape from the verbal trap in which he found himself. "If you say so," he finally managed to get out.

"My parents do stuff like this all the time," Mary pat said, snickering, "and their roles are nearly the same. My mom is a lot like Mrs. Garrison, except a tad more aggressive and prone to heap abuse on my dad at times."

"A lot of the time," Bobby said, showing his toothy grin. "My dad just goes along with what my mom has in mind. He wasn't like that when we were at the Base and he was security boss. Things were pretty chaotic, and he was trying to get what ships we had into space before the Thing hit."

"That's what your people called it, 'The Thing?'" Katie asked.

"Yes. Our people on Mars and in the Asteroid Belt – the miners – were never in danger, just those still on Earth, and there was plenty of warning, but we couldn't all escape. Just didn't have the capability to lift so many of our people off the planet. Our main base was about where Nebraska is here, so we all lived through the actual strike and a while longer. There was so much debris and clouds of stuff that we were doomed. The atmosphere was literally poisonous. No ships could get back planet-side and get any additional people out. My folks were very stoic, never tried to avoid the truth of what was going to happen to us and the other survivors. We had food and water, but air was the main problem. The filters on the underground portions of the base could only do so much scrubbing. When they gave out, we were done." As he finished speaking, his head hung down, and Mary Pat hugged him with both arms.

Katie thought she was going to cry. She looked at Bobby with utter horror in her eyes, and only her left hand over her mouth kept her from screaming. No one said a word for almost a full minute. "How awful," Gro finally said, clearly struggling to get any words out.

"Except the Garrisons, we have all died," Magnus said, running his right hand through his blond hair, "but yours sounds the worst, Bobak. When we get back to Boston, I would like to meet your parents. Could that be arranged, do you think?"

Bobby looked up at the King and smiled, one which for once looked very human and sad. "Certainly, Great King."

"I am not *your* great king. Here at this moment, in this relatively peaceful place, I am just another man. I would have saved you and your people had I the chance, and it is a privilege to know you now. You were very brave, as were all your people. I will thank Old Man for bringing you up when next I see him."

Mary Pat rubbed her eyes when she released Bobby from her embrace. "I'm *so* glad I have you for my friend," she told him, her voice quavering.

"Sorry to be such a downer," Bobby replied. "It gets to me sometimes."

"Every sad moment in our lives finds us on occasion," Magnus. "we all have such memories." His smile looked slightly painful. "Shall we find some ice cream, perhaps?"

Everyone agreed on that, and they walked silently to the nearest source, Katie keeping her right hand on Bobby's left shoulder while Mary Pat held his right hand in her left.

"Don't worry, Bobby," she told him. "You won't get mammal cooties."

"*You* would say that," Bobby replied, with a tentative smile.

"I love you, you know. We all do, and you're my best friend."

The little dinosaur's smile fled for an instant, then returned, strengthened. "Thanks, MP. You're my favorite mammal."

"Good. Now we get ice cream."

The place turned out to be 'Farrell's.

"We had Farrell's in our Boston," Katie said, looking around the place as they went inside.

"Probably the same fellow," Baker said. "It's a franchise, all up and down the west coast, except the rougher parts of California. Bob Farrell did begin in Portland, back in my day. Really great milkshakes."

Seated, service was rapid despite the number of patrons, and shortly ice cream and milkshakes were in front of each of the group. Other customers, curious about Bobby, came cautiously to the table and said a few words, mostly questions. Bobby's people were rare in Canada, it turned out. One little girl asked Bobby if he ate bugs, and he admitted he sometimes did, but really enjoyed small mammals, mostly rodents, though she was big enough to be safe around him.

The girl realized he was teasing her, and laughed, Mary Pat along with her.

That opened the door to more people coming over. The pattern was the same, greetings to Magnus, Fisca, and Bjorn, then talking to Bobby.

Will had to admit the kid handled the attention well, and Mary Pat chimed in helpfully when she thought it necessary.

Ice cream and milkshakes turned out to be as short-lived in Cockaigne as back in the other Oregon. A half-hour went by quickly, and then they were back on the Promenade, walking slowly and seeing the sights. Two Dragonships went slowly past, heading into port, and there was much shouting and waving of swords when the crews spied Magnus.

"I have a famous ancestor," Katie said, smiling up at the King.

"Here more than in most places," Magnus replied. "My fame will burgeon even more when they find out my descendant is one of The Raptured."

"The 'Rapture Babe,'" Will added.

"That needn't have been said, William," she said, giving Will a sharp elbow in his ribs.

"Justice is served," Fisca observed with a wide grin as Will winced and grimaced.

"Welcome to the Club of Forceful Women," Bjorn told Will, his expression mirroring the Gladiatrix's.

"Been there for a lot of years," Will replied, rubbing his ribs, "but thanks anyway."

"Do any larger vessels berth here?" Mary Pat asked.

"Well, there are regular appearances of cruise ships out of mostly San Francisco," Bjorn said, "more in recent years. Another sign of von Neumann and Hughes affluence. More of a 'spread out' than a 'trickle down,' but definitely going on. Lots of female tourists on those ships, too."

"With all the women, Bjorn," Katie asked, "how do you find time to write poetry."

The skald's familiar grin appeared. "You'd be surprised how many young women are seduced while watching a poet compose."

"Huh," Will said. "Maybe I should give that a try, Katie. What do you think?"

"I think you're asking for another elbow, William," was the quick response.

Even the two children laughed.

They wandered through the city's main shopping area, including some of side streets, for another hour, then returned to their quarters, tired after a long day.

Baker got on his pad for a satellite view of Nixon's berth off to the south. "Still in the same spot, and nothing looks different, except the drone must be somewhere below decks. No sign of Jape on the deck. He's probably going stir-crazy."

"First thing after breakfast, we go to the store that can build our Orca translator, then go down to the Quay and test it out," Magnus said. "Orcas will respond, and we'll find out where Keiko's hanging out. He is generally in the area, right, Baker?"

"Right. He should have a network which can contact him easily and quickly. With luck, we can speak with him later in the day. What do you want from him?"

"I need his thoughts on what, if anything, his people can do to help defeat Richard and Almaric and recover Jape."

"How will you pay him?" Katie asked.

Baker answered. "Future favors, a lot of fish, cetacean psychedelics. Hard to be certain. Orcas think like us, but only in general ways. The specifics may differ considerably."

"Orcas use drugs?" Will asked.

"Some. This is all speculation until tomorrow. Keiko may be religious or conservative, or both. We'll find out. What little info is out there would seem to be very incomplete. Orcas are not shy, apparently."

"Time for bed, then," Katie said, looking pointedly at the two kids.

"Floss and brush time, Bobby," Mary Pat told her friend.

"Are you going to write some poetry tonight, Bjorn?" the little dinosaur asked.

Bjorn regarded him suspiciously. "I don't work on a set schedule, you understand. My muse is not always there. Writing is a fulsome task."

"You are surely full of something, Skald," Gro told him, "but perhaps something other than words."

"Are you impugning my creativity, Forsberg?"

"Only suggesting a source for inspiration, Cripplehand. You know we all value your efforts to an extreme. Correct, Great King?"

Magnus waved both arms. "Do not draw me into this discussion. I cannot push the Skald's efforts. He creates at his own pace, and has always done so."

"Not much output lately, however," Fisca said, looking pointedly at Bjorn.

The Skald gave the tiniest of shrugs. "I will attempt to have some helpful dreams this night. Ask me in the morn."

"Dreams?" Katie asked.

"Our nocturnal activities with Morpheus can be very inspirational in our waking endeavors," Bjorn replied, "particularly in literary creation."

"Can you rely on your dreams for doing poetry?" Will asked.

"More times than not, but I once went some weeks dreaming of frogs, and my poetry output suffered greatly, unless the topics were amphibious in nature."

"Couldn't you dream of frog women?" Katie asked.

Now the Skald looked uneasy. "Please do not cojoin my past frog issues with human women. Down that path disaster must lie."

"Have you heard of a young woman kissing a frog who is in reality an enchanted Prince?" Katie replied.

"You understand that concepts considered while awake can manifest in the dreaming time, so your question may instill visions of aquatic oddities in the coming hours of slumber."

"Will you tell us in the morning?" Will asked

Bjorn said nothing, only looked around at his companions with an expression of forbearance on his narrow features.

"Ribbit, Ribbit, Ribbit!" chorused Bobby and Mary Pat, which did nothing for the Skald's mood, but amused everyone else.

"I am tormented by children," Bjorn said, shaking his head abjectly.

That prompted a general laugh.

"Perhaps a return visit to Newton's and his bevy of comely waitresses would help mend your damaged spirit?" said Magnus, lifting his right eyebrow.

The Skald shook his head. "Nay, Boss. We may need my operational capacities in full fettle tomorrow. A reduction might result from any time spent at Newton's."

"Such loyalty," Fisca observed drily. "A noble fellow indeed."

Bjorn gave her a wide smile. "I know my role in this adventure, Nubian Queen. We are going to be back in the thick of things in another few days. I must not falter."

Now Fisca turned serious. "In all the time we've known each other, Bjorn, you never have. Your reliability and energies have been constant and unrelenting."

"We still need to get to bed," Mary Pat said, looking at her friend.

"Right," Bobby agreed.

After hugs, the Garrisons and the two kids went to their room, flossed and brushed, used the toilet and bidet, washed their hands and faces and climbed into bed. Mary Pat vaulted easily up onto the top bunk, peering down at Bobby as he slid under the sheets. "Good night," they told one another.

"Another exciting day tomorrow," Katie told them as she settled into Will's embrace and turned off the bedside lamp.

"Quieter than the past few days, I bet," Mary Pat replied.

"The rocks were kind of neat," Bobby added in the darkness.

Mary Pat snorted. "Easy for us to say. We weren't the ones throwing them. Oog and Karl really had to work at it. We couldn't have done it."

"Thanks for telling us about your people, Bobby," Katie told the young dinosaur. "I know it wasn't easy for you."

"Thanks, but here I am, warm and dry, my stomach full and with nice people, even if, as my Dad says, you're all mammals."

"I guess that would be species racism," Will said, chuckling.

"Good night, everyone," Katie said pointedly. "Sleep tight and don't let the bedbugs bite."

They slept.

CHAPTER SEVENTEEN

The next morning found Magnus and Bjorn making breakfast in the attached large kitchen. The Neanderthals had the tables set, and both milk and orange juice were on tap. Platters of fish and ham found their ways to the tables, with eggs following shortly, thanks to Gro and Fisca. There was also toast from Oog's people.

Katie asked if she and Will could help, but they were waved off as guests, so they and the children sat near the end of one of the long tables and ate as they watched Baker bouncing around computer sites and studying the *Checkers* for signs of activity.

"Anything happening?" Will asked between bites.

"No. A sizeable bunch of them went into that part of town, but they haven't come back yet. Probably just provisions, but who knows. His two main lieutenants are in Victoria, supposedly, and they're probably as busy as bees concocting some surprises for whoever shows up in pursuit. They know Magnus and the Neanderthals are around, although Oog's bunch might be iffy. Magnus was within sight of those two ships which attacked us, but the Neanderthal canoes are low in the water and mostly kept the *Blood Wave* between themselves and the action, so who can say. Anyway, not much going on at the moment. I'll keep checking." He tucked into his food, but kept one eye on the screen. The Spy Eye sat beside him, beeping occasionally, and after a time, Sylvia spoke to Baker, wondering, the Garrisons supposed, if today would bring any excitement.

The meal, with as many people as were being fed, took considerable time, and the crew ate enormous amounts of food. Karl and Lars went back to the platters twice, and the rest were not laggers. Gro sat with Baker, but didn't have much to say except for wishing everyone 'Good Morning' and chatting with Bobby and Mary Pat as she ate.

"My Grandfather and Bjorn do a good spread," Katie said, wrapping a thick slice of ham between two slices of whole wheat toast.

"Some men can do that, I guess," Will replied, his tone of voice inviting some sort of response.

"You do okay," Katie said, "though the kids were never too thrilled with 'Tuna Surprise.'"

"Well, it achieved its goal. They *were* surprised, and they actually liked the Goulash Soup."

"You used a mix, and a blender, along with a large can of Heinz Beef Vegetable soup, which was not cheating, but not exactly from scratch, either."

"Are you picking on your husband?" Bobby asked, his feathered crest raising slightly.

Katie laughed. "I suppose I am, Bobby, but he gives as good as he gets, most times."

"She's just kidding. She sends far more grief my way than she gets back, let me tell you."

"We've watched the two of you sparring ever since you appeared in the Rapture Hall," Mary Pat said, "so we know it's an even trade."

"It is," Will agreed, "and I wouldn't have it any other way."

"Me, neither," Katie said.

"We're happy you're here," Mary Pat said, "even if you came Up in an easier and different way than the rest of the folks."

"You were born in the usual way humans are, right, Mary Pat?" Katie asked the young Angel.

"Yes. My Mom got pregnant, it took nine months, and they got a terrific reward. Me!" At the end of the sentence, the biggest smile Mary Pat had sported to date crossed her freckled features.

"Oh, *brother*," Bobby said, looking very unsupportive of his friend.

Katie laughed. "Both of you are wonderful children, regardless of your backstory."

"Very diplomatic, dear," Will assured his wife.

Katie nodded. "Thanks. I thought so. But I meant every word."

They finished eating, tidied up the area, and waited for the trip to the electronics store. After asking Baker about Reasonable Richard, Magnus led them a few blocks to the store, where Fisca explained to the owner what they needed, and within an hour the completed apparatus was ready, including an operation manual.

"Can you give me a short run-through?" Fisca asked.

"Sure. There are two communications bits, besides the microphone you speak into." He indicated a pancake-shaped metal and plastic piece about the size of a dinner plate, only thicker. "You connect this to the lanyard, put it in the water, then speak into the microphone after making certain the correct function is selected. A translation into Orcese is sent out through the water, the nearest Orcas hear it, then come to wherever you are. Good so far?"

Fisca nodded.

"Okay, you tell them what you want, but to do that, you have to select the atmospheric function, which occurs when you and the Orcas are face-to- face, them with their snouts out of the water, speaking directly to you. Make sense?"

Fisca nodded again.

"That's pretty much it. This's the first one of these gadgets I've done, but the design is pretty simple, all over-the-counter components, nothing exotic. It'll work easily. There are videos showing its use, but nothing complicated. Very cool, actually. I'll make up a packet of parts which you could conceivably need, but probably won't. It should be bullet-proof. Any questions?"

"How much do we owe you?" Magnus asked.

"With your royal discount and this being the first I've done, three hundred doubloons. That okay?"

Bjorn dug the necessary funds from a heavy leather bag and passed them to the fabricator, who unlocked a metal drawer and slipped the doubloons inside. "This have anything to do with that Richard guy?" he asked as he re-locked the drawer.

"Perhaps," Fisca told him, her facial expression one her opponents probably saw in the arena when they faced her on the sand.

"Will it be on the tube?" he asked, stepping back slightly, hopefully out of reach.

"No promises on that," Baker replied, "but yeah, maybe. What I do is entertain the public, after all, and it behooves me to do that. We'll see how things shake out."

"And if you folks could test this thing out, and it works, I'd appreciate it if you'd let me know, in case I ever need to make another one."

"Fair enough," Magnus told the tradesman. "We're going out to the other side of the bridge to see if we can reach the Orcas. Wish us luck."

The group left the shop, turned left and walked a couple hundred yards to the other side of the bridge, facing out onto the open water, Fisca carrying the lightweight device.

"Will this do?" the King asked. The walkway surface lay about four feet above the very small waves.

"Should," Fisca replied, unreeling the thick cable and dropping the disc into the water, then handing Magnus the microphone.

After giving the mic a dubious look, Magus inhaled deeply and said "Hello, this message is for Keiko. This is Magnus Barefoot, formerly King of Norway, and I have a business proposition for you and your pod. We are by the bridge in Vancouver, on the seaward side. If you are interested, we'll be here for two hours and would appreciate hearing from you or your representative. Thank you."

"Good thing the weather is holding," Baker said, surveying the relatively calm sea. "If they hear you, shouldn't take them too long to get here."

"Can we go up on the bridge and watch?" Mary Pat asked.

"We might see them coming," Bobby added.

"I don't see why not," Fisca replied, looking at the Garrisons to see if they agreed.

"Should be fine," Will said, and Katie nodded assent.

The kids took off up to the sidewalk on the sea side of the bridge, and stood where they could see the six adults.

Nothing happened for over a half-hour, then Bobby yelled that they could see something out about a half-mile, and five minutes later three Orcas could be seen coming from the north. The two children rejoined the adults.

"Guess the thing worked," Baker said. "Switch the selector to 'vocal.'"

The three blunt heads stopped about ten feet away, the one in the center began to vocalize. "Morning, Landers. I'm Guido, born in the Atlantic off the Jersey coast. You must be Magnus. Pleased to meetcha. Big K is up tending to a transitional bunch who've been harassing one of our affiliated pods, so we'll hear what you got in mind, and report back. On my right is Limey Jim, and on my left is Twitch. Twitch got into some bad alginate seaweed a while back and he's still reactin' a bit. Pay no attention to his jerking. Another week or so and he'll be okay. So, what you need?"

Magnus cleared his throat and explained that the Blood Wave needed an escort to Victoria, but the actual duties were of necessity somewhat vague. He ran through the issue with Reasonable Richard and the kidnapping of Jape.

"So, this Jape guy is like the public face and voice of Old Man? That's heavy-duty. Takes balls to do somethin' like swipin' somebody like that, huh? Big K will definitely be interested. Right Jim?"

"Bloody Hell! He'll be on top of it. Real firm, he will."

They chatted for a while longer, then the Orcas returned to the north, leaving the humans looking at one another. They had agreed to return at three o'clock in the afternoon.

"Well, it worked," Baker finally said.

"I cannot believe I held a conversation with an Orca," Magnus said.

"An *ethnic* Orca, too," said Katie, with a puzzled smile.

"Even more surprising," Fisca agreed, her expression mirroring Katie's.

"They're beautiful." Mary Pat said.

"The wolves of the sea," Will said. "The apex predator in all their range. They can even kill and eat Blue Whales, sharks hightail away from them, and fishermen have never been able to fool them for long. They're too darned smart."

"How do they manage to kill something as big as a Blue Whale?" Bobby asked.

"They gather together, about sixty of them. They harass and batter the whale in groups of twenty. When the first bunch gets tired, the second takes over, and so on. The whale is eventually weakened under the continuous onslaught and drowns. The Orcas then have a feast."

"Sounds gruesome," Katie said, shuddering.

"The law of the watery jungle, I guess," said Baker.

"We should go back to quarters," Fisca said, reeling the communications disc back in, and shutting down the device.

Still slightly amazed, the group returned to the electronics store and reported success.

"It really worked?" the proprietor asked.

"And quite well," Magnus replied. "We go back for another session this afternoon, this one with Keiko himself."

The store owner seemed impressed and pleased as the group departed.

Back in the Viking lodge, everyone sat around and talked. Oog's people were attentive, asking questions, and the ship's crew took over when the Neanderthals ran down.,

"I can hardly wait until the adventure begins again," Karl said, rubbing his huge hands together in anticipation'

"I'm trying to think how the Orcas might be an asset," Gro said, her brow furrowed. "They must remain in the water, and short of crashing into the *Checkers'* hull, what can they do?"

"Maybe we'll have some answers this afternoon," Fisca said, looking as bereft of answers as the others. "They have never worked with humans before, so we have no ground rules for interaction."

"They're very intelligent," said Baker, "so perhaps they'll think of something They can get their tails under things and fling them into the air. They do that with seals, playing with them before they feed. Hard to say, so we'll just have brainstorm things."

"How's Richard doing?" Will asked.

"Good question. Let me check." He booted up his pad and spent a few minutes searching, "Nope, still just sitting there. Tomorrow at the soonest, I'm guessing."

After more conversation, minor food crimes took place, and more chit-chat until it was time to go back out. Mary Pat and Bobby were the most excited, but the Neanderthals and Vikings were close behind. Magnus, Baker, and Fisca made a short list of questions for Keiko, although they had no idea what he was like or how receptive he might be. Baker wondered what on earth the Orcas would want by way of compensation, and nobody had any solid ideas on that. 'Play it by ear' was the final idea.

Fifteen minutes to three and the whole mob went to the meeting point, the two kids back up on the bridge. Fisca set up the translator and they waited.

Right on time, fifteen heads appeared from the north and swept up to the shoreline to form a rough 'V' formation, will Keiko presumably in the center.

"Good afternoon," the big Orca said, his voice more resonant then the earlier conversants. "I'm Keiko, and this is my gang. What do you need?"

Magnus introduced himself and the others by him, not going through all the Neanderthals and Vikings, then explained the situation with Reasonable Richard and Old Man.

"So Old Man is involved? His friend has been kidnapped, and naturally he wants that issue taken care of. We could probably sink Richard's ship." He turned to one of the other Orcas. "What do you think, Tony?"

"Could be done. We've got some steel nose fittings, so if a few of us wore those and hit the same spot on the hull, we could punch through it, and the ship would go down."

"But then Old Man's pal would drown with the rest of them."

Orcas couldn't shrug, but Tony came close. "Maybe with a description, we could get him up out of the water, keep him alive."

"Richard's advisor is the real problem." Magnus told them. "If we can neutralize him somehow, the problem might solve itself. We really don't want the whole crew of their ship to drown, so that easy solution might not be wise."

"How about we damage it enough to create a controllable leak," said Tony, "then threaten them with being sunk?"

"That's an idea," Magnus admitted, "but if Almaric is as crazy and irrational as he appears to be, he might be stubborn, and Richard seems to let him run the show."

"Don't humans generally want to go down with the ship?" Keiko asked. "That's been said over the centuries."

"How do your people know that?" Fisca asked.

"Some of the native human women – those little ones – have kind of learned how to talk to us, sort of, and those legends have come down through the pods. So common knowledge, I guess."

"Any other classic tales?" Baker asked, looking for grist for his eventual broadcast. The Spy Eye hovered over the gathering, beaming every word back to

Boston and The Oregonian. Editing would eventually produce an acceptable broadcast as events wound down.

One of the Orcas spoke up. "Well, there was the story about a giant human free-swimming penis that roamed the seas and fed on whale ejaculate, but nobody really believed that one. It was too far-fetched. Moby Dick was its name."

Only Baker, Katie, and Will reacted to that revelation, and they said nothing. Really, what could be said?

"Will your pursuit be renewed when the *Checkers* leaves port?" Keiko asked.

"Yes," Magnus replied. "We have to stop Richard and Almaric, as well as free Old Man's friend who has served him for many years. Richard's allies toil in Victoria to adversely affect our efforts. We have no idea of their plans, but their efforts in the time before they were brought up indicate they are ingenious and industrious."

"Bad combination," the big Orca said. "Dedicated enemies are the worst." The other cetaceans squeaked and clicked assent.

"So," Keiko continued, "not a lot we can offer to do other than sink the ship until some more acceptable plan is devised."

"What about Flipper?" a medium-sized Orca asked, raising a fin.

"That crazy kid?" Keiko asked.

"He can flip an adult Harbor Seal eighty feet in the air. What else could he toss that might help defeat the bad guys?"

"Some sort of bomb, maybe," said Baker. "It would damage the ship without sinking it."

"There's a thought," Magnus replied, stroking his chin. "Except how would such a weapon be detonated?"

"Like a mine," Katie said, "bursting when it strikes the ship's decking."

That thought met with general acceptance.

"Can any of you do the same thing as this – 'Flipper' – does?" asked Will.

"Flip, get over here," Keiko said.

A muscular-looking Orca swam to their leader. "Any of us can do it," he said. "It's just been a kind of hobby for me. Ariel can do it, too. I taught her. She caught on real quick. Right, Ariel?

"Any of us can do it, like you said," the lithe female Orca replied, turning over and sending thirty gallons of seawater high into the air. "See?"

"Impressive," Magnus admitted. "We will have to give it some thought."

Guido entered the conversation for the first time. "How about throwing shit? That'd piss them off without damaging them."

"Kind of a typical Jersey Boy concept," Keiko said, squeaking laughter and nodding his snout. "Make their decks slippery, too."

"Using materials at hand," Baker said. "Easily procured. Very practical. I'd say."

"You would," Fisca put in, laughing. "Similar to your professional efforts, wouldn't it be."

Predictably, Baker gave her a dirty look.

"How much time can your people dedicate to our efforts?" the King asked.

"Well, we have to eat, and some of us will be calving in a few weeks, but we can be available."

"How will we compensate you?" Fisca asked.

"Now that we can talk to each other, maybe some sort of open air theater where we could watch your entertainment programs, maybe learn about your societies. Now all we have is observing fishermen. We've probably gone to the limit on their lives at sea. What happens when they're off their ships, for example."

"Do they have sex a lot?" Guido asked, snorting rudely. The others laughed. Since Orcas were really large dolphins, sex might be very common.

"Another Jersey Boy thing," Keiko observed, his eyes cast down.

"Do you all want to talk it over and meet back here tomorrow in the morning?" Magnus asked. "Richard may leave tomorrow, but the distance across Georgia Strait isn't far, so likely it will be later in the day. Baker is keeping a regular eye on him, so we'll know when he sails."

"Fair enough," Keiko replied, and the other Orcas called out approval. "See you around ten o'clock?"

"Yes."

The pod turned and swam off to the north, several flipping their tails in farewell.

"They're nice," Katie said.

"Seem to be democratically-organized, too," Will replied.

"I never thought to have that conversation," Magnus said as Fisca brought the translator disc from the water, winding up the cable and clipping it to the device's case. "We've watched the Orcas for many years and understood they were highly-structured and very intelligent, but this was still a surprise."

"They may well be a big help," Baker said.

Gro laughed. "Throwing shit was a clever idea. That might work to our advantage."

"Throwing a two hundred and fifty pound Harbor Seal eighty feet into the air is an incredible feat of strength and coordination," Katie said.

Lars made one his rare comments. "They could toss Karl onto The Checkers. He could wreck havoc. He and I weigh about the same as a very large male Harbor Seal."

Karl gave his large friend a light blow to an exposed shoulder. "You could join me."

Lars laughed. "I kind of said that, didn't I? You would share the battle glory?" Lars replied, his expression disbelieving. "So very kind." He turned to the rest. "You are all witnesses to this unusual invitation."

"That actually makes some sense," Fisca said. "The two of you, along with some of Oog's people, appearing on their deck out of nowhere with weaponry to hand, chaos would ensue."

"I like the idea," Magnus said. "Some practice would likely be necessary, but the concept seems sound."

"Certainly something to consider," Baker said, looking up at the Spy Eye. "I hope you caught the birth of this nifty idea." The little bot peeped three time in ascending notes while bobbing in the air.

"Let's return to quarters and see to our weapons," Fisca suggested. "We're going to be in for it within another day or two. A battle at sea is never an easy task, even with the fifty calibers and the Bushmaster, but if they are firing at us from one side, and the Orcas fling a decent-sized force onto their decks from the opposite side, well, that could make all the difference in outcome."

As the conversation continued, the whole group walked to the east. back to their quarters.

"What are we going to be able to do to help?" Katie asked.

"Nothing involving throwing kids into the air, I hope," Mary Pat said. She and Bobby had been uncharacteristically quiet during the exchange with the Orcas.

"They wouldn't do that, Mary Pat," Katie told her.

"That was sure fun!" Bobby exclaimed. "I had no idea Orcas knew about what we discussed."

"They're really smart," Mary Pat said.

"I thought their Pods were matrilinear," Will said, "but Keiko seemed to be the one in charge."

"He and a few others have been Brought Up," Katie replied, "so maybe the rules are different here. On the other hand, some of them are going to calve, so most of them must be native, since the Brought Up can't reproduce."

"It probably doesn't matter in the context of what we're doing," Will said. "We only have to defeat Richard, capture Almaric, and rescue Jape."

"Three tough things," Mary Pat replied. "We'll need a lot of luck."

Walking in front of them, Fisca turned her head. "We will manage, youngling. Luck is always a factor in martial endeavors, but we shall do all we can to weight the balance in our favor. Never fear."

"Okay. I believe you."

"Fisca's been there, done that," Bobby added.

"Just as you say," the gladiatrix responded, grinning at the two children. "My experience will help, as will the King's and that of our crew members. The weavings of the Norns have kept us alive in this strange reality, and will likely again."

Those who didn't need to be in their rooms for whatever reason sat around the common area and talked, mostly about the coming confrontation, but also sharing stories and reminiscences from their current and former lives.

"Lars and I are cousins," Karl told the Garrisons and the two children. "We were recruited from our village…"

"…for four cattle and a percentage of the future plunder, if any," Lars added.

"And the promise of a good sea burial if our lives were lost in battle."

"Do the killed actually see the Valkyries?" Mary Pat asked.

"I did," Karl said. "Both looked like my Great-aunt Helga, and their handling was rather rough."

Lars laughed. "*My* Valkyries were young and kind, with gentle hands and soothing voices."

"Lars is prone to exaggerate," Karl said, placing one large hand alongside his mouth as though sharing a secret.

"What happened then?" Bobby asked.

"We woke up on the deck of the *Blood Wave*, whole and healthy again, and Gro threw a bucket of cold seawater over us to make sure we were awake."

Lars sighed gustily. "And we were immediately put to work."

"After some refreshing ale, you'll remember," said Karl, poking a thick forefinger into Lar's right arm.

"Gro would have made a good Valkyrie," Lars replied thoughtfully, "except for the seawater."

"You're lucky it wasn't warm urine, boys," Gro said from her seat beside Baker.

"You are a wicked woman," Karl accused.

"Old news, lads. I do my job when Fisca asks."

"As do we all," Magnus said softly, looking up from his copy of 'Viking News,' and smiling at the slender dark warrior.

Fisca grinned rather than frowned at the mild torment. She knew her place in the hierarchy of the *Blood Wave's* society, as well as her relationship with the King. She would protect them all, as well as the Neanderthals, the Garrisons, and the two grade schoolers.

"How good are the ammunition stocks for the rifles and the Bushmaster?" Magnus asked.

"Good," Fisca replied. "As powerful as the Bushmaster is, not a great deal of ammo was used in our earlier confrontation with Richard. Roughly eighty percent of our original supply remains. The Fifty caliber stock is at sixty to seventy percent. Even should we get into a protracted firefight, things will be adequate. Although we have no idea of the amount of preparation his minions are assembling, acquiring something as powerful as the Bushmaster is very unlikely. The mortars they used earlier went to the bottom of the Sound with their attack craft. Which does not mean they do not have more, but we shall see. Those two are clever devils, and they are doubtless busy on the mischief trail."

The Spy Eye chose that moment to beep, and Sylvia's voice sounded. "Can you people give me some notion of when we can have a broadcast of the past few days' activities. I'm reduced to talking heads speculating on what's next, without any of the rock-throwing being generally available, and that was great footage. We have to assume Richard has some access to the broadcasts put out by local stations, and we would tip him off if we show the rocks, the Orcas, or your current location. He has to be kept in the dark, but that necessity is really hobbling our duty to keep the public informed. This is high quandary, folks."

"I've got no good answer," Baker said. "You'll just have to keep it in the bag until the big sea battle in another day or two. Once that's past, regardless of the outcome, you can backstory the earlier stuff, explaining why it was kept off the airwaves. The public will see the sense of that, and they'll accept it."

Sylvia sighed resignedly. "You're right, of course. Wish you weren't, but there we go. I'll make do somehow. Thanks." She signed off.

"Anybody got any good ideas?" the journalist asked the group. "Some untraceable filler."

"How about a Neanderthal farting contest?" Oog asked.

"Too low-brow," Baker replied, shaking his head, "even though it would have good attention-getting potential. The public would be amused, but it would be fluff, as it were, not the meaty news they want. Maybe after things quiet down, a post heavy doings light piece."

"We can make it a competition with teams, going down to the final two farters for the Championship," Oog said. His listeners chuckled in appreciation. His people seemed enthused, which wasn't much of a surprise.

"We'll look forward to it," Bobby and Mary Pat said, very much the most excited of the non-Neanderthals.

Katie gave her husband a stern look. "No, you are so not going to get involved in something like that."

"I'm not even considering it, dear," Will replied. "I'm sort of surprised you would even think I would. I was under the impression I was a proper gentleman, at least most of the time."

"Just a cautionary thought, William. Now that we're young again, I tend to recall your occasionally wayward youth."

"My wayward youth pretty much flew the coop when the wedding took place, I thought." He frowned at the two grade schoolers, who wore matching grins. "Don't be enjoying this conversation too much."

"Isn't it about time you phone your folks?" Katie asked them.

Their smiles didn't diminish even slightly. "Not until after supper," the two truants answered. "They don't expect us to call until mid-evening, but we have to call each and every day. They were really concerned when the confrontation with the bear took place. We told them we stayed on the ship during the excitement, and that quelled their concern. They knew our safety was important to the crew and that we were being looked after, not thrust into danger. It helped, too, that we were below decks when the firefight took place. So they're not worried above simple parental concern."

"If they need to talk to Will and I," Katie told them, "we'll be glad to, if you think that would help."

Bobby gave his rasping laugh. "That's okay. Our folks know we're careful kids, within reason."

"Our approach to life is fairly constrained," Mary Pat added, her features far meeker than usual. "We're not careless, and nobody is going to let us run wild. We've watched the crew react when danger threatens, and every head turns toward us before the action begins."

"As it should be," Fisca said, her chin giving a sharp nod. "We all look out for you two first and foremost."

"We appreciate that," Mary Pat said, and Bobby echoed her.

"Probably a good time to get ready for the evening meal," Magus told the group.

"Did you guys get a new stock of your root?" Baker asked the Neanderthals.

We're stocked up," Oog replied.

"Good quality, too," several of others said. "Kind of a surprise, considering not too many of our kind are around these parts. We'll be able to pull our own weight for another couple weeks, and if we stay intact in the next few days, there's another provider in Victoria. So we're good."

"Excellent," Magnus said, "because you people are a major portion of our effort."

"Might even see some air if the Orcas decide to do that," Oog said, with a deep laugh, and the other Neanderthals perked up as he spoke, risk-takers every one.

Magnus folded up his paper and got to his feet. "My stomach seeks sustenance."

Bobby and Mary Pat stood in front of him. "Thank you for taking such good care of us, Great King. We'll try not to be any trouble.'"

Two head-pats and a sincere smile later, and the 'Great King' led everyone out the door and back to Newton's for more seafood and as much gossip as was available.

"Any word on Reasonable Richard?" Baker asked the genial proprietor as their orders were being taken.

A pirate's crafty smile appeared. "He's paying with gold, the grapevine says. Safe and useful. Nothing unusual is going aboard, just food stores and small amounts of ammunition. Several delivery persons have overheard conversations with someone ashore in Victoria or Port Angeles, those only with Richard and not the lunatic clergyperson. This, of course, means that his main minions both survived the earlier battle and are busily acquiring some weaponry which might serve to discourage pursuers on a formidable Dragonship."

Newton's smile expanded. "They have to assume you will sail after them, although some doubts have been raised on that regard."

"Do they have any crew on shore being treated for injuries sustained in the rain of stones?" Fisca asked, between swallows of good ale.

Newton laughed heartily. "Six, possibly seven, were taken ashore and seen to at a clinic. Three of those remain in that medical facility, but should be back on board for tomorrow's departure. Injuries were primarily of the contusion and bruising varieties, painful yet not horribly devastating."

"We did our best, me and Karl," Oog said, raising his mug. "Pity there weren't any noggins conked. That would have done the job, right enough."

"You weren't aiming," the restaurant owner stated. "Good enough to get most of them onto the main deck. Anything beyond that was fortuitous circumstance, commonly referred to as 'luck.'"

"Well put," Oog replied. "Luck is capricious to my way of experience."

Newton thought for a few moments, stroking his stubbled chin, then addressed the King. "You've talked to the Orcas, I hear. How was that?"

"Quite good," Magnus replied. "They are very intelligent and motivated. What sort of use they will provide remains to be seen. They could easily batter Richard's vessel into the depths, but that would sacrifice their hostage, so perhaps not."

The next expression to cross the actor's visage was totally Long John Silver's. He must know, Will and Katie thought, who was on the *Checkers*, and it was not who they thought they had. The interesting aspect to that was why Jape remained in his guise as Old Man. Loyalty and a contrary nature for certain, along with the probability that even if he were killed, his resurrection would again occur. A handy thing to have waiting in the wings if needed.

The meal and conversations continued until dessert and last beverages were over. Whenever Magnus, Fisca, Baker, or Bjorn thought of another question, Newton answered as best he could, his brow furrowing and his front teeth tapping together while he thought. The amount of gossip and definite information he had was astounding. Nothing seemed to completely baffle him. If what he'd learned was vague or incomplete, he said so.

When enough information had been shared, the words wound down and the *Blood Wave* crew and their guests meandered around the town while there was still enough daylight to appreciate the varieties of businesses and entertainment venues. A recent release by the Three Naughty Guys was playing at a movie theater. Will, Katie, and the kids paused to study the poster. This time the comedy trio was in Copenhagen, and the gendarmes pursuing them looked to be generic European.

"Have either of you ever seen any of these films?" Katie asked Bobby and Mary Kate.

"They're a little mature for us, our folks say," Bobby told them.

"But once when we were left on our own at my house," Mary Pat said, "we watched one, and it was pretty funny. Khrushchev was hilarious. My Dad told me he was a big-name political figure, but if that's true, he missed his calling. All three of them were really good, but he was the best, we both thought."

"We missed that part of him, I guess," Will replied, exchanging a glance with his wife.

"Maybe he had jovial moments we were unaware of," Katie said.

They walked on. The retail stores had plenty of manufactured goods, even a few familiar brands, but there were products which were clearly made by smaller family enterprises operating with fewer employees and a great deal of ingenuity. The big guns who built the energy systems were serious providers of the fusion power plants and the anti-gravity units which made society work cleanly and comfortably, but it was nice to see smaller companies in the retail marketplace.

They overtook a knot of Oog's people at a moderate-sized motorcycle shop with machines standing in front of the business on center stands, the Neanderthals quizzing the proprietors about the machines. Not surprisingly, the bikes were all off-road oriented, since most of the urban centers in Cockaigne were not connected by pavement. Knobby tires were the rule, but some of the larger-engined steeds were set up for longer distance riding, the so-called Dualsports.

"The brand names aren't the same as ours, are they?" Katie asked. "Traub, Yale, and Penton."

"Penton was a real brand," Will replied. "I remember them from when I was a kid."

"Looks like a lot of fun, don't it?" Oog asked, running his thick fingers over the seat of one of the bikes, a sleek Yale with a 350 cc. single cylinder air-cooled engine. "I'd need one with a low seat though, for sure. We might be hell for strong, but our legs ain't that long."

The shop salesperson had not had much experience with Neanderthals, particularly those wearing aloha shirts, that was obvious, but she answered their questions and seemed very knowledgeable and enthusiastic. They would go back to their stomping grounds in Germany when this adventure was ended, but no stretch of imagination was required to see that motorcycles might enter their lives at some future point. Oog was quite enchanted and his followers seemed the same.

The saleswoman gave Oog her card. Oog, being himself, tried for an archaic human discount. She laughed, told him she couldn't rule that out, but she'd need to see the color of his money before they discussed that issue. The sturdy Neanderthal, always affable, said he thought that would be fine. They shook hands, and the group headed up the street, Oog's people going on about the motorcycles to the point where even Bobby and Mary Pat were talking about the fun motorcycles would bring into their lives.

"My folks would frown me into next week if I asked for a motorcycle," Mary Pat said, with her hoyden's grin.

"My tail would be a problem, I think," Bobby added.

"Could you tuck it away somehow?" Katie asked. "It isn't that long. Does it flex?"

"Oh, yeah," the little dinosaur replied, "but maybe not enough. If I had to stand up, it would want to straighten out and that could be real distracting and difficult."

"It probably won't ever be an issue," Will told him. "Your folks wouldn't be any more enthusiastic than Mary Pat's."

"They had some smaller kid-sized bikes inside the shop," Mary Pat said, "and I bet they have motorcycle shops in Boston."

"Is this going to be a Holy Grail quest for you two?" Katie asked, laughing.

"Not yet," the pair answered. "We've got to grow some more before we could get bikes. We're both essentially ten years old, and we mature at about the same rate even with our different genetic backgrounds."

"A couple more years, then?" Will said.

"Let's say three," Bobby said, "maybe four or five. Raptureville will have to be finished and our dads will have their bonuses. We'll go from there."

"Plotting and planning," Mary Pat said, rubbing her hands together cunningly.

"The powers of children on a mission," Will said, shaking his head.

"We're listening to all that," Oog said from up ahead of them. "I'll have to discuss any motorcycle purchase with my dear wife. At some length and with many promises of behavior modification and improvements to our humble abode."

"Do your people live in caves?" Katie asked.

"Some do, but there's the problem of electricity, water, plumbing, and some kind of sewerage system. We have the same sort of bodily functions as your kind of humans. We live in a village of stone walls, slate roofs, plenty of flowers, and neat little garden plots."

"But no children?"

"Some of us were brought up with families. Old Man doesn't like to bust up parents and kids if they died at the same time. Like with Bobak here. He got Brought Up with his folks. And there are some adoptions of kids who died young. My *Frau* and me have a little girl named Bright Water who lives up to her name a fair amount of the time." He grinned at Mary Pat. "But some of the time she is like you."

"A complete and utter joy, then," the young angel replied.

Even Katie laughed at that.

"Are you people laughing at me?" Mary Pat said, scowling.

"Not me," Bobby replied, waving his arms, sending tiny rainbows along their lengths.

"Better not," Mary Pat told him, shifting to a tiny smile.

"Kids can be very entertaining," Will said. "ours certainly were."

"Some more than others," Katie added.

"How many kids did you have?" Oog asked.

"Three. Two girls and a boy. All doing well enough in the world. We did a decent job, mostly due to Katie's supervision of both them and myself."

Katie scoffed. "William, you're a good dad. The children love you."

"Barbara is involved in ordering her father around maybe more than she should be."

"She means well."

"She the oldest or the youngest?" the Neanderthal asked. His companions stood behind him, looking interested. "Has to be one or the other, right?"

"The youngest by a bunch of years," Will replied.

Katie rolled her eyes. "I was forty-four when she came along. She was a surprise. Twenty-five now, two decades younger than the others and more rowdy in most ways. She's fairly certain she knows it all, or very close to that. Advice is freely given. If you don't accept it, she will trot it back out at some future date. A relentless child. Her older siblings are consistently amused."

"She means well," Will said, "but she's in Med School and they seem to acquire powers of secret knowledge in that realm."

"She was that way before Med School, Will."

"Yeah, kind of," Will admitted, his grin lop-sided.

"She'll be fine," Oog said. "Your species isn't as upbeat as ours, but if the groundwork is there, things usually work out. Med School! That's gotta be cool."

"When we get back home," Katie said, "the big problem for all three children will be their parents' recovered youth. How will we explain that?"

"Divine intervention?" Mary Pat said.

Will regarded her sourly. "That answer, while true, may not be very convincing to modern offspring, especially ours."

"Bobby and I could come with you and explain things." A maximum gamine grin accompanied her words. Bobby looked at her in mock horror.

Mary Pat gave him a light swat. "You would totally want to do that, Bobak. Together we could make it happen!"

Bobby nodded slowly, probably thinking his friend had a lot in common with the Garrison's youngest.

"First we gotta get Jape back home," Oog said, and the other Neanderthals growled assent.

"They told us there's a T-shirt place up ahead," Mary Pat said. "Bobby and I could use new T-shirts, right?"

Bobby gave her a guarded nod.

The group walked on, and in another half-block discovered the shirt emporium. The children trotted in, followed by the rest.

"Look, Bobby!" Mary Pat exclaimed. "They've got Orca shirts!"

"'Orca Dorks,'" Will said. "Keiko's gang would like to see those."

"Can they read?" Katie asked.

"We can tell them what the shirts say," Will told her. "And the shirts do have Orcas on them."

"Okay, but will they know what a 'dork' is?"

"That might be tough. I don't imagine they have Dork Orcas. They all contribute to whatever they're up to, no slackers or goof-offs."

At that juncture, the kids were trying on the shirts, certain Katie and Will were going to finance their endeavors. Which would happen, of course. The Neanderthals watched with interest.

When their results were acceptable, Mary Pat and Bobby paraded around in the shirts with the young salesperson looking on. Katie and Will nodded and brought their debit cards out. The new shirts were bagged , thanks were given, and everyone went back outside and continued their amble.

"Keiko will be impressed with these shirts, I bet," Mary Pat said, beaming happily.

"He'll probably try to figure out a way to market Orca-related products," Will replied. "Maybe they have copyright laws in Cockaigne that will favor the subject of the products, in this case the Orcas."

The two children shared a long look, apparently trying to come up with a way to help the cetaceans.

An ice cream parlor interrupted that unspoken exchange. The Neanderthals turned as one and went in, and Will, Katie, and the new shirt pair followed. The little store immediately became crowded, with orderly aloha-shirted patrons giving their orders. The servers were organized enough to get cones and sundaes distributed quickly. The Garrisons and the kids watched patiently, Bobby and Mary Pat less so.

The debit cards came out again, and shortly four cones were in four hands. Then it was back outside.

"This is good," Katie said, "but maybe not from cows."

"What else?" Will asked.

"Mammoth, Mastodon. Who knows?"

"Mammoth don't like to be milked," Mary Pat told them. "It's been tried, with mixed results. Mastodon will put up with it without fuss, but the milkers have to be women or teenage girls. Nobody knows why,"

Are there Mastodon dairies?" Katie asked.

"I'm not sure," Mary Pat replied. "Do you know, Bobby?"

"No, but I like ice cream."

"Baker might know," Will said. "We can ask."

They passed a news stand, and Oog noticed a magazine called 'North,' with the Garrisons on the cover. "Lookit that!" he said, pointing. "You should get a copy and take it back home when you go."

Will had enough change in his pockets to do just that. The young guy who ran the stand asked them to autograph the remaining copies, and the Garrisons did that also.

"Thanks, Oog," Katie told the sturdy Neanderthal.

"Don't leave it around the house where your kids can see it," he replied. "Too many questions, no good answers."

"You got that right," Will said, smiling at the thought of the potential questions the magazine would create. His wife's expression mirrored his.

"Wonder what Richard's up to?" Katie asked, addressing no one in particular.

"Playing cards with Jape, maybe," Will replied, thinking that was unlikely, but his remark got a few grins.

"We got an issue, speaking of that," Oog said. "So far we ain't been firing on Richard's ship except above decks. Should it happen that we're firing at the hull, I'm guessing the Bushmaster would go right through below decks, which might not be healthy for Jape."

"Good point," Will admitted. "I'm sure Fisca and Magnus have taken that into consideration."

They walked on, with no more morbid thoughts on oncoming battles or the death of Old Man's understudy. Eventually they reached the outskirts of the commercial area, then crossed the street to go down the opposite side on the way back to quarters.

"There's a comic book store," Bobby said, pointing into a medium-sized storefront with a very colorful grouping of displays in the window.

"Let's go in," Mary Pat said, looking a Will and Katie. "Can we?"

"Sure," the Garrisons replied, following the children in. The Neanderthals joined them.

Will remembered comic book stores from his own youth, and evolution had not changed the basic layout at all. The two people greeting them from behind the counter were solid counter-culture. Even here.

"Can we help?" the emo young woman asked.

"Do you have new work by Carl Barks?" Will asked, dredging up a name from many years in his past.

"Oh, yeah," the girl replied. "He and Walt reconnected when Barks was Brought Up, and new work has been ongoing for the past twenty years. Do you fancy the ducks?"

"Uncle Scrooge?"

"Plenty of that. It's over here. Barks is prolific, and Disney Enterprises has backed him to the hilt." She led Will. Katie, and the kids over to a full rack. "You like the Beagle Boys?"

"Their battles with Scrooge were legendary."

"Quite a lot of that."

Behind them, the Neanderthals were asking about Stone Age comics and Burrough's Tarzan. The other staffer showed them what was available, to great excitement. 'Turock, Son of Stone' created a few yelps of joy. 'Ka-Zar' also got them going.

"These are all new, aren't they?" Will asked of the shopgirl.

"Oh, yeah."

Will studied what they had, which was quite a bit. "The Beagles never win, do they?"

"You remember the comics from sixty years ago, don't you?"

"Longer than that. I read the ducks from the mid-sixties. Never liked Gyro Gearloose all that much, but the Beagles and Gladstone Gander were enjoyable."

"The comics nerds have been trying to get Old Man to bring up some pristine copies from the Forties and Fifties, but Johnathon Albunn is solidly into Marvel and DC, so it's an uphill battle." She paused, looked more closely at the Garrisons. "You're the Raptured, aren't you?"

"We are," Katie told her.

"Neat. You're in with Old Man, then. He's got to send you back. Maybe you could bring him around on the comics. Word is he fishes a lot, so if you convince Albunn to be helpful to us, that'd be bitchin'."

Mary Pat and Bobby hung onto every word, probably not realizing Will might have been young many years ago and had interests then which matched theirs now. Times change, but kids don't.

Will actually bought copies of all the new Uncle Scrooge material while his wife regarded him skeptically, but Mary Pat and Bobby were excited.

"Can we read them?" they asked.

"See how they're in mylar covers?" Will told then as he got to the cash register and the girl checked him out and bagged his selections. "That's to keep them pristine for collectors."

"We'll be careful," Bobby said, trying to simultaneously look responsible and plaintive.

Will grinned down him, noticing that Mary Pat duplicated his expression and that Katie was having entirely too much fun with the situation.

With Will clutching his treasures tightly, they left the store, the Neanderthals trailing behind with their purchases. Neanderthals and comic books seemed a stretch, but they were clearly dedicated fans.

"Here's the deal," Will told the kids. "You can read these, but first you have to wash your hands and be very careful with them, okay?"

Emphatic nods followed.

"Will, if these are unknown back in our world, they are still the work of the genius of Carl Barks, and reproduction would be worth a small fortune, right?"

Will thought about that as they walked along, ignoring the excited Neanderthals, who seemed to be squabbling over who was going to read what they'd bought first. "You're right. Barks' style is unmistakable.

There's no question of their authenticity. How to explain their sudden reappearance twenty years after his death, and under the Disney label is an issue. Scrooge is perhaps the most popular of Bark's creations. Enthusiasm will be incredibly high. Perhaps if I approached Fantagraphics Publishing with these, a deal could be done."

"Some large dollars, then?"

"Definitely. Might require some real inventive backstory to explain these unknown works reappearing, but the upside would be something special. Plus the ducks are incredibly popular in Europe, so there's a true goldmine waiting there."

"We still get to read them, right?" Mary pat asked.

"We made a bargain," Will told her. "You will live up to that, so yeah, you two get to read these, within my rules of care."

"Oh, boy!" the two exclaimed, high-fiving.

Few other distractions presented themselves during the remainder of their stroll back to the Viking quarters. The sun had set by the time they arrived, and they sat and watched Baker study the *Checkers*. "Close enough to actual darkness so I can't see much," the columnist said, looking irritated. "In the morning, after breakfast, I'll get back to them, and I'd expect them to set sail by mid-day, unless there's something we're unaware of, which there could be. We'll just have to see how it goes then."

"We'll follow as close as we dare," Fisca said, her dark features concerned.

"The Orcas will be with us," Magnus said, "and we can hope Nixon and Almaric see their proximity as mere co-incidence."

"They will not be alarmed," Fisca said. "Orcas are a natural thing which won't be seen as oceanic spies stalking evil in the service of Old Man or a shipload of Vikings."

"Keiko is intelligent and Orcas are both powerful and adroit in their element," said Baker. "They are just part of the scenery, the natural world. How could they betray themselves, hold up signs reading 'You're Screwed!' or something similar?"

Magnus chuckled. "There will be no problem on that level. Keiko will send one of his pod members back-and-forth from The Checkers to us, and then back again. No problem will arise."

"They just turned lights on their deck," Baker said, frowning. "Bodies are moving around, but not in any kind of hurry. Just normal activity."

"Do you want to get up during the night to check on them?" Gro asked Baker. "I'll be glad to rouse you."

The columnist considered that for a few moments. "No, we should be okay. They've still got their gangway down to the dock, so we're not looking at departure at daybreak or anything like that. They may still have people ashore recuperating from the rock attack, so we're probably good. Of course, we have no idea what his two main minions are doing in Victoria. Readying some sort of nasty surprise for us if we prove to be persistent, one would think."

"Too bad we have no foreknowledge of their endeavors," Fisca said.

"Perhaps in the morning we could ask Newton to reach out to his sources in Victoria to determine what may be going on there," Magnus said. "Any sort of unusual activity of possible violent nature. I am concerned of the possibility of some type of ariel assault. A helicopter gunship, perhaps, or a bomb-carrying drone."

"A drone would be vulnerable to the Bushmaster," Fisca said, "and drones armed with missiles are not available in Cockaigne, so it would have to get close and kamikaze in on us. I can take out anything which has to strike directly. Never fear."

"More than one, perhaps," Magnus replied. "Multiple flying bombs might prove daunting."

The gladiatrix shrugged. "We also have the nine millimeters and good accurate trained personnel handling them. The Bushmaster will not be alone, Great King. I worry about some sort of torpedo, but then we can rely on the Orcas to steer torpedoes away from the Blood Wave."

"Wouldn't the Orcas trigger the torpedoes?" Katie asked.

"No," Fisca replied. "They would simply give the weapons a nudge off in another direction, but not turn them back on their origin. The safety of Jape is of paramount importance. Telling Old Man that we recovered the larger pieces is not a desirable result of any interaction."

Nods all around.

"We'll do whatever we can," Oog assured the group. "We're awfully low targets, and if things get into close quarters, we can move rapidly into boarding position. On the other hand, the Orcas can get us onto their ship without much fuss."

"You'd do that?" Katie asked. "Let the Orcas toss you onto the ship's deck?"

"You probably noticed we ain't easily hurt. We can take a lot of bumps and bangs. Landing on a deck surrounded by hostile sapiens is doable. Even sounds like it might be fun. Right, guys?"

The other Neanderthals grunted loud approval.

"You and your hubby could join us."

"Maybe not," Katie replied, smiling at his bold insanity.

"Well, we have the day behind us," Magus said. "I think our pre-hashing is done. Tomorrow will happen. When Richard and his ship of fools set sail, we will pursue at a safe distance, the Orcas closer to them, so as not to create a connection with us. Are there any questions before we retire?"

No one said a word, merely shook their heads.

CHAPTER EIGHTEEN

Breakfast was a carbon-copy of the previous day, Baker eating slowly while studying the *Checkers* for predeparture activities.

"They're still not hustling around," he said, sipping coffee without taking his eyes off the screen.

"We can safely meet with our aquatic allies, then," Fisca said, while tucking into her eggs and sausage. "Their voyage to unite with their allies will be short. The strait is not horribly wide at this point. The Orcas will be forthcoming, and I expect them to have arrived at some consensus which will aid us."

"The moment Richard and Almaric sight us and are certain of our identity," Baker said, "something will hit the fan. How hard and in what amounts is questionable, but we can expect some sort of attack. They might have some speed on us, but not enough to leave us dramatically behind. We will be able to maintain contact."

"Agreed," said Magnus around a bacon sandwich. He seemed eager for their pursuit to begin, and Fisca, while still looking focused and calculating, seemed much the same.

You're a lot more action-oriented than we are," Will said. "Back home, this time of the week, I'd be mowing the lawn and Katie would be baking cookies for the grandkids' next visit."

"I cannot imagine such activities," Fisca told him, looking dubious and amused.

"We can," Oog said. "Sounds soul-fulfilling and meaningful." He shrugged his heavy shoulders. "Gotta do what we gotta do, but cookies sound real fine."

As usual, his burly companions agreed.

Magnus chuckled and scraped his plate with a piece of toast. "Perhaps when this excitement is completed, we can go to Godsend and have cookies with Old Man, the Vicar, and the rescued Jape. That would be a fitting finale for the endeavor."

"What will Old Man do with Richard and Almaric?" Katie asked.

Magus cocked his handsome head at his descendant. "Probably not cookies, but my thought is that his main anger will be directed at the Papal Legate and not the wily and duplicitous Richard."

"Maybe a cage fight between Jape and Almaric," Baker said. "That would be worth watching, though Jape is a solid and muscular guy, and the battle might not be lengthy."

"Jape was in his prime when brought up," the King said. "Almaric has been described to me as a smaller, sneaky fellow who insists on getting his way. None of the Popes which have been brought up wanted him back with them. His track record with the Cathars made him undesirable. So his contest with Jape would not go well, I am certain."

"Still fun to watch," Fisca said, smiling while draining her coffee cup. "Assuming we will head out sometime in late morning, all travel gear should be aboard the *Blood Wave* prior to our meeting with the Orcas, in the event we leave shortly after that."

All agreed that would be smart.

"Still no action from Richard," Baker said, grinning, "but using the highest resolution, I think I can see several Orcas out away from the *Checkers* berth. So Keiko and company are on the job, keeping tabs on the enemy."

That's smart," Katie said, tapping Will on his nearest thigh. "We should re-pack for the next leg of our adventure, dear."

"Right. Us and the kids."

The four took their plates and utensils to the sink, rinsed everything, the stuck then into one of the dishwashers.

Back in the room, only a few minutes of effort got everything in good order.

"I wonder why Magnus and Fisca simply didn't go to the *Checkers* and finish things in port."

"Against the rules," Mary Pat said. "Vancouver and Victoria are Free Ports. Aggressive actions are not permitted. Once out to sea, then the battle can begin, but not until then. Richard knows this, and while he and Almaric may not know where we are, they know they are safe as long as they're in port. It's clever the Orcas are keeping tabs on them, though."

"Smart cetaceans," Bobby added, placing his neatly-folded new T-shirt into his go-bag.

"We'll know a fair amount more when we talk to the Orcas in another hour or so," Will said, zipping up his bag.

"Did you put your new comic books in a safe spot, William?" Katie asked, giggling.

"Absolutely," Will replied. "Can't be too careful with my new treasures, you know. They're in the middle of several surrounding layers of clothes."

Mary Pat and Bobby said nothing, merely smiled.

After checking the bathroom over carefully for anything they might have missed, they went out into the main hallway, shutting the door behind them, the proceeded to the main room, joining most of the others.

"Maybe we have time for lunch before the sailing," Karl told them, and the crewmembers present echoed that thought.

"Karl," Katie said, "we only just finished breakfast!"

"*Ja*, sure, but Viking warriors must have sufficient energy levels available when the weapons come out, and we never know when that will happen. Later today, maybe tomorrow. We must be ready." He raised one meaty arm. "Am I right?" The crew members responded as one, roaring their approval. "Sure enough, then," Karl added, looking Viking-proud.

Everything going to sea went onto and into the Dragonship, and while the excitement and anticipation mounted, there seemed to be no anxiety. Viking concern, certainly, but this portion of their lives was their norm, going lustily into battle and smashing the enemy.

Even Will, Katie, and the children were not worried. After the sea confrontation, with bullets flying and Fisca carving up her foes with the Bushmaster, that had been their baptism of fire. Surviving the giant bear had, in retrospect, been more dangerous, and they came through uninjured.

Still, Will asked if Katie and the kids were worried as they walked with the others toward the Orca meeting place. They just laughed and shook their heads.

The skies were quite clear, only lines of fluffy clouds traversing the blue vault. The weather report, according to Baker, was promising for the next few days, so there would be no questing through fog banks searching for an elusive enemy.

Shortly after they arrived at the meeting spot, the Orcas appeared, with Guido and Tony having a complete update on doings to the south. Though they couldn't understand what Nixon and company were saying without the translator, their observations were enough to determine that the *Checkers* would be departing for Victoria in the early afternoon.

"What we'll do," Keiko told the assembled crew of the Blood Wave, "is keep in the general vicinity of the enemy. Not too close, just within visual range so as not to make them suspicious. We'll just be part of the scenery, typical for the Georgia Strait, happy Orcas doing their thing, getting some fish and cavorting around. Nothing to be worried about."

"Seems a good plan," Magnus agreed.

"A very good plan," Fisca said, her gladiatrix' smile totally lacking in warmth.

The Orcas decided they would hang about a ways offshore and wait for the *Checkers* to go to sea. The *Blood Wave* would sail out at that point, with a goodly distance between the two vessels, with Baker keeping watch over the enemy's progress toward Victoria.

"If we stay completely out of sight, they will see no reason to act aggressively" Fisca said. "So at some point we must overhaul them, to see what comes from

Victoria or wherever to attack us. My thoughts are that both Richard and Almaric are paranoid enough to call their allies on shore to come into battle the moment they are aware of our presence."

Magnus merely nodded, looking thoughtful.

"We have no idea what resources they may have," Baker said. "Every weapon needs to be ready for whatever comes at us, be it afloat or aloft."

Fisca regarded the journalist with her gaze narrowed. "You have spoken the possibilities which the King and I have considered. All hell may break loose and we are on our own, though the Orcas can deal with any sort of torpedo quite handily, the rest is up to us."

"I can get the children below into what safety that will provide," Katie said.

"That's reasonable, Granddaughter," Magnus told her. "Your husband certainly performed well during the earlier firefight, and something like that could easily happen again. He proved to be quick-handed and dexterous." The King smiled at Will as he spoke, and Will couldn't think of any sort of response to the praise, even with Katie and the two kids grinning at him.

"I've got a thought," Oog said. "If they come at us with a buttload of aerial drones which are darting around and difficult to fire on accurately, we have fishing nets which could capture them if we were airborne."

The Orcas instantly saw what the Neanderthal was driving at. "How much do you weigh?" Keiko asked.

"Around a hundred seventy-five pounds."

The Orcas held a quick conference in fast clicks and trills which took place so rapidly the translator could barely make sense of it. "Okay," Keiko finally said. "We can toss you up to nearly a hundred feet. If you can unfurl the net quickly, then the drone can be snared and dragged down into the water, which should incapacitate it almost instantly. This is provided that they have only a few drone operators controlling several drones apiece, which makes sense if you think that's how they'd do it. Can the drones be autonomous?"

"Maybe," Baker said, "but probably not. All this is assuming they'll use drones at all."

"One attacked us in the forest," Oog told him. "It was clearly controlled, but weather conditions were kind of murky, so its operator couldn't really be sure where we were hiding and retreated back toward their ship after blowing the hell out of the general area."

"I was nearly frightened," Karl said, "being a larger target."

Oog slapped the taller man on his lower back. "You found a good shelter and hunkered down out-of-sight. *Maybe* you were scared, but I don't think so."

"Regardless," Fisca said. "if they come at us with small lightly-armed drones, we have a response which may work well. If they settle down into an exchange of rifle fire, the Bushmaster gives us the advantage, excepting we cannot fire into their hull, whereas they can fire into ours. Probably they will fire at our riflepersons, as before, but who can say."

"If they use torpedoes," Keiko said, "we've got that handled. A bump here, a nudge there. and the torpedo is useless, going off into the distance until it runs out of power."

"We may have the gamut of their actions covered," Magnus said, turning to Baker. "Any news, wordmaster?"

"Still there. People going into the town and returning, probably picking up provisions. No sign of the recovered victims from the rocks, but they'll be the last to come aboard and may or may not be fully functional. I'll stay on observation mode, and the moment they set sail, we need to be not far behind."

"Any further questions?" Fisca asked the cetaceans.

"No, but keep the translator in the water all the time. Developments may be rapid and require quick response."

"Tony and I think throwing humans into the air would be lots of fun," Guido said.

"We'll see how that goes," Oog replied, laughing. "If it goes."

"Righto," Guido and Tony said, smiling at the Neanderthal.

Talk and attack variation possible speculations went on for a while, then adjourned for lunch, while the Orcas swam slowly out into the Strait to await the enemy.

Back at Newton's, the man himself spent time listening about the preparations, finding the concept of flying Neanderthals delightful.

"Will there be some good footage?" he asked Baker, after giving Oog and his contingent an expression of mock horror which had no effect on them whatsoever.

"Definitely," Baker replied, tapping the Spy Eye on its carapace, which caused it to beep affirmatively. "Can you hear me, Sylvia?" the journalist asked.

"Yes," came the reply. "I listened to the conversation, and have to say that if we cannot dominate the viewer base with airborne Neanderthals, we should lose our broadcasting license immediately."

Before responding, Baker glanced at the Neanderthals and saw only wide grins. "I think we're covered," he told Sylvia as he signed off.

The meal progressed slowly with Baker glued to his screen. Even Gro couldn't distract him significantly. Finally, just after one in the afternoon, the gangway slid back aboard the *Checkers*, and shortly thereafter, the schooner began to move.

"Here they go," Baker said, snapping his fingers.

"And ourselves also," Magnus said, beckoning for the bill. A few minutes later and they were back on the street heading for the Dragonship, and twenty minutes after that lines were loosened and the *Blood Wave* took her leave of Vancouver, moving slowly until they had passed the bridge.

"Oh. Boy," Bobby and Mary Pat said in unison.

"Are you two editing what you're telling your parents?" Katie asked from their seats at the ship's prow.

"Yes!" they replied emphatically. "If we told them all the dramatic stuff, they'd shit bricks. We stressed the interaction with the Orcas, didn't mention that there would be a pitched sea battle sometime today, with an uncertain outcome."

"We'll come out on top," Will assured them. "Good will triumph."

Twin expressions of mild doubt spread over young features. "This isn't an adventure movie," Mary Pat told him. "It could get grim."

"I expect it will."

"We are with good and skilled warriors," Bobby said. "The last encounter was worse. We weren't that prepared, and continual improvisation was necessary."

"Fisca and the Bushmaster made the difference," Katie said, "and that could happen again. Of course, now they know about it, which caught them by surprise last time."

"We are warriors," Gro said from ten feet away. "They are ragtag and bobtail wannabes. They have weaponry capable of subduing lightly-armed or unarmed foes, but that's it. Unless Richard's two main minions are more ingenious this time, we will prevail, mark my words,"

"They had some short distance howitzers last time," Will said, "but Fisca acted rapidly and to devastating effect. If anything, we're more prepared now, thanks to the Orcas."

Gro reverted to her pigtailed teenager persona, grinning broadly. "Plus, they cannot know about the Orcas, which is advantage in our court. As I said, we will prevail."

The mighty Dragonship surged to the west. Baker's binoculars swiftly found the *Checkers*, and Magnus closed slowly, well aware of the encounter needing to be some distance prior to Victoria. Haldeman and Erlichman had doubtless been busy while Richard and Almaric meandered through the channels and islands on their way to Vancouver, uncertain of pursuit until the skies rained rocks, and even then a bit of a mystery. Still, they had to know the *Blood Wave* was out there somewhere, and if they had anyone scanning the waters around them, any hope of completely fooling them was clearly impossible. Hard to disguise a large Dragonship, and *Blood Wave* was very large.

"This is such a pretty day," Katie said, looking up at the lines of fluffy clouds and a single vapor trail coming in from the west. "What's that?" she said, pointing up.

"Interfloat," Mary Pat replied. "Probably from Victoria to the eastern Provinces, maybe going to Banff first, then Calgary. Thanks to von Neumann and Hughes, travel is cheap and easy. Cockaigne is truly the land of the perfect life."

"Cockaigne was a thing during the Middle ages, wasn't it?" Will asked.

"That's what they told us in school," Bobby said. "It caught Old man's fancy at some point, and he used the name to define his creation, even though this world already existed and what we have now is a sort of grafted-on reality."

"And Zongo's people and the Little People were already here?"

"Exactly."

"How does Old Man decide who to Bring Up?" Katie asked.

"He relies on Jonathon Elbunn to provide a list of potential candidates," Mary Pat said. "If He doesn't recognize the person's name, He asks for a thorough background check. The Vicar is always ready, and rarely does Old man reject an individual, though He took some convincing for some. He likes entertainers like Harvey Korman and Tim Conway, and Robin Williams came up in a heartbeat. Political figures receive more scrutiny, because their motives are more questionable. Lyndon Johnson was nearly rejected, John Kennedy was heavily scrutinied, but Bob Dole was easy. It can be a bit of a crapshoot, my Dad says. Sometimes a single speech or good deed is enough."

"What about Fred Rogers?" Will asked.

"He breathed his last, and was here almost instantly. His children's show is seriously popular in Cockaigne."

"He's sincere and completely believable," Bobby added. "No questions about his motives and intentions."

"That's very comforting," Katie said, sighing.

"A truly amazing man," said Will.

"Our kids certainly liked him," said Katie.

"I watch him sometimes," Mary Pat said, "but he's more for younger children. Still, he's great."

"How did Old Man get involved with Jape?" Will asked.

"Good question," Bobby said. "They look a lot alike, so that has to be a factor. After we rescue Jape, you can ask him."

"You folks have a song about the plane crash, 'The Day the Music Died,'" Mary Pat added.

"'American Pie?'"

"That's it."

"He was on the plane?" Will asked.

"So we're told."

"I'll be darned."

While the ship was not rapidly overhauling Nixon's vessel, the distance between the two was obviously closing. Baker gave updates every fifteen minutes or so, and the crew locked shields into place after bringing out the heavy sniping rifles and loading them. Ammo boxes were placed at intervals along the port railing, and Lars told Will to be ready for a repeat performance as the magazine monkey. Will nodded, but didn't smile, and Katie patted him on the back.

"Our weapons have the range on theirs," Lars assured Will, "but chances are good that some type of armored vessel will eventually appear to confront us. Lady Fisca and her fire-breathing monster will handle that possibility. They have not had time to truly equip some sort of heavily protected ship, so we'll see what they have hired. A vessel crewed by hirelings not strongly allied with either Richard or the psychotic Papal Legate may be a frail reed for the task at hand."

"Lars," Katie asked. "you don't speak as roughly as Karl does. Why is that?"

Lars laughed. "Karl is a German, a country bumpkin by his own admission. A wonderful human being and a fighter with few peers, but still a German. I was a school teacher in Oslo, so my speech was more couth and cultured, even with a somewhat German background. My family were landowners and several generations away from the sea lanes. When I was Brought Up, I decided to revert to the old life, trained hard, learned the ways of weaponry and even became fairly proficient, thanks to Karl and some of the other reckless warriors. King Magnus believed in me, I taught my companions some school knowledge, so my use in our endeavors has been adequate, I believe."

Katie moved closer to the huge school teacher and lowered her voice. "How good a fighter is Gro? If I can ask."

"One of the best. She is called the 'Female Yingling,' and not for nothing. Lightning fast, supple and deadly. A cheerful killer, and her cousin Gudrun is nearly the same. A truly nasty pair of young ladies. They tend to fight side-by-side in any melee. One works clockwise, the other anti-clockwise, so they protect one another without danger of accidental injury. Any foe faces an impenetrable wall of razor-sharp steel." He grinned, exposing some very non-academic incisors. "Gudrun is also admirably heterosexual, much like Gro. The Forsberg Frolic, we call it."

"Oh," Katie replied, blushing.

"Sorry to embarrass you," the huge ex-academic said, his smile reduced by fifty percent. "We Vikings are most open about such things. As a revered descendant, you understand that. Remember, too, we have all seen the video of your sudden arrival in the Rapture Hall. It was most revealing and delightful. The Viking stamp of approval, for sure."

Will knew enough to keep his mouth shut at that juncture.

Katie's blush slowly subsided, and they moved on to less embarrassing subjects.

"I can see something approaching from the west," Baker said. "Looks like a large twin-engined tugboat. Somewhat armored perhaps. There may be another behind it."

The gradual pursuit continued, and it was clear that the Dragonship was closing the gap. A half-hour passed, and the moment they'd anticipated happened.

"Here are the drones," Baker said. "A dozen so far, carrying what look to be small missiles."

"We got 'em," Oog called from the canoe contingent, and Will and Katie heard splashes as the Neanderthals dove overboard.

Fisca had the translator in the water, its cable trailing over the deck. She spoke into the microphone, but from the sound of things. the Orcas were collecting Oog's people and heading for the low-flying drones.

Katie gathered Mary Pat and Bobby. "Let's go below, children." She kissed Will on his cheek and left. Will went to the line of snipers and situated the ammo boxes for quick access, then crouched down slightly so he could watch the proceedings between the stationary shields.

The *Checkers* was still over a half-mile away, the other vessels that much more distant beyond that.

The drones swept over Nixon's ship, and ten seconds later, the first Neanderthals soared into the air, spread nets clasped in powerful hands, and dropped in among the drones, snaring most of them and falling back down into the water with their captured prey. The surviving drones seemed to falter, and the second wave of bulky bodies arrived to ensnare them. Within a few seconds, no enemy remained aloft.

"They've got torpedoes," Baker said. "Just tossed three of them overboard."

"Commence firing at what of their crews you can see!" Magnus yelled, waving *Legbiter* over his head.

"Get down, Great King," Fisca replied from behind the Bushmaster, "out of my field of fire. Keep your hands on the wheel. Bring us broadside facing The Checkers, or as near to that as possible."

The snipers opened up, choosing their targets carefully, and those on Nixon's ship who remained on their feet went down. The remainder hit the deck.

The *Blood Wave* swung to starboard, giving the fifty-caliber handlers good fields of fire. Targets were few, mostly heads peering over the schooner railing, so shots ceased for the moment.

An explosion blasted against one of the tugs, and it lost headway.

"The Orcas have redirected the torps," Will observed, as a second blast exploded against the same vessel.

"Not as much damage as you'd think, though," the nearest sniper replied. "They must be heavily armored, or else the torpedoes are small."

"They've got deck guns on the tugs," another nearby sniper said. "Nixon's ship is a bit in the way, but it's moving out to starboard."

"I'm on it," Fisca said, and fifteen seconds later the Bushmaster roared to life, lighting up one of the tugboats.

"Armor's heavy," one of the snipers said, everyone holding fire for the moment as they watched the Bushmaster get to work.

"What about the upper control deck?" Will asked.

As if the gladiatrix had heard him, Fisca shifted her attention to the control deck and there the armor only impeded the Bushmaster rounds without stopping them. Pieces flew, and whoever might be directing the ship either took cover or died as twenty-two millimeter rounds penetrated the ship to dramatic effect.

As the *Checkers* moved well away from the Tugboats, Fisca turned her attention to the second ship and systematically shot it up, using her ammunition judiciously but with good results. Both tugs lost direction, and the *Checkers* fled toward the south, leaving its supporting cast to the doubtful mercy of Fisca and the Neanderthals.

The Orcas swam slowly toward the disabled tugboats, and shortly Oog's contingent were on the decks, doing their axework with their usual dispatch. Will heard the screams from his location on the Dragonship.

"The Cavies are doing their jobs," the nearest snipers said, laughing. "Brutal little buggers."

Meanwhile Nixon's schooner was under full power, speeding to perceived safety on the U. S. coastline.

Occupied with the stricken tugs, *Blood Wave* could not immediately move in pursuit. Magnus brought the big vessel alongside the smaller ships and those on the Dragonship watched as the Neanderthals mopped up the tug crews. A few surrendered, which Will thought was prudent under the circumstances.

When the battle was completely over, the captives were brought on board the Blood Wave for interrogation.

"What were your orders?" Magnus asked the cowed survivors.

"Use the drones to incapacitate your ship. Would've worked handily, too, if your secondary force hadn't taken down every drone so quickly."

"We done good, huh?" Oog said, grinning.

"Damned Orcas! We didn't think of them even being part of this."

"A mistake, then," Oog said, his good cheer growing.

Their captive shot the sturdy Neanderthal a begrudging look. "Yeah, no shit."

"Do you have enough survivors to crew both tugboats back to Victoria?" Fisca asked.

"Yes, barely."

"Good, then we'll remove your weaponry and head after the former President when that's done."

Not a simple task, as it turned out. The deck guns were heavy and bolted down. Getting their bases free and the guns aboard Blood Wave took Karl and Lars some time, while rifles, pistols and other weapons were far easier, simply confiscated and tossed from one ship to another.

Keiko and the other Orcas watched the time-consuming operation with interest, clicking and squeaking questions which Baker did his best to answer.

Katie and the kids were back up on deck by that point, Bobby and Mary Pat paying close attention to the goings-on, not asking questions since the process of disarming the tugs and their crews was obvious.

When the job was done, the survivors of the brief battle were put back aboard their vessels and *Blood Wave* headed west. The *Checkers* was completely out-of-sight, vanished toward the either Victoria or the States. Baker got into the satellite view and began searching for the schooner.

Not quite on maximum speed, the big Dragonship plowed southwest after a long conversation with the Orcas, who agreed to keep within underwater hailing distance. They'd had fun tossing Neanderthals, and fun was a large part of their lives. More fun could happen.

The distance to Victoria wasn't that great, but the islands dotting the Strait gave the *Checkers* the possibility of finding a hidey-hole somewhere. However, Baker quickly found the ship and felt that Victoria might not be the goal. "They're maintaining a course that won't take them to Victoria unless they slant around the city itself and enter on the south."

"Where else might they go?" Magnus asked.

"Good question," the journalist replied. "As long as we can track them, they can't escape. They're going to realize that at some point, that we can find them as long as they stick with the ship."

"They won't abandon it, will they?" Katie asked.

"No, but they hired the two tugboats, so other welcomes may await us in our pursuit. Nixon's two main minions could easily have been busy with other efforts while the tugboats were sent out to intercept us, and we have no idea where they might be lurking. The tugs were probably given a good chance of success, and our aquatic allies were unknown to them. There was some luck involved on our part, for sure."

"Will they pass by the San Juans?" Will asked.

"Seems likely at this point," Baker replied. "They may be heading for Port Angeles, leave the ship, and trek inland, though that seems unlikely. What can they do with Jape? At some point they've got to realize he isn't Old Man, but with two crazy people in charge, that may take a while longer."

"They will not come to the conclusion that they kidnapped the wrong man," Fisca said, "unless the actual personage confronts them and they realize their mistake."

"I've been in contact with Jonathon Elbunn on most days " Baker said, "and Old Man remains convinced we will eventually recover Jape. How much longer he will retain that attitude has to be seen. Also, Jape may tire of his situation and blow the gig, though I doubt that. He's very loyal."

"If Haldeman and Erlichman are still preparing a surprise for us," Magnus said from behind the wheel, "one wonders what that might be."

"Helicopter, submarine, guided missiles," Bjorn said, entering the conversation for the first time. "Maybe commandeer a Floater and attack us with that."

"Assorted lawdogs would be after them in a heartbeat if they did that," Baker told the skald. "Still, some sort of airborne assault is possible. Hard to say how liquid their finances are. How much can they afford to do?"

And what are their plans?" Katie asked. "Are they just going to sail around waiting for Jape to do some sort of something? Is he just being stubborn and refusing to demonstrate some power or other? Nixon and Almaric must be frustrated."

"Oh, for shit's sake!" Baker suddenly exploded. Every head within hearing distance turned his way.

"A new message from Elbunn. Old man wants us at Godsend. Apparently Jape's absence has complicated his existence. The Saturday evening radio show can't happen because that would blow the gig, as they say, and that bothers him."

"Is Old Man set in his ways?" Katie asked.

Baker shrugged and nodded. "Yeah, to an extent, I guess. When you're thousands of years old and responsible for the welfare of the Afterlife…"

"Along with Old Woman," Katie added.

"True," Baker admitted. He addressed the Spy Eye. "Sylvia, you there?"

"Yes. Heard every word. Sounds like the excitement is about to rachet up."

"Something like that, for sure. We'll find out shortly." He looked at Magnus. "Where are you on this?"

Smiling brightly, seeing potential action ahead, the tall blond hauled on the wheel, bringing the Dragonship around to port. "We're on the way. Tell Elbunn."

Fisca appeared with the Orca translator and hurried to the starboard side of *Blood Wave*, dropping the communicator over the railing and speaking with the Orcas.

"You don't have to go with us," she told Keiko and the others.

"Try and stop us," the pod leader replied, and the listeners to the exchange could hear the other Orcas clamoring their approval, all seemingly eager for a good time, at least by Orca standards.

"Are you getting adequate nourishment?" Fisca asked.

"Could be better, but we're not starving."

"We'll see what old man can manage, then," Fisca said.

Katie laughed softly. "Maybe instead of loaves and fishes, just the fishes."

"Our religious myths might be different than here," Will said, "but the Orcas need several hundred pounds of fresh food every day, and that's their reality."

"Something will work out," Baker told them. "Old Man is out on his boat several times a week, so he'll have some notion of where the schools of fish are."

"He'll help," Bobby and Mary Pat said. "He's benevolently inclined."

"Can he make something from nothing though?" Katie asked.

"Let me get back to Elbunn," Baker said. "Tell him about the Orcas' plight, or potential plight. They'll come up with something."

Fisca told Keiko's pod that they were going to see what Old Man could do. The Orcas knew there was some sort of human deity, but were ignorant of just who and where. They could sense His presence to an extent, so they had some vague feeling of power extant when He was in their area, but beyond that, not a lot. The Gladiatrix spent considerable time trying to give them some notion of His nature, but since she wasn't at all certain on the extent of His powers now, things were vague. The Orcas were not dismayed or discouraged, even looking forward to meeting a mystical human. Fisca reassured them, and they took her word for it.

A bit over two hours later, *Blood Wave* neared the broad landing below Godsend. Old Man's fishing boat was moored to the edge of the landing, and the big Dragonship slipped into position on the main stretch of concrete, just as before, and just as swiftly tied down.

Old Man, wearing clean shorts, T-shirt, and socks, stood with Elbunn and two other men, dressed similarly to Old Man.

The crew and the Neanderthals left the vessels and greeted Old Man.

"What do you have in mind?" Magnus asked, "and I apologize for not devising a decent plan for rescuing Jape."

Old Man shrugged and grinned, looking apologetic. "Jape is a hostage, and they have only to bring him on deck, revealing him to be unable to rescue himself, and threatening violence, perhaps terminal, to frustrate your actions. They may not actually realize that Jape is somewhat mortal, but he could be killed, something I will not tolerate."

"You could bring him back, right, your Grace?" Oog said, and the other Neanderthals muttered agreement.

"Of course, but the pain of his dying is not desirable, Oog. We have been friends for nearly seventy years. He is a good man, and faithful."

"Gotcha," the Neanderthal replied, nodding.

"So we have devised a plan to get our revered deity on the *Checkers*," Elbunn said. "It will involve the Orcas." While speaking, he glanced at the attentive cetaceans, who clustered by the quay. Fisca had set up the translator while Old Man spoke, and not an Orca eye left the Vicar.

"What do you have in mind, Revered Human?" Keiko said.

"Let me introduce these two gentlemen," Old Man said, indicating the two tanned fellows who stood with him. "This fine chap is Ralph Samuelson, and next to him is George Blair."

"Call me Banana George." Blair said, smiling as the two shook hands all around.

"What do bananas have to do with all this?" Katie asked.

"We're water-skiers," Samuelson said, "and Old Man asked for our help finding a way to get him on board Nixon's ship without being flung into the air."

"A bit undignified," Blair finished, grinning at Old Man. "An as for the banana thing, I used to ski with the end of the tow line between my teeth and a banana in each hand. Showmanship!"

"Oh," Katie replied, still looking puzzled.

"What we have in mind is to have our god water-ski toward the *Checkers*," Elbunn told them, "and, using the Orcas both as towers and as ramps, soar gracefully into the air, landing on the deck of Nixon's vessel and rescuing Jape."

"Can you water-ski?" Old Man asked the Garrisons.

"Years ago," Will replied, giving Katie a worried look.

"Good, then. As our surprisingly-raptured innocents, you can join me in the daring rescue."

"Sounds good to me," Oog said, with a deep chuckle.

"Us, too," Keiko agreed, his other pod members chittering and chirping with him.

"Saying 'no' would be inappropriate, I suppose?" Katie replied, "considering the circumstances."

"How soon do we leave?" Will asked, his tone resigned.

"Three things to do first," Old Man said, anticipation clear on his features. He lifted his right hand over his head, producing a disturbance in the air above the Orcas from which fish cascaded down into the water. "Say when," he told them, as the water roiled and the fish disappeared into the hungry cetaceans.

When the Orcas appeared satisfied, He gestured again, and five pair of water skis suddenly lay on the quay. "All right, let's board the Dragonship and sail in pursuit." He turned to Magnus. "Do you have enough fuel to move at maximum speed, Great King?"

"Indeed. We brought in several bags of fusion pellets at Vancouver. We may be able to overhaul The Checkers in roughly a day, allowing the assault you have in mind to take place around noon tomorrow."

Elbunn entered the conversation, addressing Baker. "Can you track Nixon during the hours of darkness?"

"I think so, if the moon shines through the clouds enough. The ship could be hard to spot, but the wake can be seen easily enough. While you've been talking, they seem to have realized we aren't still after them and have slowed. At their current speed, they won't make port until early evening tomorrow. We can catch them before then."

"And off we go," Old Man said, gesturing again. A large cooler appeared. "Sandwiches, enough for myself, Jonathon, George, and Ralph."

"What are George and I going to do for the effort?" Samuelson asked.

"Simple enough. The Vicar and I will take point, the Garrisons on either side of us, and you two experts on the ends of the speeding quintet."

What's our purpose, then?" Blair asked, puzzled.

"Merely to draw their fire as we approach our quarry."

"What!" the veteran skiers exclaimed incredulously.

"Fear not. I will cast a glamour which protect all six of us and the involved Orcas. We will be unharmed. It may be slightly unnerving, but no damage whatsoever."

"What about the kinetic energy?" Katie asked. "If bullets strike us, even though we don't get injured, won't the energy affect us."

Old Man grinned. "Good question, but that energy will be dissipated by the safety precautions I will have provided. Your progress to the deck of Nixon's ship will be accurate and true."

"How will we stop on the deck?" Will asked, looking worried.

"Also not an issue. Simply turn one way or the other, and slide to a halt. At that point, they will have to cease firing, since all six of us will then be surrounded by Nixon's crew. Further discharges would strike their own people. At that point, I will deal with them."

"If I am to be of some help," Elbunn said, "how do I get onto the *Checkers*?"

"You will cling to my back, Jonathon. Tightly, I hope. The extra weight will mean little, and you will address Almaric while I stand with arms akimbo, looking imposing and Godlike."

Elbunn had only a slight tan, but he blanched enough so that the tan was gone. "You aren't joking, are you?"

"Oh, no, this is serious business, Jonathon. We must rescue dear Jape and stop the evil of Almaric. The former President is of less concern, but I am confident he will see the error of his recent ways once he is confronted by our righteous selves."

"But riding on your *back*..."

Old Man's answering smile was warm and confident. "Not to fret, please. All will go well, I assure you."

Elbunn did not look more confident at that point, but he stayed quiet, realizing he was being dragged along against his will, but could do nothing about his situation.

Katie tried to reassure him. "We'll be fine, Vicar. Don't worry needlessly.

"One can only hope," Elbunn replied, glancing up at the hovering Spy Eye, which had captured the entire exchange for future broadcast.

"May we go aboard, then?" Old Man asked.

Grinning about as widely as she could, Fisca gestured to the Dragonship. "As you wish, Blessed Creator."

"In the past, perhaps," Old Man said, looking modest, "but this journey will give me a chance to revisit those thrilling days of yesteryear and flex my skills for the first time in many years."

"Except when you are upset, Lord," Elbunn said, speaking from years of experience as Old Man's right hand.

Samuelson looked at Blair. "Sounds like fun, huh, George?"

Blair smiled. "A total blast, Ralph. A total blast."

The group went aboard, the Neanderthals springing into their dugouts while chewing on handfuls of root. They'd brought supplies of both root and food aboard in Vancouver, along with jugs of water, so their ability to keep up with Blood Wave would be no problem.

The gangway was brought onto the ship after Karl and Lars untied from the quay and came aboard. Magnus, with Old Man at his side, steered away from the shore and hit the throttle while Fisca spoke with the Orcas and Baker kept up his scrutiny of the *Checkers*. The Spy Eye slowly moved above the deck, spending more time recording Magnus and Old Man than the others.

"What do you two think of all this?" Will asked the children.

"I couldn't be more excited," Bobby replied, his feathered crest elevating.

Mary Pat smoothed it down, tut-tutting. "Just relax, Bobak. We'll be able to see everything from our vantage point here."

"Like you're not excited?"

Mary Pat grinned. "We're going into battle, or near enough, so yeah, I'm tuned. It'll be maximum fun."

"One way or another," Katie told them, "you two are probably right. It will be the adventure of a lifetime, even here, where adventure is a way of life."

Baker looked up from his screen. "The truth, for sure, and the Spy Eye will get it all. Our paper and the affiliated broadcast stations will totally rule. Old Man,

Magnus Barefoot, Fisca, and the rather reluctant Jonathon Elbunn, heroes all."

"Don't forget the noble Vikings," Gro said, standing beside him and poking his neck.

Baker looked up at her, his gaze more serious than usual. "So here we are, you and I, and the big adventure is drawing toward closure. Where does that leave us in the future?"

"Could I get a job as a cub reporter, learn the ropes from the master? Perhaps an option?"

The reporter's expression brightened some. "The paper doesn't have a lot of need for a swordswoman. There are mild arguments, occasional shouting, but nothing going to death or flying from shattered windows on the upper storeys of the building."

"Is there a YWCA in Boston? I could hold evening classes, teach my trade to newbies."

"Can't rule that out. It might work. A few hours a week. Sounds good." His brow furrowed. "What about your cousin Gudrun? Without your company, how will she be?"

Gro pursed her lips and frowned. "She'll want to be with me. I got her on *Blood Wave*, so this would just be another plateau in our lives. She's very vigorous and a good worker. Are your quarters large enough for two young female Vikings and yourself?"

Now Baker began to look distressed, but not much. "There's an extra bedroom, plenty of closet space, and my entertainment stuff is more than adequate. I can see it working out. Do the two of you squabble?"

"No, but Gudrun is as active as possible sexually…" One eyebrow raised. "But she walks both sides of sexual preference boulevard, so our relationship isn't completely cousinly, if you get my meaning."

"Oh," Baker replied.

"Sounds like a win-win to me," Katie said.

"Sounds like mammal magic to me," Bobby added.

Katie studied the young dinosaur seriously. "You're a little young to suggest such things, Bobby."

Mary Pat stepped into the conversation. "Bobby thinks his understanding of Cockaigne culture is very advanced, and he likes to show that off."

Bobby wilted a bit. "Don't think I'm wrong, though," he finally said stubbornly.

"I suppose we'll see," Gro said, smiling brightly and flipping her pigtails.

"Let's go listen to Old Man and Magnus," Mary Pat told her friend. "Maybe we can learn something."

Jonathon Elbunn had drifted over in their direction as the children departed. "They'll be plotting and planning by the wheel. My very senior colleague has not gotten himself into a situation like this for many decades, and how things will unfold once we are on the deck of the *Checkers* will require considerable mental preparation."

"You're going to confronting Almaric is our understanding," Will said.

The slender Vicar nodded. "Yes, but I believe my sermon experiences during my time in my clerical life will provide sufficient background so I can express myself without being strident or needlessly confrontational."

"Almaric doesn't sound horribly reasonable though," Katie said. "He may bite back at you."

Elbunn nodded, looking rather smug. "Then I step aside and let our deity deal with him. Old Man will have watched our exchange and be ready to have words with Almaric. Almaric will be on the receiving end of some strong language, and possibly some strong deeds. For now, however, on we go."

Magnus didn't have the Dragonship at maximum throttle, but close. The deck stayed level, but the sensation of power remained. Oog's people kept nearer the prow of the ship, away from the beginning of the wake, and held their own.

"Are we closing, Baker?" Will asked the writer.

"Yes. Because they have slowed, we should catch them by late morning, before noon perhaps."

The day wore on, not boring exactly, but Nixon had kept moving while *Blood Wave* was at Godsend, and the distance between the ships had increased.

In the meantime, Blair and Samuelson played cards and Baker composed text while keeping one eye on his viewscreen. The Spy Eye loitered around, picking up what would probably become filler for the eventual triumphant broadcast. Occasionally Sylvia would speak with Baker, deciding how to present the oncoming confrontation to the public. Regardless of how events played out, it would be one of the biggest happenings in Cockaigne's history, and the media knew that.

Mary Pat and Bobby stayed near Old Man, and their conversation seemed to go in equal ways, mostly the revered god asking questions which proved Bobby's original thought that Old Man had no memories of anything like a childhood, and thereby found kids fascinating.

Evening came and food appeared, thankfully not hardtack and salt beef. Coffee was abundant, even handed over the railings to the Neanderthals, who said it jacked up the effect of their root. Fisca spoke with the Orcas, and their conversation with the two old water skiers went on at some length, questions being asked and instructions given.

Everything seemed ready. Tomorrow would tell.

CHAPTER NINETEEN

The next day dawned with high clouds and diffuse sunlight, but the air warmed quickly and the *Checkers* was not that far away. Baker's estimate of late morning seemed accurate. *Blood Wave* was in the open sea, any land barely visible on their horizons.

Old Man gave every appearance of keen anticipation for the eventual action, speaking with Jonathon Elbunn, Magnus, and Fisca at length, in low tones. Blair and Samuelson went over instructions with the Orcas, even sharing some jokes, though the contrast between aquatic life and solid land required explanation. The legend of Moby Dick took the skiers aback, to say the least. They described the book about the white whale, and Keiko's people were fascinated but skeptical. They knew about whale hunting, since some of them had been Brought Up, but since Cockaigne had no history of such a thing, it remained an unfamiliar tale and nothing more than that.

Around ten in the morning, binoculars showed the *Checkers* in the distance, clearly heading toward Port Angeles. "They have to see us," Baker said, "but their speed hasn't picked up."

"Maybe they have another surprise on tap for us," Will said.

"Maybe not in caparison to the one we have for them. Have you and Katie any doubts about attacking the schooner on water skis?"

"We did it a lot when we were first married and the kids were small. Muscle memory should get us there to the point where we jump onto the *Checkers*. Once we're in the air, most bets are off. Understand that we jumped as younger people, and that was fun, though Katie was better at it than me. In fact, she's generally more athletic than I am."

"I'm glad it's you going out there instead of me," Baker replied.

"Think of the fun you'll be missing."

"I am. I have."

"Don't blame you. We'll probably survive free of any physical distress, thanks to Old Man. We'll see, I guess."

Katie had overheard the last parts of their conversation. "It'll be fun, William. Wait and see."

"Good thing Bobby and Mary Pat didn't hear that remark," Will replied, grinning at her.

"I did," said Gro, "and I think you're both very brave. I need to learn to water ski. Do you know how, Douglas?"

"No, my life has been free of even moderate amounts of danger."

Gro slung one long arm around his shoulders and hugged him. "Gudrun and I will have to do something about that, won't we?"

"Do I have a choice in that?"

Gro gave him a smug close-lipped smile and shook her blonde head, squeezing him harder.

"We'll probably be back home before any of that happens," Katie told the sinewy blonde, "but maybe there'll be a way you can let us know how it works out."

"Maybe Old Man will set us up with some kind of pathway from here to there, so we can be notified of current events," Will said.

"Maybe you could come back for the Rose Festival next year," Gro said. "Old Man knows that your being here was due to a glitch in fulfilling his wishes, so He'll likely pay special attention to your welfare, grant you some good stuff."

"He certainly doesn't have to do anything special for us," Katie said. "Getting back home will be enough."

"How are you going to explain to your children how you got younger-looking than they are?" Baker asked. "That'll be interesting."

"Don't be snide, Douglas," Gro admonished.

Baker shot her a dirty look. "It's a legitimate question, young lady, don't you think? And just because you look like Pippi Longstocking doesn't make you a dominant authority."

Gro's freckled features settled into an expression of grim acceptance, which didn't bode well for Baker's short-term wellbeing.

Will and Katie smiled at him. "Trouble is brewing on Baker street," Katie told the columnist, stepping back in case the young Viking warrior went from a simple glare to direct action.

Instead, Gro grinned. "Not to worry, Mrs. Garrison. I have no intention of punishing this wordy rascal until after today's excitement is over and night has fallen. *Then* I will do as I wish, and devil take the hindmost."

"You think you're the hindmost, Baker?" Will asked. "That might mean getting your ass chewed, huh?"

"Maybe you should sleep up on the deck tonight, Douglas?" Katie said, laughing.

The journalist was undaunted. "First we have to get through the day with ourselves and the ship intact." He beckoned to the Spy Eye, and gave a low whistle. The little device scudded down onto his shoulder, beeping twice.

"Sylvia, you there?"

"Yes, and I'll be close to the communicator for the duration of the action. You folks better come through this all hale and hearty."

"Old Man will keep us safe, Sylvia. He seems very invested in what's being attempted."

"The rescue of poor Jape, and the punishment of evil, right?"

"There's probably a method to the madness, though," Baker replied, "But at the moment, that's a bit vague and elusive."

"It'll work just fine," Will said;

"We remain positive," Katie added.

"Water skiing seems somewhat ragged, don't you think?"

"We remain positive," Katie repeated, smiling to reinforce her words.

"I'd pray, if the person in charge of this experiment in terror weren't the person I'd be praying to," Sylvia replied, chuckling.

"Well, you'll have it all first-hand in a couple more hours." Baker assured her.

"I'll be ready."

"Talk to you then, I think."

"Bye."

Blood Wave continued to encroach on the *Checker's* lead. The water skis were set out for the moment when the attackers hit the water. Blair and Samuelson grew visibly more excited, but checked out the ski's fittings carefully and calmly. Everyone shucked their clothing and got into swimsuits, though Elbunn seemed reluctant. Keiko and the other Orcas stayed close on the port side of the ship and Oog's dugouts hugged the starboard.

The on-creep drew closer to the surprisingly unruffled *Checkers*. Baker noted that some of their crew were making rude gestures in the Blood Wave's direction.

"They don't seem terribly worried," Old Man told Magnus.

The tall king shrugged, his hands steady on the wheel, anticipation of coming events showing brightly in his blue eyes. "I expect something to happen soon, your Grace. Their sleeves hide something."

"Would you, under the circumstances?"

Magnus guffawed. "I do. I have you and Jonathon. They don't know that. They believe they face a shipload of Vikings eager and ready for battle, nothing more."

"That would ordinarily be enough," the Vicar said, his smile pensive, clearly worried.

"Jape is hostage to blunt our aggression," Fisca observed from her seat at the Bushmaster.

The distance between the two vessels continued to close. A lot of waving and shouting went on between the two crews. The *Checkers* bunch waved rifles; the *Blood Wave* swords. At around three hundred meters, Fisca and Baker yelled simultaneously.

"Incoming from the southwest!"

Three rocket trails rose from the now-visible shoreline kilometers distant.

Two things happened. Fisca brought up the long barrel of the Bushmaster and thunderous fire flamed from the muzzle. Old Man raised his arms and began to gesture.

"Shit, He's *manifesting*!" Baker cried. The Spy Eye rose to a good vantage point.

Lightning flared from Old Man's fingers. One of the missiles exploded, one more went down to the Bushmaster, and Old Man took out the third.

"Odin!" the Blood Wave crew screamed, brandishing their longswords wildly. "Odin!"

"Holy jumpin' shit!" Baker exclaimed, ducking away from Gro's waving sword.

In the aftermath of the downed missiles, the *Checkers* crew went silent while Blood Wave continued to near riot.

"Time to go," Old Man said, gesturing to the water skis. The designated skiers hurried to get over the side. With Elbunn death-gripping his torso, Old Man, Katie, Will, and the two professional skiers floated down into the water. Old man gestured again, and metal collars appeared around their necks. "These will keep us safe during our efforts." His features were both deadly serious and exulted, apparently the use of his powers after so many years held some real joy.

The Orcas positioned themselves and gripped the ski lines in their teeth while Katie, Will, and the others got their feet into the skis, and then they were off, rising up and skimming over the water.

Whatever protected them from gunfire apparently extended to the Orcas. Occasional flashes sparked against the protective layer surrounding them, but they quickly closed on Nixon's schooner, and other Orcas, all female, positioned themselves to the front, ready to be ramps for the jump to The Checkers' deck. Will glanced over at his wife and saw her fierce smile. She was ready. He hoped he was.

The towing Orcas planed off, freeing the path to the ramping cetaceans. Will bent his knees, ready for flight, flew up the dark back, keeping the dorsal fin between his feet, and soared up over the railing, alighting on the deck, already turning sideways to cut his speed, Katie and the two pros beside him.

Old Man had apparently added some extra impetus to his flight. He and the wailing Vicar arched across the entire deck ad disappeared over the side. Every head turned in that direction, most mouths agape.

In the following silence, Old Man and Elbunn, both dripping wet, rose up over the port railing, the god's countenance a mask of embarrassment and rage. He landed on the deck with the Vicar going to his hands and knees behind Him, choking and spitting out water.

"Are you all right, Jonathon?"

"Barely. Let's not do that ever again," the Vicar said, climbing to his feet, a slender smallish pale figure in a grey swimsuit, an unimposing individual at best.

"Which of you is Almaric?" Elbunn asked, though Will and Katie thought that was obvious, a short, robed man standing by the former President. He looked surprised and taken aback, apparently realizing that the tables hadn't just turned, but vanished entirely.

Nixon, blue-jawed as usual, had a suspicious, fearful look

Still, Almaric put on a show of something like courage, used to power and unwilling to relinquish it. "I am he," he said, his tones pompous.

Elbunn jerked a thumb over one shoulder at Old Man, who stood silently glaring, his brawny arms folded across his thick chest. "And who do you suppose this is?"

"I don't know. Some burly old fool, perhaps."

"While I deal with the situation," Old Man said, turning to Will and Katie, "would you two go below and free Jape?"

"Certainly," Katie replied, nodding curtly to Almaric and taking Will's hand. "Lets go, Sweety."

Though the former President said nothing, merely looking nervous, Almaric started to protest. "Wait! You can't just go down below decks and..." He trailed off.

The Garrisons just grinned and headed below, through an open door. No one moved to stop them.

"I think that went well," Katie said as they descended the stairs.

"Wonder where he is?" Will asked.

"Don't worry. We'll find him. He'll probably look a lot like Old Man. Behind some door." Above, on the main deck, conversation continued.

The fourth door they tried, on the right side of the hallway, housed their quarry, who did, indeed, look almost the same as the old god.

Jape sat in a chair, playing solitaire on the small table in front of him. "Hey, you the rescue party? Heard a bit of ruckus from upstairs, thought my boss might be here."

"He's dealing with Almaric, I think," Katie told Jape.

"Almaric's a little turd."

"Why don't you have chains or shackles?" Will asked.

The responding smile spread over Jape's whole face, altering his resemblance to Old Man. "Where would I go? Almaric figured I was just a washed-up old creator who'd lost what little skills I ever had. I didn't contradict him. Knew the boss would be pissed and somebody would show up. He up there?"

"He is," Katie replied.

"Lets get on up, then." He stacked the cards, stuck them back into their box, and got to his feet.

"You sure look a lot like Him," Will observed, taking in the heavy shoulders and thick arms.

Jape laughed. "He can't play guitar or sing. Well, he will sometimes *try* to sing, but it doesn't go well. Can't carry a tune."

The trio climbed the stairs, back to the ongoing confrontation.

Once there, Jape put his hands on his hips and glared at the flustered Papal Legate. "Now you're in for it, you little pissant."

Almaric returned Jape's glare. "You turned out to be a fraud."

Jape shrugged. "Yeah, but I fooled you, didn't I?" He studied Nixon, who was trying to smile. "You probably figured it out, didn't you, Richard?"

"I suspected at some point," Nixon replied. "Your personality seemed wrong, somehow."

Jape went to Old Man and the two friends hugged. "Good to see you, your Excellency," Jape told the burly god. "And you, too, Jonathon."

"We're all glad you're safe," the Vicar replied, shaking hands.

"Well, then," Old Man said, recrossing his arms. "What shall we do with you, former Papal Legate?"

A voice came down from the heavens, faint with distance. "I have an answer."

Every head craned to take in the sight of two figures dropping smoothly toward the schooner, their garments shining in the noon sunshine.

As they watched, *Blood Wave* came alongside, grapples were placed, and Magnus, Fisca, Baker, and Gro stepped onto Nixon's vessel, along with Mary Pat and Bobby. The two kids were visibly astonished.

"It's Old Woman!" Bobby exclaimed, as the two figures dropped onto the deck.

"She looks like Cate Blanchett," Katie said, her lips close to Will's left ear. Will nodded.

Old Woman turned to the much smaller woman beside her. "All right, Pat, see to your husband. He needs you."

Pat Nixon walked slowly up to her husband, who seemed to be trying to decide whether to leap overboard or embrace her. He settled for the latter, and Old Woman smiled beatifically at the pair.

Then She turned to Old Man. "Have I arrived at a good juncture, great god?"

"You have indeed." His smile matched hers. "Quite perfect."

"Nice swimsuit, by the way, but Jonathon, I just don't know about yours."

Elbunn tilted his head. "I didn't pick it, my Lady."

"Good to know."

Now all eyes turned to Almaric, whose earlier bluster had vanished. He stood meekly, eyes down.

"I have made arrangements for this troublemaker's disposal," the tall goddess said, shaking her head, sending ripples of sunlight through the curls of her long blonde hair.

Everyone waited for her next words. "He should be here shortly." She grinned at Old Man. "You will approve, I believe."

As she finished speaking, a black floater appeared above the vessels, descending rapidly to hover ten feet above The Checkers' deck. A slim dark figure came down a rope ladder.

"It's The Hound," the kids said, their voices filled with awe.

"Setanta," Old Man said, nodding to the great warrior.

"Glad to be here, in front of so much importance, and to be of service once again." He gave Almaric the once-over, his brown eyes narrowing. "Is this him? I recognize everyone else, so this miscreant must be my task. Are you ready for a long voyage, Legate? This great lady has requested a boon, which I was quick to grant."

Two other men had come down the ladder, the same pair from the Rose Festival capture of Borkan. They took Almaric by his arms and stood waiting.

"Any last words?" Old Man asked the quavering captive.

"Am I to be killed?"

Both gods laughed. "No," Old Woman replied. "You will serve Setanta for a period of time, the actual number of years depending upon your diligence and devotion to the tasks he sets for you."

Almaric regarded The Hound fearfully, his features only somewhat hopeful.

Setanta chuckled. "I expect your clerical hands are soft. I will toughen them up, never fear. I have considerable plantings back in Ireland. I hope you like potatoes. You will see to their procreation. For many, many years."

"Better than what I would have given you, you little weasel," Jape added, grinning.

"What about the originators of the missiles?" Old Man asked.

Setanta's smile turned grim. "Once we have this cargo stowed, we go to Port Angeles and deal with them. Perhaps more exciting than this. Right, lads?"

"We look forward to it," said the two men holding Almaric. One patted him on the butt. "Up the ladder with you now, good fellow."

As the three went up the ladder, Setanta looked down at Mary Pat and Bobby. "I remember you two from the Rose Festival. Did you put my autographs away for safe-keeping?"

"We did," the kids replied.

"Of course," Cuchulainn said. "but it is most surprising to see you again under these circumstances. When will we meet again, I wonder?"

Mary Pat and Bobby glanced at one another, then grinned. "You'll have to wait and see, great warrior."

"I promise not to be surprised when it happens. Until then, fare you both well."

"Thank you."

Setanta bowed to everyone else, then disappeared up the rope ladder into his floater, which rose swiftly into the sky, heading southwest toward Port Angeles.

"A very useful person," Old Woman said, shielding her eyes from the sun as her blue gaze followed the vessel as it dwindled into the distance. Then she turned to the Nixons. "Have you forgiven him, Pat?"

"Somewhat. He seems quite contrite."

"There needs to be some payback with Levinsk," Old Man said. "Magnus assures me there was considerable damage to their city. That cannot stand. It must be made right."

"It shall," both Nixons assured him. "We have considerable funds to hand, enough to pay for damages and forgiveness. Almaric brought gold aboard with him, sufficient to take care of the issue."

"Along with copious pleas for forgiveness," Richard continued.

"Don't make me sorry I Brought you Up," the god said, frowning.

"I won't." The former President promised.

"Good," Old Woman said. "Sail directly to Levinsk, deal with that, then resume your business in San Clemente. Keep a low profile, and I expect you to keep him in line, Pat. No more harrying off in pursuit of power, treasure and adventure."

"Consider it done," the diminutive woman replied, her features resolute.

"Sorry I wasn't who you had in mind," said Jape, with an evil grin. He turned to Jonathon Elbunn. "Is my guitar still around?"

"Yes."

"Some playing when we get back to Godsend, then."

Both gods, Magnus, Fisca, the water skiers, Baker, Gro, Katie, Will and the two children climbed back aboard *Blood Wave*, cast off from the *Checkers*, waved, and reversed back toward Godsend.

"Did we let him off too lightly?" Old Woman asked as the Dragonship gained speed.

"No," Old Man replied. "We are, after all, gods. We can be magnanimous as occasions demand. I have been dubious about Richard over the years, but his wife is a wonderful person, and I believe we shall have no more issues from San Clemente. A lesson has been learned."

"Are you ready to speak with the Orcas, goddess?" Fisca asked. "They are quite excited about you."

Old Woman walked to the ship's railing as Fisca dropped the translator into the water.

"What do I do?"

"Talk into the microphone. They will answer."

"Hello," the goddess said. "Which of you is Keiko?"

"I am," said the pod leader, jiggling his snout up and down. "Call me 'Big K.'"

Old Woman smiled down at the eager cetacean. "All right, Big K. What shall we talk about?"

"We have arrangements made with the Vikings for the things we'd like to have. We don't want to burden either of you gods with specious requests. You probably have more important things than us to deal with."

The goddess' features formed a more knowing smile, tinged with fondness. She looked quite lovely. "You are noble creatures. I can see that. We have perhaps neglected your wellbeing owing to the difficulty of communication. That is now history. Give your needs some thought amongst yourselves. We will speak again soon, I assure you. You have my word."

The Orcas churned up the water wildly. "All right," Keiko replied. "That's good enough for us. Thank you!"

"Soon," Old Woman repeated, reaching down and patting Keiko on his snout. The cetaceans sped off, leaping and splashing.

"That was wonderful," Katie told the goddess.

"Communication is the key to my work. They are really quite marvelous creatures. With all my skills, I could never speak with them. Now, thanks to this wonderful new device, that obstacle is gone. Technology! Who knew?"

"I could use another hug," Old Man told her.

"Your needs are so simple. Fishing and hugs. A good life, free of turmoil and trouble."

"Remember that Jape was kidnapped. My stress level was elevated."

"Pshaw! You were afraid you were going have to do his weekly program, playing good music interspersed with lively commentary. Difficult tasks for one so set in his ways, hidebound and resistant to change. Don't you think?"

"Don't be too hard on Him," Jape said, laughing. "Not that you're wrong, truth be told, but perhaps I can do some in-person training in the near future, in case something like this happens again."

Old Man shot his friend a hard look. "Will this happen ever again? One hopes not. On the other hand, I appreciate you allowing yourself to be carried off into harsh circumstances and not revealing who you really are."

Jape laughed even louder. "What choice did I have? They wouldn't have believed me. Almaric was so certain that I was the key to power and fame he was blinded to reality. He deserves his new job as a potato farmer. Might clear his mind."

"Good enough," the sturdy god replied.

"Now I must speak with the mighty Oog and his stalwarts," Old Woman said, going across the deck to the starboard railing. "Are you good fellows faring well?"

A loud roar answered Her. "We be *fine*! Ready for an evening of food, song, story, and copious drink!"

"Did you hear that, Jonathan?" Old Woman asked the Vicar, who had gone below to re-don his robe and sandals and now looked perfectly normal again.

"I will phone ahead to our usual suppliers," Elbunn replied. "I have a rough headcount and will order in excess. The Neanderthals will doubtless be very hungry after a long day and night of exertion."

"Right you are!" the rowers called up over the side.

"They didn't exactly feed me well during my captivity, either," Jape added.

"As I said," the Vicar replied. "We will have enough for all, and then some, I assure you."

"A fitting conclusion to our endeavors," Old Man said. Then he addressed Bobby and Mary Pat. "Are you children satisfied with the day?"

"Oh, yes," they assured him. "A lot of fun."

"Glad you think so," the god rumbled, a broad smile on his bearded features. "It was just right, I think. How are you doing, Baker?"

"Composing the best commentary I can manage," the reporter replied, his head down over his screen, the Spy Eye hovering beside his right ear, with Sylvia's voice interspersed with Baker's. "This is a major story. We will kill the opposition. Can the Eye record our evening at Godsend?"

Old Man pulled on his beard, momentarily lost in thought, then sighed. "I suppose." He turned to Old Woman. "Any objections?"

"No, old dear. The public needs to see us in a normal human light on occasion. Eating, drinking, normal conversations, personal observations of our adventures, these all bring our lives and their lives closer together. Baker is right, though this isn't just about his ratings and the paper's success. This will all be very important. You will get back to your beloved fishing soon enough."

"How long will you stay at Godsend, my Lady?"

A coy smile. "Until we tire of one another or we drive Jonathon and Jape crazy."

"Won't happen," Jape assured her, and Elbunn echoed his sentiments.

"We will be back at Godsend tomorrow morning early," Magnus said from behind the wheel. "A brief meal, good cleanup, then an afternoon and evening of festivities."

The gathered Vikings, who had until then been quiet, murmured polite agreement, then went back to sharpening swords and minding the sails' rigging. Gro knelt by Baker, taking in every word and keystroke, smiling at his occasional muffled oaths and minor expletives.

The rest of the day went well, with no issues beyond the interchanges between Sylvia and Baker. Food appeared at intervals and naps were taken.

* * * * *

Elbunn's orders had been delivered when *Blood Wave* tied up at the base of the broad steps leading up to the spacious buildings at the crest of the tall ridge. The Neanderthals dragged their dugouts up onto the concrete wharf to dry out, then joined the procession uphill.

The Vicar assigned rooms, of which there were many, and Katie, Will, and the kids found themselves in a room whose broad windows overlooked the sea, with scatterings of lesser islands and sunny vistas.

"This is beautiful," Katie said, pulling aside the curtains and looking out the windows.

"It's all been good," Bobby and Mary Pat said, bouncing on the beds.

"Did you two phone home last night?" Will asked. "I forgot to ask."

"We were proper children," the pair replied, their bouncing slowing down. "We won't be able to tell them everything until we get home."

"Not to ruin your tale for your folks," Katie told them, laughing. "You'll probably concoct something like the truth, but remember Baker and Sylvia will have put the whole adventure on the airways and in print before we get back to Boston, so whatever you tell them will have to jibe with that. A lot of the footage will have you two in it."

Both kids looked thoughtful and a touch puzzled for several moments, then high-fived. "We can make it happen!" they chorused.

"There maybe some interest in a children's perspective, too," Will said. "Make sure your stories match, although you'll almost certainly be interviewed together."

Another exchanged look and smile. "No problem!"

"Now that's settled," Katie said, "you two can use the bathroom first. Will and I will wait until you're finished."

* * * * *

By the time the quartet went out onto the crowded plaza abutting the huge home, food and drink were well underway. The Neanderthals were into the wine and in a party mood. Oog waved a half-empty bottle. "My team!" he yelled. "We done good and had some fine times, didn't we?"

Katie, Will, and the kids waved back as they headed for the food-laden tables. Jonathon Elbunn presided over the spread, something most clerics probably found an unknown skill.

"It all looks so good!" Katie told the vicar, who smiled benignly.

"A large gathering, even for here. We have plenty of everything, though the Neanderthals and the Vikings are denting our supplies of alcohol. Fortunately I had some mead laid aside for just such an occasion. Our Nordic guests prefer that in amounts that daunt the imagination."

"It all looks good," Will said, loading his plate with Salmon and greens.

"Where did all the seating come from?" Katie asked, looking around at the array of chairs.

"We made sure when the place was constructed to make certain we could accommodate large gatherings, so it was just a matter of bringing it all outdoors. Our godly pair used their powers."

"Where are they?" Will asked, looking around at the crowd.

Elbunn smiled suggestively, elevating an eyebrow. "Indoors for a bit longer. This happens when they haven't seen each other for a while."

The Garrisons found some seats beside Baker, Gro, and Gudrun. The latter had a particularly large glass of wine.

"No mead?" Will asked.

"Too heavy for my taste," the rangy blonde replied, her grin identical to her cousin's. "Besides, I need to learn how to deal with wine if I'm going to settle into Boston."

Bobby and Mary Pat were close enough to converse with.

"You kids okay?" Will asked them.

Vigorous nods. "This is *great*. Great adventure, good food, and everybody looks out for us. Best ever."

"We'll need some quotes from everybody who traveled on or with *Blood Wave*, which also means you two young people," Baker told them. "Too bad we can't get any from the Orcas, but the Eye did record all the interactions with them, so Sylvia can use that. Should have the whole package done by tomorrow evening. We'll likely be back on the ship by then. Sylvia will have a rough cut at that point. It would help if both of us were in a studio at that point, but that can be worked around."

"Will circulation increase?" Katie asked.

"Does the Pope shit in the woods? It should nearly double, and viewership on television will go through the roof. 'The Raptured,' the mighty Magnus Barefoot, and the Neanderthals, all together on your home screen! Huge, and that's putting it mildly. Wait and see. Just actual interviews with Old Man and Old Woman will be enough, but the total package will be the biggest thing ever."

"That big?" Will asked.

"Oh, yeah, simply enormous."

"It's been fun overall," Katie said, coming back from a second trip to the serving tables. "Couldn't imagine water-skiing off an Orca's back, but they were all female, with a smaller dorsal fin, so we could pass right over it on our way to The Checkers' deck."

"Keiko's bunch are plenty smart, for certain," Will added. "We saw history being made, even here."

The amount of alcohol being consumed was beginning to increase the volume of the goings-on. Vikings and Neanderthals seemed to be nearly competing as to who could be the loudest. Things hadn't quite gotten the point where singing had begun, but close. Oog and his lads had produced small drums from somewhere and were thumping away, chanting softly for accompaniment.

"They're good, aren't they?" Katie said. Mary Pat and Bobby began to clap along with the Neanderthals, and the result was quite pleasant.

"More musical than I would have expected, for sure," Baker said, briefly looking up from his screen.

"Can't you take a break for a while, sweetheart?" Gro asked.

"What d'ya think, Sylvia? Can I take a breather?" the journalist asked. "A couple hours?"

Permission was granted, and Baker visibly relaxed. "Good. My fingers were getting tired."

"Get some food and something to eat," Gro told him, kneading the back of his neck with her right hand.

Baker nodded and climbed to his feet, stretching out the kinks. Then headed to the food, returning a few minutes later with a laden plate and a glass of wine.

He just sat down when a clean-shaven and suit-and-tie-wearing Jape walked out the main door and raised his guitar over his head.

Katie covered her mouth with one hand. "Now I recognize him, Will! He's J. P. Richardson!"

"You're right," Will agreed, as Jape walked over and tugged Gudrun to her feet.

"I need a good-looking girl to sing to, sweetheart. C'mon!"

The two walked to a center point in front of the group, and Jape spun Gudrun around to face him, and began to play and sing.

"Hello, baby

Yeah, this is the Big Bopper speakin'

Ha Ha Ha Ha Ha

Oh, you sweet thing.

Do I what? Will I what?

Oh baby, you know what I like!"

It went from there. Most of the crowd had no idea what the song was, but as kids, Will and Katie had heard it often enough and were familiar with it. Baker started laughing when the song began, as did Jonathon Elbunn. Despite their ignorance, the listeners lit up anyway, shouting and clapping. Oog and his companions drummed in time to the words. Richardson sang it twice, and Gudrun played along, looking coy and swaying provocatively, a surprisingly seductive young Viking warrior.

A few other songs followed, and the evening progressed. Old Man and Old Woman eventually appeared, looking like they'd been doing what they had probably been doing, and joined in the festivities.

A nice end to this stage of the adventure.

Tomorrow *Blood Wave* would head back to Boston, and Katie and Will's time in Cockaigne would draw to a close shortly after that.

CHAPTER TWENTY

A long two days at sea brought them back to Boston. Baker and Sylvia interviewed the Garrisons and the children at length while on the ship, and the full program was ready for broadcast when *Blood Wave* docked at the seawall. Then it was hugs, thanks and tears as the return journey to Raptureville commenced. Their walk up to the Floater station was a constant round of Boston residents asking questions and giving congratulations. Most asked if Katie and Will really wanted to go back to their old lives in Portland, and only the existence of their children and grandchildren stifled those conversations. People understood that, but then the idea of their occasional return visits came up, and of course Mary Pat and Bobby encouraged that possibility.

"Well, we sort of escaped," Katie told Will when they were on the Floater and headed southwest. The little airship was sparsely filled, and while their fellow passengers clearly knew who they were, no lengthy conversations took place. Bobby and Mary Pat wore their Orca Dorks T-shirts and looked forward to home and their parents.

"We haven't let any cats out of any bags," the two agreed. "Our folks won't get stirred up, even though we were in some semi-dangerous moments."

"The stone-throwing episode might worry them," Katie said, "And that'll be on the big program."

"The fact that we're both in one piece with no damage should deflect their concerns," Bobby said. "My dad will be pleased I behaved well and that Mary Pat and I acted in a trustworthy manner."

"The Garrisons will take some credit for that," Mary Pat added. "You both should accompany us to our homes. Give us some backup."

"We'll be glad to do that," Katie told them.

Both sets of parents awaited them at the Floater stop in Raptureville, a bit of a surprise. Greetings and hugs commenced, followed by stern gimlet-eyed examinations in case things were not as proper as appearances indicated.

"Thank you," Siobhan and Serpent Woman told the Garrisons. "They look none the worse for wear. We hope they weren't too much trouble."

"They were fine," Katie said. "They're terrific children, very sensible and well-behaved."

Twin frowns appeared on two very different faces. "Are we sure you had the correct children?" Angelic expressions graced both kids at that point.

As parents do when obvious difficulties aren't apparent, they gave up.

"Ball game and grilling tomorrow evening," Michael O'Connor said. "Good eats, good beer, and we'll look for some good stories."

"We'll have some good stories today," Bobby and Mary Pat assured them, now that they were sure they were safe from any parental repercussions.

After more hugs, the Garrisons walked back to their temporary home and collapsed on the patio chaise lounges with soft drinks.

"I'm not sorry it's over," Katie told Will, barely able to keep her eyes open, "but it was still a great adventure with some unusual and fascinating people."

"And the Orcas," Will said. "That was unexpected. Keiko and the others were both helpful and amusing. Free spirits and kindly and terrific support when asked."

"They enjoyed themselves and a door into Cockaigne's human society opened. They'll rapidly learn about the land walkers, and that two-way cross-pollination will be mutually beneficial."

Will didn't respond immediately, thinking things over. "You think we might want to come back once in a while, see how things are? Maybe at the big opening for Raptureville?"

"Oh, maybe before then. I'd like to see how Bobby and Mary Pat are growing up, and if Gro and Gudrun are behaving and learning journalism."

Will chuckled after another long swallow of cola. "Those two will always be on the lookout for a good time, but Gro at least will be dedicated and serious. She'll drag her cousin right along with her, I expect. They'll drive poor Baker crazy, or I miss my guess."

"You're probably right, Will. Youthful energy and high sex drive will make Baker's life maybe not more difficult, but more complicated."

"Frankly, I'm still trying to get my head around the fact that Old Man's stand-in is The Big Bopper."

"Plus the most popular film comedy team is Zero Mostel, Benny Hill, and Nikita Khrushchev. Three Naughty Guys. A real surprise, that."

"We're probably going to be here another week or so, and they have Streaming on the TV. We can probably catch one of their movies."

"For sure," Will agreed. More silence followed. "How are we going to explain our youth to our kids? We can't possibly tell them the truth. They'd never accept that."

"Simple. We take a DVD of the big program back with us, sit them down and make them watch it. That'd do it."

"Maybe, but our grandchildren will want to be with us when we come back. They're about the same ages as Mary Pat and Bobby. They'll push hard."

"I don't see why not, really. Our grandkids are well-behaved and in a strange environment like Cockaigne they'll not try any shenanigans."

"Oh, like Bobby and Mary Pat won't have activity suggestions? William, you need to realize that children, given the opportunity to influence others their own age, will do so. Mary Pat is a bona fide troublemaker and Bobby is close to that. They would form their own little gang and figure out how to work around parental and grandparental parameters."

"Sure. That would happen. We'd just have to be ready to tamp it down." He opened a copy of *The Oregonian* he'd picked up at the Floater stop. "Hey, here's a Tom Peterson ad on page three."

"'Free is a very good price.'"

"Gives me a warm feeling to know that he and Gloria are here, though."

Katie didn't reply, merely smiled softly and leaned her head back against the lounge, closing her eyes.

"I wonder how the Nixons are doing in San Clemente?" Will said.

"Well, if they're back by now, Dick probably still has his tail between his legs."

"He really loved her. I remember his sobbing through her whole funeral. A very sad occasion."

"We've avoided that possibility, haven't we?"

"Yeah, we have, an accident created by a computer glitch."

"I don't mind looking young again, and you probably don't either."

"No. For sure."

"I'm going to take a nap. Then some food, and then…"

"That occurred to me also."

* * * * *

The next day was relatively quiet. Interviewers from the broadcast media came by after setting up times. Katie was more the focus, but Will got in a sentence now and then. As it should be, he figured. Katie was the more animated and photogenic. Cameras of every sort had always loved her. Will sat back and appreciated the situation.

They walked around the housing area and hiked up into the forest, then came back and put together food and drink for the evening get-together, filled a wheeled cooler and headed to the picnic area and playing field.

"More mammals," Bobby's father said, his clicking laughter accompanying his words.

"Maybe Old Man and Old Woman will Bring Up more of your people," Katie told him, lifting an eyebrow.

Serpent Woman shook her head. "Perhaps not. He likes being the odd creature out, not necessarily the center of attention, but something akin to that. He was once a figure of influence and power, and those old ways still exist in his head at some level."

Red Claw gave his spouse a hard look and said, "William, are females always so judgmental?"

"I can't answer that, RC. We'd both get in trouble."

"So very true. Let's escape and find some beer."

The women exchanged superior smiles as the two males walked away.

"We seem to have a few things in common," Katie told Serpent Woman.

"Indeed. I have heard that you and your husband may return here on occasion? I would enjoy that."

"You would?"

"Yes. Your life in your reality has been long and fulfilling, and because of that, your mannerisms and approach to life here are different from the angels and the people Brought Up after their deaths. You are more recent and contemporary. 'Up to date,' or similar, plus you have children and grandchildren who are unaware of what you and Will have experienced here. How will you handle that when you return?"

"Will thinks we should take back a DVD of the adventure and simply show our family."

Serpent Woman's golden eyes widened. "Isn't that taking an incredible chance, or something similar?"

Katie shrugged. "Can you suggest something more effective and less disturbing?"

The tall dinosaur looked off into the distance and stroked the border of her lower jaw, sending the beautiful rainbow effect across her scales. "No," she said finally. "It's a chance, but I can think of nothing better, though we have a few days to consider other options."

"Any suggestions are welcome."

"Well, Bobak and his little hoodlum friend are already proposing visiting your world. Their time with Old Man has given them the courage to consider such unlikely endeavors, framed as a request."

"We'd be glad to have them."

"That is not the sole issue. They tell us you have grandchildren their age, and my imagination conjures up all manner of mischief such a group could come up with, should your descendants be anything like Bobak and Mary Pat."

Katie grinned. "They are a lot the same. But they're children. We should expect and accept that. They *will* get into trouble. It's the nature of the little beasts, particularly in groups."

"True enough. You and Will didn't let Mary Pat and Bobak do anything foolish…"

"We had a lot of help. The Vikings and the Neanderthals really helped."

"…indeed. I understand that. But my son is clearly not mammalian, and would that not be a problem?"

"Maybe if we wait until Halloween. Bobby would simply be a terrific costume on a normal child."

"Yes, but that is months away. They are going to begin their efforts well before then. Let's say they decide on a month from now, and they get Old Man or Old Woman to grant their wish. Suddenly there they are, standing in your living room with your grandchildren. What to do?"

"Old Man and Old Woman won't go against their parents' wishes, will they?"

"No, but then we become the villains, standing in the path of a new adventure."

"I see what you mean. Accommodations must be made which will satisfy the kids."

"Could you bring your grandchildren here?"

"That would be easier. If we show them the News video and ask if they'd like to meet Bobby and Mary Pat, that would be a solution."

"How old are they?"

"Ten, eight, and six. The oldest is a girl. The other two are boys. The oldest and the youngest are our son's, the eight-year-old is our older daughter's. Our youngest daughter is still in Med School, no children yet."

"Continue your consideration. Speak with William. See what happens. Also, I have another question."

"Fire away."

"Tell me about Nordstrom."

* * * * *

When the evening was over and the Garrisons were back in their temporary home and in bed, they lay on their backs and discussed things.

"So we bring the grandkids here and they get to experience Cockaigne?" Will asked.

"Yes, if Old Man and Old Woman go for it. We seem to be special, at least in their eyes, so Serpent Woman thinks it's a done deal."

"Kind of a can of worms, isn't it?"

"Well, we're retired, so we have the opportunity and freedom to do what we want. The grandchildren will benefit from the experience, don't you think?"

Will smiled in the darkness. "Tabitha will go all the way in, Chad will be fine, but Bobby is only six, so hard to say how he'll respond to a young dinosaur who's only maybe two or three years older and has the same name."

"They'll bond. 'Here Bobby' and 'There Bobby.'"

"Clever."

"Why not take advantage of the opportunity, Will?"

Will shook his head. "Can't see how it could go really wrong. *The Oregonian* here would go nuts over the incursion of three kids from the current Earth, the kids will adapt quickly with us along to ease their ingress to this society."

"Sounds good. We should talk to Michael and Siobhan, since Mary Pat is going to be involved." Katie snuggled up against him. "Can we quit talking for now. I have another idea."

"I suppose," Will replied, understanding what was next.

* * * * *

The next day had television crews with interviews. They'd given the Garrisons a day or two to recover from their adventure, but in the aftermath of the two hour Special program, this would be more personal. A lot of time was spent on the bear episode, understandably since the footage showed both Garrisons only inches from real damage.

"Weren't you terrified?" their interviewer, Holly Gustafson, asked.

Katie laughed. "We really didn't have time, did we, Will?"

"Most of the part with the shaking and fear came afterward. I don't mind admitting I was scared, but Karl was confident and encouraging, telling us to keep our heads down and push for all we were worth. It worked out."

"What about the firefight with the cigarette boats?" Holly asked.

"I was out of the picture on that," Katie told her. "I was below decks with the children. Will had to keep the family name in the mix,"

"Your ancestor commanded the Dragonboat, though. He's a handsome devil, isn't he? I can see him in your features."

"We have the same coloration, fair-skinned and blond. He has the better smile, I think."

"I disagree," Will said, stroking Katie's right cheek and getting a look of mild reproval in return.

Holly chuckled. "The viewers call you 'The Rapture Babe.' And those autographs you gave on the way aboard the *Blood Wave* are getting some big prices on Craigslist." She grinned. "Not surprising, really. You two were involved in a mega-adventure, and not something you asked for, either."

"We just played it by ear," Will replied.

"Played very well, I'd say. High-level heroics with no experience. I've studied the water-skiing clip onto Nixon's ship, and that was flawless. You did better than Old Man and poor Vicar Elbunn. You cannot imagine the replays that gets on YouTube. A mess-up by a god, always worth a good laugh. And the Vicar looked like he inhaled a gallon of water. A great scene."

"They both recovered nicely," Katie said. "I felt sorry for Jonathon, though. He looked so miserable."

"He didn't think that should be part of his job description, that was pretty clear," Will added.

The interview went on somewhat longer. The Garrisons apologized for not having any family pictures, and Holly said it wasn't surprising considering the method and manner of their arrival. Still, there had been thousands of views of their initial nocturnal appearance on the floor of the Rapture Hall.

"Really?" Katie asked, embarrassed.

"Oh, yeah. There's even a rumor going around that the two of you will be asked to appear in the next Three Naughty Guys film, set here in Boston."

"They wouldn't!" Katie exclaimed.

"Would that up the profits?" Will asked, grinning at his wife. "'The Rapture Babe'."

"You can just keep quiet about that, Mister!"

"Just a thought."

"The rumor is pretty solid, I think," Holly said, enjoying their reactions, "but I'm through with my questions, so unless you have some additional thoughts, we can all relax and I can go back to the station and edit this interview."

Thanks and handshakes followed, then Holly and her lone camera person departed in *The Oregonian* floater.

"Think that was maybe the last of our fame?" Will asked when they were alone.

Katie smiled at him, chuckling. "Until we join The Three Naughty Guys cast, anyway. I cannot envision that."

"Might be fun, don't you think?"

"After what we've been through, it might be okay, William. We'll have to see."

* * * * *

A few more unexciting days and it came time for the Garrisons to return home. A group gathered in the Rapture Hall for what amounted to a farewell ceremony, with the Garrisons, Mary Pat, Bobby and both sets of parents.

Old Man, Old Woman, Jonathon Elbunn, and Jape popped into existence alongside the small group. Jape wore a false white beard and clothing identical to his boss' outfit, which this time was a dignified white robe with golden trim and new sandals. Old Woman was decked out in the same fashion, but looked far more comfortable than the two men. Elbunn grinned widely.

"TV people should be here in a minute," Jape said, glancing at his watch.

Indeed they were, two camerapersons and Holly Gustafson.

"So we are all ready?" Old Woman asked, both eyebrows raised.

Bobby and Mary Pat started to tear up, and Katie put her arms around them. "Don't cry. We'll be back."

"Indeed you will," Old Man assured them in his deep bass voice. "I envision many happy years and returns. You came here by accident, so you are owed. Perhaps not so exciting next time, but there will be plenty of surprises in your future. Mark my words."

Old Woman's flawless smile joined His. "I agree completely. We have enjoyed your company and our world – our Afterlife – has benefitted from your presence."

"It's been a joy," Will and Katie said together.

"Hold hands," Old Man told them. He looked over at the TV crew. "You folks ready and situated?"

"We are," Holly replied. "Lighting is perfect."

Old Woman held up her arms. "Tap your heels together, Katie."

Katie did, and they were gone.

EPILOGUE

They appeared in the kitchen rather than the bedroom, and their clothes remained in place. The exterior windows showed only darkness, but the dim light of dawn touched the eastern horizon.

"Several hours later than when we left," Will said.

Katie released his hand, put her arms around his neck and kissed him. "I love you."

"I love you," Will replied, closing his eyes.

When their kiss ended, some time later, Katie headed for her computer to check the calendar.

"We're back on the same night we left," she said. releasing a sigh. "That's one good thing."

"Sure is," Will agreed. "Should we duck back to bed for a couple hours."

"Take up where we left off?" Her smile was devastating.

"If you want."

"I want." She grabbed his right arm and they went rapidly to the bedroom. Young bodies responded and things progressed.

* * * * *

Well after ten o'clock, breakfast done and Will had rinsed the dishes, Katie asked him to go out into the garage and bring in some ground chuck to thaw. When he came back in, his face was puzzled.

"There's a motorcycle in the garage."

"What? Where'd that come from?"

"Allied Motors in Boston, on SW Powell. A 350 cc. air-cooled Yale, a box of parts, complete set of manuals, boots, helmet, gloves, a jersey, and other riding gear. All my size."

Katie put down what she was doing and went to see, came back in five minutes. "You haven't ridden since we were first married. It has an Oregon plate and current stickers." She cocked her head at Will. "You don't know anything about this?"

Will spread his hands. "Nothing. I'm as surprised as you are."

Then, nearly an hour later, they heard voices from behind the house, near the pool.

"That sounds like the Jensen twins," Katie said.

"Well, we did tell them they could use the pool when they wanted." The twins were tall, short-haired, muscular young women who played basketball at the University of Oregon. The Garrisons had watched the pair grow up, had always liked them, had even baby-sat them when they were small.

"I'll go take a look," Will said, heading for the back door.

"Ask them if they want lunch," Katie called after him.

Will was back in ten minutes. "Well, they're not alone." He held out a folded sheet of paper. "Here's the schedule."

"For what?" Katie asked, taking the paper from Will. As she read it, her mouth fell open, and her brow furrowed. "Karl and Lars are out there with the girls?"

"Yup, and I wouldn't have thought what was going on when I first walked out was something you could do in a pool. Filters'll probably be able to handle it, though."

Katie read down the page. "They're here until next week. Then we have two days off before Gro and Gudrun arrive. Then Old Man and Old Woman will be here after that. Good God in Heaven, Will!"

"The kids'll be here on Sunday, right? Chad and his family? They'll like Karl and Lars, especially the kids."

"How will we feed them? You've seen how Vikings eat."

"There's a bunch of new stuff in the freezer. Shouldn't be a problem. Could take them out to eat; they'd fit in the SUV, I think."

"I never thought of anything like this. We can handle it, but goodness sakes! We're a way station for something like Heaven!"

"We could take Old Man and Old Woman to church with us."

"Sure, William, two Elder Gods at Saint Apollonia's, with Father Mendenhall. What could possibly go wrong?"

"Okay, maybe not that, then."

"Is there anything positive in all this?"

"I have a new motorcycle?"

"You would say *that*, typical male."

"I suppose," Will said as they embraced.

ACKNOWLEGEMENTS

This is a rather short book by my standards, and fairly low key. Catholic education from Grade School through most of College is to blame. More specifically, the very entertaining and free-thinking Fr. Meinrad Gaul at St. Martin's College, whose idea of Church History didn't gloss over the downsides of Catholicism, the 'bad things' as he put it. Hard to say what his lectures would be like today, after the horrendous revelations of the past couple decades, but they were unsettling to the students of fifty years ago, for certain. Fr. Meinrad resembled Andy Rooney in both appearance and lecture delivery, so that helped. He made Church History fun.

Cockaigne, The Land of the Perfect Life, was a popular concept in the Middle Ages, with assorted tales of the good life and preposterous circumstances designed to make the poor and downtrodden feel better about their pitiful existences. Probably wasn't real.

Nuns were the real deal. You never knew who was going to show up at St. Francis De Sales High School in Eugene. One afternoon I walked out of the Men's restroom and Louis Armstrong stood talking to the principal and vice-principal. Another time the student body sat in the gym looking at a folding divider. No one in sight. Then Marcel Marceau walked around the end of the divider and gave his performance. Nuns had powers, for sure. They treated us well, and we had fun. Also learned stuff.

Some members of the now-defunct Lucky Lab Rats Writers' Group will recognize themselves in the text, but all are portrayed in positive ways, so hopefully there will be no later revenge. Good people every one.

The next book will be back with Megan and Farrell and their ever-increasing band of do-gooders with bad habits. A German research vessel, the *Planet*, heading for Antarctica and the German secret facility from WWII, hoping to get there before the North Koreans, led by Kim Yo Jong. Two dinosaurs in tow, the German KSK, and Heide Knecht from the BND, plus the first Japanese member of Team Blood, Sayoko Bizen, who loves to cook. The Vril legend and Maria Orsic will be on hand, but whose side will Natalia Rokconskaya be on? Regardless. a good time will be had by all survivors.

Some discerning readers of 'Krampusnacht' wondered why Jordan Burke was even in the book, since she is an Oregon law-dog (cat, actually). Easy to answer. Before the events in the book began, Jordan and Annike, being friends with privileges, planned to get together for the Holidays. In the Summer, Annike goes to John Day if she can, so this was the Winter trip. The activities in the book intervened. Because Jordan is a fun-loving and action-oriented young woman, she was on-board. No surprise there.

As to the early Change for Liesl, those already Changed are more confident and comfortable with their own kind, and the Change gives Liesl as much protection as possible. The Changed can be killed, as the Aztecs in 'Other Blood,' but it is difficult. With their durable bodies and vastly-heightened senses, they are instantly part of the team, so to speak. Liesl turned out to be more action-oriented than I thought going in, but I let her have her way.

The usual thanks for inspiration, organization, and persistence go out to John H. Quiner, Mike Contris, all the nuns I ever had, the mysterious and reclusive Keith Tittle, Steve Perry, Dexter Chapin, Big Ben, Sandra

Hazard (no snakes, please), and the ultra-communicative Maryann Congreves (a joy at every level).

Made in the USA
Middletown, DE
29 October 2022

13679114R00189